EYES OF THE
OCEAN

Sherry,
May all you do
be blessed!

DANIEL MORTON

EYES OF THE OCEAN

BOOK ONE

TATE PUBLISHING & *Enterprises*

Published by Tate Publishing & Enterprises, LLC
127 E. Trade Center Terrace | Mustang, Oklahoma 73064 USA
1.888.361.9473 | www.tatepublishing.com

Tate Publishing is committed to excellence in the publishing industry. The company reflects the philosophy established by the founders, based on Psalm 68:11,
"The Lord gave the word and great was the company of those who published it."

Book design copyright © 2010 by Tate Publishing, LLC. All rights reserved.
Cover design by Kristen Verser
Interior design by Joel Uber

Published in the United States of America

ISBN: 978-1-61739-495-9
1. Fiction; Suspense
2. Fiction; Christian, Suspense
11.01.26

To my wife, Beverly, and all our children for encouraging me as I poured so much time into this endeavor.

1

August 18

As Jim sat on the beach with his head in his hands, it was hard for him to believe all these things had come to pass. It had only been two weeks since life seemed right. Everything was as it should have been. He had the perfect job, the perfect home, the perfect wife, and the perfect daughter. God had smiled on him. He couldn't have asked for more.

That was before. Now everything had changed.

The crash and roar of the waves rang in his ears as they rose and fell before him. The nightmarish images that replayed in his mind tormented his thoughts. As the sun disappeared below the horizon, he cried.

His mind wandered to that sunbathed morning when it all began, less than five hundred yards from where he now sat. He turned his eyes that direction, only to see the charred remains where his home once stood. A few blackened two-by-fours stood ominously pointing toward the purple sky like solidified remnants of a bad dream.

August 4

As Jim finished his breakfast and paper, he looked across the table at Susan. She had been there for him through a lot. He couldn't help but think of everything he had put her through while in college and all the little jobs that finally had brought them to this point. It had been a long, hard road, and now it was beginning to pay off.

Susan's hair was a dirty blonde and her skin tan. Her blue eyes set off her face as if they were precious jewels set in place by a master craftsman. Jim thought she was the most beautiful woman he had ever seen.

Susan rose to her feet, took Jim by the hand, and kissed his cheek.

"I'll be back soon. I've got to give the bod a workout," she said as she turned to go out the door.

He watched her as she walked away, allowing his eyes to soak up the beauty of her form as it was highlighted by the morning sun shining in around her.

She turned and blew him another kiss and said, "You're a good man, Jim Fender, and I am proud to be your wife. I promise I'll be back in time for you to go, but you need to head to the shower or you'll be late."

If ever a man felt blessed to be married to any woman, Jim did. Before he headed upstairs to shower, he stopped at the window to watch her stretching. Even after years of marriage, she was still the one he longed to see. John Hall had expressed just how he felt when he preformed "Still the One." He found himself in a frozen stare until she started off on her southward trek.

Jim thought about when Susan had been pregnant with Kristy, how she was so afraid that she would be fat and ugly after delivery. She had promised that she would try to get back in shape as soon as she could.

Jim would smile and say, "I will always love you no matter what your shape."

Her caring spirit was one of Susan's greatest qualities as far as Jim was concerned. She cared about her looks, yes, but more so, she cared about Jim and what he thought. She cared about Kristy. She cared about people in general. She was a person love radiated from.

She had started running and swimming three weeks after Kristy was born. On the days that the weather did not allow her morning routine, she would usually put on some music and dance. If Jim was there, he would get a dancing workout as well.

After Jim finished his shower and his morning shave, he took a moment to pray about the events the day promised and to thank God for his wife and daughter. As he prayed, he was filled with an unusual feeling—not fear, not joy, but a strange mixture of the two. A cold chill ran down the length of his spine and sent tingles throughout the whole of his being. He shook it off to the best of his ability and slid his watch on his goosebump-covered arm as he headed downstairs.

The feeling that something was not right followed Jim into the kitchen. He looked out the window and saw Kristy on her swing. He stepped out the door and walked toward her.

Kristy jumped from the swing and ran toward him with her arms open wide.

"Daddy, do you have to go today?" she said. "Can you please stay and play with me and Mommy?"

Jim wanted with all this heart to stay, but he knew he couldn't. Today, he would close the deal that would put his name in the books: Jim Fender, Mortgage Broker Extraordinaire.

Jim was a relatively tall man, around six foot three with dark, brown hair. His eyes were brown with a few specks of hazel in them. He wasn't exactly muscular, but he wasn't fat either.

He picked Kristy up, held her over his head, and spun around, making it seem as though she were flying. They both loved playing this game. He helped her come to a safe landing and knelt down in front of her.

Brushing her hair back from her face, he looked into her eyes. "You know I would stay with you if I could. I just can't stay this time."

The tears welled up in her eyes. Jim pulled her in close and slipped the watch off. "Kristy, I have something I want you to do for me. You keep this for me today. When the little hand's on the seven and the big hand is on the three, I will be home. Okay?"

He carefully slid it onto her arm and adjusted the clasp. That brought a smile to her face. Jim thought of Susan as he placed the watch on Kristy's arm. Surely she would return from her swim soon. She had been so proud of him when he told her about the deal he was about to close. Ninety-two million dollars was the agreed price. There was sure to be a large bonus in it for him.

Jim turned and faced the water and realized how blessed he and his family were. How many men, excluding those who had it given to them, could afford a house on the beach at age twenty-eight? The ocean was calm this morning—not glassy, but relatively smooth. He could see a couple of dolphins racing back and forth in the water. About a quarter of a mile out, a sailboat sat drifting along. Up closer to shore, he could see something, but he was not sure exactly what it was. It appeared to be something fairly large. Suddenly, he could tell that it had a human shape. The reality caused him to jerk as if he had stuck his finger into a light socket. It was a body. Not swimming, not moving, not doing anything except bobbing slightly with the small ripples of waves that rocked it.

"Kristy, stay here!" he shouted as he ran toward the water.

The closer he got, the more clearly he could see the body. As the image became increasingly visible, the more familiar it became.

It was Susan.

His mind raced as he jumped into the water. Had she drowned, been attacked by a shark? Surely he could revive her with CPR.

The water around her had a pinkish tint, and some of the foam that decorated the surface of the water appeared to be the eyes of some hideous creature lurking just below the surface.

Jim grabbed Susan's body from the water and carried her to shore, moving quickly and looking over his shoulder as if to make sure that whatever it was was not after him too.

Her limp body felt as though it had doubled in weight. Her arms flopped back and forth as Jim carried her clear of the water. He carefully lowered her to the sand. While placing his hand on her cheek, he tried to say her name, but the lump in his throat would not allow it. Rising to get a better look, he froze in disbelief. His eyes, fixed on the gaping hole in her chest that now oozed fresh blood, filled with tears.

One word forced its way past the lump. "No." It came out soft and labored. And then again with more force, "No!" Once more, this time with a shout, "No!"

No CPR, no cardio massage, nor any lung manipulation would revive her. She was gone.

"What is it, Daddy? What did you find?" he heard Kristy call from the yard. He did not know how to answer. "Stay there, honey. It'll be okay."

Over and over again, his eyes scanned his wife's body . His mind refused to believe the truth of what he was seeing. His hand held tightly to hers. Tears streaked his face while his heart pounded in his chest. Was it possible that such a thing

EYES OF THE OCEAN

could truly be? A million questions crossed his mind, and none had answers. Nothing made sense.

The wound was not one that would have come from dashing against a rock. It was too clean, not like that from a shark attack. It was a hole that you would expect to see in some horror film when some loon gets a knife and goes crazy.

Jim placed his fingers on Susan's neck in hope to find a pulse. What he felt was the cold lack of one. He looked at the face of the woman he loved so much. Her radiant tan had faded to ash, and her lips had lost their color. He drew her close and kissed her forehead as he had so many times. This time, she didn't lift her eyes and smile.

In the distance, he heard a car racing its engine and tires squealing as it raced off.

Gulls were beginning to congregate overhead, hoping for the usual free popcorn, potato chips, or stale bread that Susan brought to them on mornings like this. Some of the gulls were diving or landing in close and then flying off again as if to say, "Hey, don't forget me."

The sun was growing brighter and hotter. Jim was numb and unable to move. Shock had carried him into a different dimension—a dimension in which nightmares are the only reality and time can slip by without a trace.

"Sir, do you want me to call an ambulance?" a voice came from behind him.

Startled back to reality, he jumped to his feet.

"Should I call an ambulance, or have you already called?"

"No, I haven't called. I just found her floating."

The rising tide was bringing the waves to the body. Slowly, the water crept up closer and closer. Jim looked down the beach and noticed that the footprints that Susan had made jogging down the beach were all but washed away.

Reality began to impress itself into the wrinkles of his mind. How long had he sat here? He glanced at the empty spot on his arm where his watch belonged. Why was it so quiet? Where was—?

"Kristy!" he screamed as he ran toward the house.

The swing that held the object of his search just a short time earlier now sat empty. The yard was void of life. His eyes quickly scanned the beach. He cried out again to no avail. Surely she had gone inside for a drink. He opened the door.

"Kristy!"

No answer.

2

The police and the ambulance had arrived by the time Jim had searched the house for some sign of Kristy. The three Port Suni police cars lined the south side of the drive, and the ambulance sat backed in on the north with the rear doors wide open.

"Jim Fender?" The question came from a remotely familiar face that was approaching him. "Tommy Sutton," he said with his hand outstretched. "Remember me? We played basketball in high school and graduated together."

He did remember Tommy. As a matter of fact, he remembered Tommy very well. He had changed, but he still had that crooked red nose he had acquired in his junior year playing basketball. Tommy was the one person whom Jim had to work hard not to hate. They had, at one time, been friends in school; but things change. Susan had been his girlfriend through most of high school. It was only the last few months of their senior year that she had begun to date Jim.

Susan had told him about Tommy, how he had treated her gentle and sweet most of the time. Every time they were together he made her feel special. He would buy her flowers or candy on almost every holiday. She said she was really head over heels with him until the night of senior prom. Susan's eyes had filled with tears as she recounted the way Tommy had driven her to the beach "just for a walk." As they walked barefoot in the sand, Tommy took her hand and pulled her in close. He stopped and kissed her. "Let's make love right here on the beach, right now," he said.

"Tommy, stop kidding around. We've talked about this before."

"Come on," he said with a twinge of firmness in his voice. "It's dark, and no one will see us."

"This isn't funny anymore. Let's just go back to the car."

Tommy's voice became cold and harsh. A grimace overtook his smile. "I'm serious. I've been waiting a long time for this, and I do not intend to go home disappointed again."

Susan felt the hair on the back of her neck beginning to rise. "Take me home, Tommy!" she demanded.

His grip on her arm grew tighter. "No! I told you I don't intend to go home disappointed. I have waited long enough."

She tried to break free from his grasp but could not. "Stop it, Tommy. I'm scared!"

As hard as she tried, she was unable to prevent him from raping her.

She had been wearing Tommy's ring on a chain around her neck. The chain broke, and the ring was lost and had never been found. He took her torn clothes with him and left her naked on the beach. When she got to the road, Tommy's dad, Officer Sutton, was waiting with her clothes. She was about twenty yards from the police car when the spotlight came on. She stopped and attempted to keep herself covered with her hands and arms as best as she could. Her eyes, already blurred from her tears, now throbbed from the stab of the light.

"What's goin' on here, runnin' round naked like that?" Officer Sutton asked with a chuckle in his voice.

"Tommy has my clothes," she said with a tone of apprehension.

"I guess he did, but I do now. Want 'em?"

She started toward him.

"Don't be such a spoilsport. Put your hands up and turn around for me."

"What? No! Just give them to me, please." She wanted to just run away, but it was a long way home. She wanted to scream, but who would hear? "Please, just give me my clothes."

"You can have them. All ya gotta do is slide those hands up and turn around a couple of times for me."

Susan just stood there, unsure of what to do. If she did, what would he do? If not, then what? Was she about to be raped again?

Officer Sutton raised his hands over his head. "Come on now. I'm not gonna hurt ya. I just wanna see."

"Please," she begged, "just let me have my clothes."

He brought his hands back down to his side. "Do it, and you'll get your clothes. Don't and I wait till you do. Now which is it gonna be?"

Susan slowly raised her hands and started to turn.

"Slow now. No need to rush it."

Before it was over, he had her turn completely around at least three times. Then he said, "Listen girly, if you ever say a word to anyone about this, I can make life really rough for your whole family. What shame would come on the whole lot of ya if I were to find something that would tie your old man to that murder down at the inlet last week. I wouldn't mind seeing old Alfred sit behind bars for a while. I might even have a chance to drop in and comfort your mom a bit." Thomas paused, and a smile replaced the stern expression he wore for a brief moment and then vanished as quickly as it came. "Just keep your mouth shut, and that won't have to happen."

On several occasions, she had considered talking to a lawyer or a police agency away from Port Suni; however, there was no doubt that Thomas Sutton had enough clout that she would not be believed. Susan loved her mother and father deeply, and the thought of her dad in jail was enough to squelch any desire she had to talk to anyone about it. He could have easily stopped with that, but the image of Thomas doing to his mother what Tommy had just done to her was the clincher. Jim was the only breach in her secrecy.

"What's going on, Jim? The call I got says someone found a body on the beach in front of your house? Anyone we know?"

Jim stared at Tommy for a moment or two before answering. His anger swelled up inside of him. He wanted to pick up a baseball bat and knock some sense into him. He swallowed hard. "Yeah, Tommy. It is Susan. She has a hole in her chest about the size of your fist," he said as he pushed Tommy to the side. "But what I need now is to find Kristy."

"You're messin' with me, right? About it being Susan? Right?" he questioned as he followed Jim.

"No. It's Susan."

"Then why in the name of all that is good are you not down there with the body? Is it a weak stomach? It's okay if it is. I still get a bit nauseous sometimes when we have to deal with bodies and stuff. Y'all were still married, weren't you?" He continued to talk as Jim continued his search.

"Jim, what are you looking for?" he asked with that same blank look on his face that Jim remembered so well from school. It was the look that always arrived on Tommy's face when a teacher would ask a question that he had no clue how to answer.

"I'm looking for Kristy," he said sharply. "I need to know where she is."

"Who is Kristy?"

"My daughter. Susan's daughter. She is gone too. She was outside. Now she is gone."

Jim walked back to the swing set. On the top of the slide, he saw a piece of paper taped down. He hadn't noticed it before. Confused, he pulled it off the slide and looked closely at the typed page.

> Susan is one.
> Kristy is two.
> Two is alive
> If this you will do.
>
> When the cops come
> Tell them she's with friends,
> And I will soon call
> To tie up loose ends.

Tommy took the note from Jim and said, "Looks like she has been kidnapped. Also looks like whoever left it means business."

Jim dropped to his knees and cried. The question that kept running through his mind tormented him. *How could I have left her here alone?*

Jim prayed. In his heart and mind, he reached out to the Almighty, the Creator. "Oh, God, keep my little girl safe. Forgive me. I should have kept my eyes on her. I let her…God, forgive me. I don't understand how any of this can be real. Lord, wake me from this nightmare. Let me open my eyes and find everything the way it was."

The words of the sermon that he and his wife had heard the previous Sunday came back in vivid clarity. Dr. Eller had talked about the time when Christ was pleading for all mankind and then for himself in the garden of Gethsemane. And then he had said, "Nevertheless, not my will, but thine be done." Jim tried to pray the same thing. With all that was in him, he wanted to submit his will to the one who knew the end before the beginning, but he could not. His prayer was that he would wake up and see Susan sleeping and that he could walk to Kristy's room and pick her up and hold her.

Tommy took Jim by the shoulder and helped him to his feet. "Jim," he said with a certain confidence, "if we are going to find out who did this, we need to get started ASAP. The longer we wait, the more evidence we might miss. We're going to have to take prints, and we will need to ask you some questions. Do you think you can handle that?"

Within just a few minutes, Jim's home had been sealed off with a three-inch-wide strip of yellow plastic that reached around the perimeter. Jim couldn't stop the questions in his mind. How could such a small strip of crime scene tape wield the power to keep out the unwanted when he was unable to keep it out himself? How could he have let the two things that mattered most to him be taken so quickly? What had he done to deserve such a horrid punishment?

Jim walked alongside the gurney as the paramedics brought Susan's body to the ambulance. The sheet that covered her face added a touch of the unreal to the situation. It could have been anyone under there, but it wasn't. It was Susan. When the gurney was loaded, it was as if his heart was being ripped out and placed in with her. His knees began to tremble as he watched the ambulance turn northward on A1A.

3

Kristy stood looking at her daddy's watch. She had been disappointed when he said he could not stay home, but then he had given her his watch to hold. It was so pretty, especially the numbers 7 and 3. They held a special meaning today. That was when her dad had promised that he would be home.

She looked up from the watch and saw her dad carrying something out of the water. He had found some pretty neat things out there before, but he usually did not go in the water with his shoes on. This one must be really special.

"What did you find, Daddy?" she asked.

"It'll be okay," he answered. Whatever it was, it couldn't be as special as the watch she held. She looked at it again and pulled it close to her heart.

She looked back at the watch. She noticed that she could rock it back and forth and the sun would reflect off of it and flash across her eyes. She started twisting it around and causing the reflection make circles on the side of the house.

It was going to be a good day. She had been swinging in the warm morning sun. The cool breeze was blowing in off of the ocean. She had the best mom and dad in the world. Kristy could hardly wait to tell her mommy about getting to keep her daddy's watch. She started back toward the swing when she saw him again. She almost screamed, and then she felt that she could trust him. She had seen him earlier, talking to her mommy down on the beach. She remembered seeing him a few other times jogging up and down the beach while she waited for her mommy to come in from swimming or her daddy to finish getting ready for work. He would smile and wave, look at his watch, and keep on going. This time, he was in the yard with her.

"Hi, little girl," he said. "That sure is a pretty watch. Is it yours?"

"No. It's my daddy's, but he said I could keep it today. He has to go to work, but he'll be home when the little hand's on the seven and the big hand's on the three."

"What's your name? You sure are a pretty little girl."

"My name is Kristy. That's spelled, K-R-I-S-T-Y F-E-N-D-E-R."

"Your mommy's name is Susan, and your daddy's name Jim?"

"Yep. Susan Fender and Jim Fender, and I'm Kristy Fender. What's your name?"

The man looked down the beach at Jim kneeling over Susan's body. He smiled and looked at his watch. Kristy thought his eyes looked happy and friendly.

"I am just an old friend of your mommy and daddy. By the way, I have a present for them in my car. You wanna help me get it for them? We'll tell them it is from both of us."

He held out his hand toward her. His smile was warm. She placed her hand in his and walked with him, full of excitement, to the car. He opened the back door on the driver's side. The driver's door was already open, the motor was running, and the car was backed all the way up the drive as close to the garage door as it could get without touching it. She looked in. The seat was empty and scary-looking. He grabbed her, threw her in, and slammed the door. He jumped in the front and slammed his door. Dropping it into gear, he floored it. A couple hundred yards away, the loud squalling of the tires could be faintly heard over the sound of the ocean.

Kristy held tightly to her daddy's watch as she was thrown across the backseat by the force of the car turning onto the road. She noticed that the door handles had been removed from both doors. She tried to understand what was going on.

"Mister, did you forget the present? Is that why we are going?"

"Shut up, and sit still! There is no gift. Your mom has already gotten hers, and your dad will get his soon enough."

Kristy looked at his eyes in the mirror. They were dark and cold, not happy or friendly like they were a few minutes ago. Her mommy and daddy had told her many times about bad men that stole little girls. They said she should never trust strangers. But she thought she could trust him. Her mommy had.

Fear induced adrenaline poured into her system. Her trembling hands grabbed tightly to the wire cage that separated them and shook it. It was firmly in place. Throwing herself back in her seat, Kristy screamed, "Daddy!"

"Shut up, Grub!" demanded the driver. "He can't hear you. You're mine now."

"I want my Daddy! I'm scared! Take me back!"

The man hit his breaks, bringing the car to a crawl. Turning in his seat so he could look at Kristy. "Grub, I said to shut up. I'm gonna have to do somethin' bad to ya if ya keep on yellin'. I really don't want to hurt ya, but I'm gonna have to if ya keep it up." With that, he turned and sped back up.

She stared out the back window and watched her house fade from sight, her tiny lips murmuring a prayer. "Dear God, please be good to Mommy and Daddy and make this bad man let me go home. Amen."

The flood of tears that had been held back by fear and anger broke loose and streamed down her face. She curled up in the seat and squeezed her knees into her chest as she held tightly to her daddy's watch.

4

Officer Larry Phillips stayed behind when the rest of the police finally left to be there in case a call from the kidnapper came in before the lines could be tapped. He had been one of the first to arrive.

"Mr. Fender," he said with his hand out inviting a shake, "I'll be hanging around in case of contact with the perpetrator. If there is anything I can do for you, answer any questions, whatever, just let me know."

"Just call me Jim. Thanks for the offer, and I'll keep it in mind," Jim said as he accepted the invitation.

"I'll stay as much out of the way as possible. Oh, and most people just call me Larry."

Jim prepared to call Susan's parents. He wasn't sure he would be able to tell them what had happened, but he had to try. Mr. and Mrs. Harwood had treated Jim like family and loved him ever since the first time he and Susan had dated. Jim had come to admire Susan's parents. In every situation and struggle, they seemed be able to maintain an even keel. The only time they seemed irritable was when they had any discussion in which a Sutton was mentioned. Jim was sure they knew about the rape. He wasn't sure how, but they knew.

Jim wished he could call his own parents, a brother, a sister, someone; but there was no one. His parents had divorced a year before. He knew the pharmaceutical company his father worked for had transferred him to Germany to be a sales rep. His mother had moved to a small town in northern Virginia not too far from DC. It had been months since he had heard from either. He had contacted his father's employer about a month ago and told them he needed to talk to him. They said they would make sure he got the message, but he hadn't received a reply. He had checked back several times, but all they would tell him was that his dad had gotten the message. He had tried to find his mother's information on the Internet but had come to the conclusion that her phone was unlisted or possibly she only had a cell phone. He had even considered asking down at the police station to see if they had an address on her, but that would mean getting a favor from a Sutton. It was almost funny that he wouldn't ask a Sutton to help find his mother, but he had to rely on one to find his daughter.

Jim's only brother, Jerome, had been killed in a freak car accident about a year and a half earlier. It looked as if someone had run him off the road, but there was never any evidence. Thomas Sutton had done the investigation himself. His final report said that Jerome had most likely fallen asleep at the wheel and hit the tree.

"Hello." A cheerful female voice came from the other end of the receiver.

"Inez?"

"Yes, Jim. Is that you? What's wrong?"

Jim was trying not to show any emotion in his voice, but it wasn't working. "Inez, is Alfred there? I don't want to talk to him yet, but is he there?"

"He is, Jim. What's wrong? Tell me."

"I need to talk to you guys about something. I want you to promise you will do your best to listen before you say anything. It will just be easier for all of us."

"I don't understand. What's wrong?"

"Can you both get on a phone at the same time and be near each other?"

"Jim, you're scarin' me. What's wrong?"

Jim could hear the fear rising up in Inez's voice. He wished there was some way he could go to Houston to tell them in person. But that wasn't possible. Jim heard the click and the rustle of the second phone as Mr. Harwood picked up the line.

"Alfred?"

"Jim, what in the world is goin' on? Inez is all upset and says you won't tell her...whatever."

"Inez, Alfred, I want you to just listen for a minute. I can't answer a lot of questions right now, but I'll tell you what I can. Susan went out for her swim this morning and when—" Jim began to cry and wasn't able to speak for a moment.

"She's dead, isn't she?" Alfred's voice quivered.

"Yes."

The sound of Inez's voice as she burst into tears cut straight through Jim's heart. The lack of response from Alfred told Jim that he was crying too.

"Please, Jim. Tell me it isn't true. Tell me...it can't be true."

"Inez, I wish I could do that. And I wish I could go back and change it, but I can't."

Alfred's voice came back on the phone. "Jim, how did she drown? She was a great swimmer. Rip current? Big wave? How?"

"Alfred, she didn't drown. She was killed. Someone stabbed her."

Inez was crying, almost to the point of hysterics.

"Did the police get whoever did this or have any idea of who they are looking for?"

"No. They just started the investigation. We really don't have much to go on."

He wished he had a better answer for Mr. Harwood, but the cold, hard truth was they had nothing.

"Jim," Alfred asked, "can we come stay with you and help watch Kristy and help with the arrangements?"

"Alfred, you are welcome anytime. You know that. But…" Jim swallowed hard. "Kristy isn't here."

"What do you mean she isn't there?"

"When I found Susan's body, someone kidnapped her."

Between the sobs, Jim could hear Alfred and Inez's cries of denial.

5

Never in his life had Jim felt so alone. The house was bigger and quieter than he had ever noticed before. An occasional pop or crack would bring him to his feet.

Jim waited anxiously for the kidnapper to call. Every creak brought him to his feet. He paced from window to window, looking for anything unusual, and then dropped back into his seat. The realization that Larry was sitting on the deck after the note said not to involve the police brought Jim back to his feet.

As he stepped out on the deck, Jim's eyes were drawn to the spot where he had found Susan's body. Heaviness filled his chest as a tear crept down his cheek. For a moment, he was captured as the scene replayed on the screen of his mind.

"Jim?" Larry spoke up. "Is there anything I can do for you?"

The sound of his voice reminded Jim of why he was out there. "Did you read that note I found out by the swing?"

"Yeah, I saw it. Not much there to go on though."

"No, but it pretty much says not to get the police involved. Don't you think it would be best if you don't sit out here where you can be seen?"

"Really, with my car in the drive, I don't know that it would make that much difference."

"I forgot about your car. You can put it around on the side, if you would, and that way it won't be as easily seen."

Larry stood to his feet. "Good idea. Anyway I need to stretch my legs a bit."

Jim watched as Larry started down the steps.

When the phone rang, Jim almost knocked over the end table in his rush to answer it. Disappointment and relief filled his head when he heard Mr. Hyatt's voice from the receiver.

"Hey Jim, I just wanted to check in. Jackson did great, and everything went off without a hitch on this end. Still a few papers to file and lawyers to pay."

"That's good to hear. Be sure to tell him I said thanks for filling in like that at the last minute."

"I would have rather had you there, but in the light of your situation…Jim, have they heard anything yet?"

"Not yet. I need to keep the line open though."

Mr. Hyatt was never considered a caring person unless money was involved. He was all about business and big bucks. On the wall of his office was a laminated poster that read, "Never mix business with feelings." One of the men who worked for him said it should have read, "Never mix feelings with anything." Up until now, Jim believed that was true of Mr. Hyatt.

"I'll keep you posted."

"Thanks Jim. If I can do anything at all, I want to know."

"Okay, I'll keep that in mind."

He hung up the phone and walked to the back door that opened to the deck and looked out. Larry had not returned from moving his car. It worried Jim that he had received that call and the officer that was supposed to be there listening did not even know the call came in.

Looking out the door, Jim wanted to walk down to the beach again. Maybe he could find something that had been overlooked earlier. Even so, Tommy had said he needed to stay near the house in case the kidnapper called. He had said that they would be back that evening to set up a phone tap.

He went up to Kristy's room and looked at her toys. The stuffed animals all sitting on the shelf above her bed only added to his loneliness and hurt. It had been no more than two or three months ago when he had put up that shelf.

Kristy had been having bad dreams about a bad man setting fire to the house. She said in the dream that she always felt cold, scared, and alone. She could never see the bad man's face, but everyone else always thought he was a good man. Jim had prayed with her and told her that everything would be okay. She had begged for someone to stay with her and keep her safe in case the bad man came back. After he and Susan had taken turns going in to calm her a few nights, he had come up with a plan. At first, he put a few of her stuffed animals around her bed and told her they were to remind her that there were angels around the room and they were her friends and would protect her. That seemed to help. So he had put up the shelf, set the animals on it, and said that from up there they would have a better view.

On Kristy's dresser sat an eight-by-ten photo of the family in a ceramic frame. Jim picked it up and looked at the smiles on all the faces. He noticed how close they all were sitting. It had been no more than a month since this picture had been taken. Jim had not been happy about going and wasting the time and money when they had plenty of other pictures they had taken. Now, in retrospect, Jim was so glad Susan had insisted.

Kristy had picked out the frame for this picture because of the dolphins on it. Earlier that year, they had gone to Grand Cayman Island, where she had swum with the dolphins. She had been so happy. She said it was like the best dream ever had come true.

Jim was shocked back to the present by the ringing of the phone. He ran down the stairs, taking three at a bound. He leaped across the coffee table that marked the center of the room and grabbed the phone.

"Hello?"

A gruff voice spoke back from the receiver. "Jim?"

"Yes. Who is this?"

"Not for you to know. I have a problem with you, Mr. Fender. You let the police see the note, didn't you?"

"Yes. They were right there when I found it. I couldn't help it."

"So I am assuming they have your lines tapped, and the police are there right now, aren't they?"

"No. They haven't gotten here to set up yet."

"Don't lie to me, Jim. I am not stupid. Some people think I am stupid, but I am not. After seeing the note they *are* there. By the way, your little girl is very pretty. She reminds me of her mom."

"Listen. I don't know what you want, jerk, but I know this: I want Kristy back. Is she okay?"

"Oh, she's fine. I had to get her attention a time or two so that she would know not to get on my bad side. I think she understands now. Want to speak to her?"

"Yes, and you had better keep your hands off her."

"Daddy?" Kristy's voice was soft. It had a quaver to it that told Jim she was scared.

"Sweetie, are you okay?"

"I'm okay, Daddy. The bad man from my dream got me, Daddy. Was my angels not looking when he came?"

"They are still with you. Please don't make him mad. Just do what he wants. I am going to get you away from him."

"He told me that Mommy is dead. Did he do something bad to her, Daddy?"

"Yes, he did, Kristy. Do you know who he is?"

"I don't know his name, but everyone smiles and waves at him like he is a good guy. He is not good, Daddy. He is a very bad man. I still have your watch. He wants me to give it to him, but I won't let him have it."

"Kristy—"

The gruff voice returned to the receiver. "Listen, Mr. Fender. She can keep the watch. When you get her back, it will be in her grubby little hand. By now, they have begun searching your house because they have discovered that this call is coming from your number. The beauty is I am three blocks from your house. They will find a telephone company van on the side of the road north of your lovely home. Inside the van is a man. He is tied up right now, but you can get him to give you a present."

"Don't do anything to Kristy. You hear me? Don't lay another hand on her!"

Silence.

Jim looked at the picture he still held in his hand and cried. He sat the picture on the coffee table and turned it to face his favorite recliner.

Jim tried to call the police, but every time he picked up the phone all he got was the fast beeping sound that comes when you leave a receiver off the hook. He pulled out his cell phone and dialed 911. Just as the call went through, Larry walked in.

"Who are you calling?"

"The police. The kidnapper called while you were... wherever."

6

About thirty-five minutes after Jim's 911 call, Tommy pulled into the drive, followed closely by a minivan. He watched as Larry walked up to Tommy. Jim could tell by the expression on Tommy's face that he was not happy. Larry kept pointing at the car he had moved. Tommy shook his head a few times and tapped his watch. Larry got in his car and left.

Two men got out of the front of the van, and Tommy joined them as they unloaded several suitcases. Jim watched them from Kristy's window as they came to the door. He thought about letting them wait. After all, they had missed the call; but the thought that the kidnapper might call again any second wouldn't let him. Jim helped them get set up as best he could.

"Jim, this is only a precaution just in case he does call back. I really don't think he will after the last call. I don't know how he might try to contact you, but I doubt it will be by phone." Tommy had a look of doubt on his face as he spoke. "We really haven't had a lot of dealings with this kind of stuff around here. I just want you to be prepared for whatever might happen."

Jim knew exactly what he meant. He knew that whoever had Kristy might find that making safe contact was too difficult. He knew the next time he saw Kristy she might not be alive.

That evening, Jim and Tommy sat watching the Channel 7 News at seven. As the anchor spoke of Susan's death, she said,

"A source from the Port Suni Police Department has informed us that there are as of now no leads in this case…"

Tommy stood bolt upright as if hit with a thousand volts. "Who could have been talkin' to them? It ain't like we don't have any clues. We have the note, we have the knife, and we are checking the van for prints."

"What knife?" Jim asked as he stood to his feet. "You didn't say anything about any knife."

Tommy's frustration could be heard in his voice as he spoke. "The guy in the van had a knife in his pocket. He said the guy who had knocked him out and tied him up had put there. He said he was told it would match what we were lookin' for. We also have the van. The guy drove the van to the relay, where he tapped into your phone line to call you."

Ring!

Jim spun quickly to grab the phone, striking his shin on the coffee table in the process. The jar from the impact caused the family picture to fall off the edge of the table and hit the floor, breaking the glass and the ceramic frame.

"Hello," Jim snapped.

"Jim, Alfred and I will be flying into Sanford International tomorrow."

"Inez, it's good to hear your voice, but I can't come pick you up. Let me make some calls, and I am sure I can find someone."

"No. We already have a rental lined up. I am thinking we will be there no later than about four thirty. We will stop and bring some dinner with us."

"Thanks, Inez."

"Is there anything else we can bring or do?"

"Not a thing. You just be careful on the way."

"Jim, I know this is a tough time for you. If we need to, we can get a room."

"No. I could sure use someone besides the cops to talk to, and you know I have lots of room. But don't feel you have to stay here. There are a lot of reminders here."

"We'll see you tomorrow."

"Inez, I love you and Alfred. Susan was such a lucky person to have ya'll for parents."

"We love you too. I really was trying not to ask, but have you heard anything from Kristy?"

"Yeah. I got a call before the phone tap people got here, and I was able to talk to her for a minute. She was okay then."

"Do they know who they are looking for?"

"Not yet."

"I love you, Jim. Alfred and I will be praying for you."

"I love you too."

When Jim hung up the phone, he took the pieces of the frame from Tommy, who had picked them up during the call. Jim got angry and kicked at the table, striking the same place on his shin that he had hit earlier. He pulled up his pant leg and found that it was bleeding quite heavily. He went to the bathroom, where he cleaned it up and coated it with a triple antibiotic ointment. He wrapped it with gauze and pulled his pant leg down. *Good as new,* he thought as he limped out of the bathroom.

As Jim hobbled back toward the living room, he noticed a few vehicles outside near the road. There were a couple of news vans and a police car or two. Along with them were a few other cars that looked like they were probably just onlookers and thrill seekers. He walked around to the ocean side of the house only to see a news crew busy shooting something he assumed to be for the morning edition.

It wasn't long before the knock came to the door. Some brave reporter asking for an interview stood there with a smile and a microphone.

"Mr. Fender, John Billings, News Nineteen. May I ask you a few questions?"

Jim looked at him for a moment before answering, "Not right now."

"Is there anything we can do to help? Maybe show some pictures, give a description or something?"

Tommy stepped up to the door. "Not right now," he said firmly as he closed it.

"I had hoped we would have a little longer to get things together before the press got hold of this," Tommy said, shaking his head. "I really wanted to have some more information before we started talking."

The rest of the evening was quiet, except for the occasional car door or the distant sound of voices.

7

August 5

Tommy arrived at his office at 7:00 a.m. sharp as he had for five to seven days a week for the past nine years. Police work was all he had ever known or even considered. His dad had been the police chief most of his life. It seemed only natural to follow in his footsteps. His dad had covered for him on many occasions when he was sowing his wild oats; but for the most part, people had liked his dad and considered him a good police chief.

Now Tommy was the chief and his dad, Thomas, had retired. He had big shoes to fill, and he felt that his feet were too small to fill them. No one could ever live up to a man like the great Thomas Sutton.

Tommy now faced the biggest crime he had ever had to solve; and on top of it all, his high school sweetheart was one of the victims. When he called on the voice of experience, Thomas just laughed and said, "You're a smart boy, Tommy. You'll figure a way out."

Tommy opened the bottom right drawer on his oversized desk, reached way in the back, and pulled out his high school yearbook. He placed it on his desk and opened it to the page that had seen the most use, the page that held the pictures of Mrs. Johnson's homeroom. The picture in the center of the page circled in red and having small hearts drawn around it, was Susan Harwood. Just three pictures to the left of that, with a big red X over it, was the picture of James Fender. Two rows down was Thomas Sutton Jr. His picture had a badge drawn on it. Around his name under the picture he had sketched in a knife to give the appearance that his name was written on the blade of the knife.

Tommy thought back to the night on the beach when he had forced Susan to have sex with him and wondered how much would be different if he had just waited until she was ready. He thought of how his dad was always pushing him to have sex with Susan; how he had told him that if he really wanted to, he would make sure nothing happened; that if she said yes it would be okay, and if she said no he should make her. She had, after all, been his girl long enough that she needed to start meeting his needs.

A knock at the door caused Tommy to jump. He slammed the book closed and placed it back in the drawer. Tommy signaled Larry to come in.

"Tommy, I have some good news and some bad news for you. I can't give you one without the other, so hang on."

"Go ahead. Tell me."

"You remember yesterday, that knife I got off the phone guy?"

"Yeah. I remember."

"Well, I thought it looked familiar. It wasn't a store-bought knife. It was one of those custom-made knives that we come across from time to time. You know the biker that we arrested at the public beach area a few months ago, who mugged that girl at knife-point?"

"Yeah. I remember."

"The knife he had was made by that guy over in Orange City. The guy who made it said he received the order over the Internet a month or so earlier, and the dragon inscription on the base of the blade was the customer's request. Well, the knife we got yesterday had that same dragon on it. So I came back to compare other features before heading over to Orange City, and guess what."

"Okay. I give. Tell me. Were they the same?"

"You could say they were the same, exactly the same."

"So have you been to see our friend, the knife-maker, yet?"

"Don't need to. It is the same knife."

Tommy stood to his feet. "What do you mean the same knife?"

"Just that. The knife we had in the evidence room is the same knife. Whoever gave that phone guy the knife got it from here. The lab is checking the knife to see if it could be the murder weapon used on Susan Fender. My guess is yes."

Tommy fell back to his seat. "How could that be possible?"

Larry pulled a chair up close to Tommy's desk and spoke softly, "Tommy, you didn't do this, did you?"

The shocked look on Tommy's face was mingled with fear. "No. Larry, how could you think such a thing?"

"Tommy, most everyone on the force knows you have never forgiven Jim Fender for taking your girlfriend. And who else could have gotten the knife without being noticed? No one."

Tommy sat and stared at Larry in disbelief. He had loved Susan so much that he would have given anything to have her. But that was then, and now he was married.

"If you had anything to do with this, I will do everything I can to help you. Just tell me."

"Larry, no. No, I didn't do anything. How could you even think like that?"

Larry got up and headed toward the door. "Tommy, if I can do anything to help you, just tell me."

Tommy was afraid. He was afraid because of things he had said over the years. He was afraid because he *was* the only one who could have gotten in and out of the evidence room without being noticed. He was afraid because his dad couldn't help him this time.

Alex Carver came to the door and knocked softly. Alex was the only mechanic on the Port Suni Police Department staff. He was not considered the brightest guy in town; but he was an excellent mechanic, and he had an eye for detail. Not only did he keep all the cars running at peak, but he also kept all them washed, waxed, vacuumed, and smelling good.

Tommy and Alex had been good friends for years. Most everyone in town knew Alex. Tommy had pulled him from a burning car after an accident several years ago, and Alex had never forgotten it. Tommy had encouraged Alex to get his mechanics certification and helped him get his job with the department shortly after that. Alex would have gladly done anything Tommy asked.

"Tommy, is this a bad time?"

"No. I was just thinking about a case."

"Let me get your keys for a minute, and I'll go gas up your car for you so you'll be ready."

Tommy unhooked his keys from his belt and tossed them to him. "Thanks, Alex. You're a good friend and a thoughtful employee to boot."

"No prob, boss. I'm just doin' my job. If you ain't in too big o' hurry, I'll run the vacuum over it too."

"I will need it back before too long, but if you wanna take time to vacuum, that'll be okay."

"You got it, boss," Alex said as he turned to go.

Port Suni, being a small town, was not blessed with the most state of the art equipment. But they did have four surveillance cameras set up on the police station property. One of them monitored the public parking lot out front. Another kept watch over the fenced lot where the police fleet was kept. The third watched the reception area. The last camera watched the hallway that supplied the only entrance and exit to the evidence room. Tommy went to the surveillance video machine to check the tape from the evidence room. When he got there, he noticed the tape had already been changed. He went to the shelf where the tapes were placed. August 1, 2, and 3 were all in their places, but August 4 was nowhere to be found.

Tommy was furious. He turned with a jerk and stormed down to the desk with the Larry Phillips's name plate on it.

"Give me the tape, Larry."

"What tape?"

"Don't be stupid, Larry. Give me the tape."

"I don't have a clue what you're talking about. What tape are you looking for?"

There were only two other people in the room, but Tommy noticed he had their attention. He glared at Larry and went back to his office.

The phone rang.

"Chief Sutton."

"Hi. This is Andrea Everson from Channel 7. I was hoping to set up an interview with you today to get an update on the Fender case. People want to know what is going on."

"I know they do. And so do I, but I can't tell you anything right now."

"Oh, so it is true that you really don't have any clues so far."

"No, that is not true. Just none that I am at liberty to speak about right now."

"You know, Chief Sutton, you are going to be under the spotlight until this case is solved. With that Kristy girl still missing and your people apparently doing nothing to find her, you can expect the pressure to just worsen. I can be your friend or your worst nightmare. I prefer friend."

"So do I, but right now, I have an investigation going on."

"Okay then. Let me talk to the dad. Let me run some pictures of the girl. Let me give you some positive coverage so we can scare the creep who has her into making a mistake."

"Okay. I don't see any real harm in that. I'll call Jim and tell him to talk to you. Do you have a number … "

8

Alex returned to his own office and laid Tommy's keys down on the desk. He turned and took the clipboard off the wall that was marked, "Boss's Car." After reviewing the recent entries, he put the date in the first empty box in the left column. He then went out to the parking lot and walked around the car, checking it for any dents or scratches. He reached for the door and remembered that he had left Tommy's keys on his desk. He looked around for a minute, pulled a set of keys from his pocket, put the key with the red plastic top into the door of the car, and unlocked it. He drove around to the gas pump and filled it up.

After recording gallons and mileage, he checked all the fluids. He then pulled up by the vacuum canister and turned it on. He meticulously worked on the floor, getting every speck of sand he could find. Then he continued to suck crumbs out of the seat.

He knew that Tommy was in a hurry, but some things just couldn't be rushed. He never wanted to hear Tommy say, "You missed something." Tommy meant the world to him.

Just as he was about to finish the backseat, he saw the hair on the deck under the back glass.

"Gee, Tommy. I didn't know you picked up anyone yesterday. You must o' picked you up a little girlfriend," Alex said to himself as the long, blonde hair was sucked into the vacuum.

Alex finished the vacuuming and returned the car, clipboard, and keys to their proper places. Taking a look around the lot, he wiped his brow with an exaggerated sweep and proclaimed his day's work to be satisfactorily underway.

9

The interview was underway when Tommy arrived. Jim and Andrea were sitting in the living room.

Jim continued, "...old cliché but she really was my best friend. I could always count on her. It's so hard..." Jim tried to force out the words, but they would not come. Overwhelmed with emotions, he began to cry.

Andrea signaled for the camera man to stop filming. "Jim, You don't have to say anything else if you don't want to. We can take what we have and go with that."

Standing to his feet, he said, "Maybe if we go out on the deck."

The ocean breeze helped him regain his composure. He took a few deep breaths and told Andrea he was ready. The camera resumed filming.

"Every morning Susan would jog down the beach and swim back. She loved the ocean. Yesterday she went..." Jim pointed to the southeast. "She went but did not come back. I found her there, floating."

"Had either of you received any threats or anything that would have given any indication that someone wanted her dead?"

"Nothing. No one. Everything was perfect."

"If you can, tell our listeners what you found when you returned to the house."

"When I saw Susan's body floating, I left Kristy playing in the yard. When I got back, she was gone. After the police arrived, we found a note that confirmed that she had been kid— " He broke into tears again. He paused for a few seconds and then continued. "...She had been kidnapped."

They walked to the side yard and looked at the empty swing set. They looked at the monkey bars that now set monkeyless. They walked up to Kristy's room where the animals kept watch over an empty bed. They stood in the doorway of his bedroom where Susan's side of the bed was still made and his pillow lay damp with tears.

The interview ended with several pictures of Kristy and a plea for anyone having information to please call. Andrea put the pictures in a large envelope and set them with her purse. She then turned her attention to Tommy.

When Andrea had finished the interview, Jim felt a sense of relief, a new hope, and still, a newly reinforced fear that Kristy would not be found. His head was numb, and his eyes felt as if they had cried so much that it would be impossible to shed even one more tear. Even if the interview accomplished nothing by being aired, the process had been good therapy.

Andrea asked Tommy to give her a short interview, and before he could answer, she nodded to the cameraman and began asking questions.

"Chief Sutton, you and I spoke on the phone last night, and you indicated that you do have some clues concerning the Fender case. Can you elaborate on that for me?"

Tommy was completely caught off guard. The look of confusion that highlighted his face spoke out, saying, "I am clueless."

After a couple of moments of silence, he replied, "We do have a couple of things that we are looking at. As I said before, I am not at liberty to discuss them now."

"Have you heard anything else from the perpetrator?"

"No. I have a..." He wanted to say he had the weapon and some fingerprints, but he knew that both were a dead end. "I am not at liberty to say, okay?" He felt like a fool. He couldn't say anything that sounded like he knew anything.

With that, Andrea ended the interview.

Tommy and Jim were both glad when the television crew finally left. Tommy felt better because at least until noon, when the *7 News at Noon* aired, he was off the hot seat. Jim felt better because there was now a point of hope. There was that small possibility that someone would have seen Kristy.

That morning, Jim had spent extra time in prayer. He had asked God if he was being punished. He had begged God to watch over Kristy. He had pleaded with God to show the law enforcement whatever clues they needed to find. He had prayed long and hard; but for the first time in years, he felt as if his prayer was useless. He felt that even the great God who had created everything had no control over this situation. He felt as if Satan himself had stretched out a blanket of sound-proof insulation between the created and the Creator.

"Jimbo, you had breakfast?" Tommy asked, trying to shake off the embarrassment of the interview.

"No. I'm really not hungry."

"You didn't eat lunch yesterday or dinner last night either. Ya can't go on like that. Starvin' yourself to death ain't gonna get either one of 'em back."

"I really don't feel like I could eat anything."

Tommy handed Jim a sausage, egg, and cheese biscuit wrapped in wax paper that he had picked up on the way over from the deli in the grocery store. Jim was surprised that Tommy would have thought to do anything for him.

"Thanks, Tommy."

He opened the wrapper, and within a couple minutes' time, the contents were gone. He really hadn't felt hungry; but when he started eating, he realized his hunger was just numbed by his pain. He felt better after eating.

The two men walked out to the deck and sat facing the ocean. After a couple of minutes of small talk, Tommy began discussing the clues and the lack of them.

"Remember I told you about that knife that was got off that phone guy?

"Yeah."

"We are fairly certain it is the murder weapon. We don't know who used it."

"Somehow I expected that. I guess your response to Andrea's questions led me there."

Being around Tommy brought back some old memories. He thought about some of the basketball games they had played in high school. He remembered a shot that had won the game.

"Tommy, you remember that game we played against New Smyrna where you made that ridiculous shot that saved the game?"

"How could I forget? I amazed myself. You grabbed the ball and ran it almost to half court and passed it to me."

Jim chuckled. "I had no idea you would try a shot from there."

"Truth is, I didn't plan to shoot either, but I tripped and just threw it. I was as shocked as anyone."

"Maybe so, but talk about hero for a day…that was you for sure."

They talked about a lot of games, a lot of plays, and good times in general. They spent time looking back at the bygone days that held little responsibility and less concern. Days when the biggest problem was how to set up the next shot.

There was one particular game that they tried not to talk about. It was an away game where they played Deland High. They were ahead by seven points coming into the second period. Deland stole the ball and ran down court. Deland's best player had the ball. Tommy was running in from the left side of the court and Jim from the right. The ball was up. Jim jumped to block the shot, and so did Tommy. Jim was on his way down and Tommy was on his way up when Jim's left elbow made contact with the bridge of Tommy's nose. Jim went down on the flat of his back, and Tommy went to the local hospital.

They had never been close after that. Both had been benched several times over the next couple of months because of friction between them. Their anger had cost the team a game or two and points almost every time they were on the court together. One game, they had even gotten into a fist fight when the game was over.

As much as he tried to avoid it, Tommy had to say it. With all that was in him, he tried not to mention it, but the anger within him had to come out.

"Do you have any idea what it's like to be called Rudolph all the time? I'll just be walkin' down the street, and some kid will whisper to his friends, 'Hey look. There's Rudolph. I wonder where the other reindeer are?' Every time I look in the mirror, I have a reminder of you."

"Listen, Tommy. You know as well as I do that you were as much at fault as I was. It was an accident. I have told you at least a hundred times that I was sorry. Let it go."

"I can't let it go. You had to rub it in by takin' Susan. Every-thing was just fine, and all of the sudden she was your girl. I had planned to marry her."

"I didn't have anything to do with her dropping you. You just had to be a jerk and force yourself on her. You piece of scum. She loved you, and you had to hurt her like that. You have no idea how much that hurt her."

Tommy felt sick to his stomach and almost blind with anger at the same time. He wished he had just kept his mouth shut, but it was too late to go back and change it now. He wanted to use his night stick across Jim's head or at least practice a few of the things he had learned in his self-defense classes.

By this time, Jim and Tommy were standing face to face, both men so full of rage that one more word would have been all they needed to push them both over the line. They stood and stared into each other's eyes for what seemed an eternity, waiting for a reason to make the first move. Jim was suddenly overwhelmed with emotions and began to cry. He felt as if all his strength had been taken from him. He collapsed to his knees on the floor. The sudden movement startled Tommy. Fueled by the rush of adrenaline and ignited by the rage, Tommy kicked Jim in the chest. Jim fell to his side and began to gasp for air.

Through the kitchen window, Norm and Dale, the two officers assigned to man the phones, had been watching as the events on the deck unfolded. They were listening for the phone, but this was more exciting. The phone taps were in, the tape machine set; all they needed was a call. But a fight would break the boredom without a doubt.

Dale ran out to the deck and grabbed Tommy by the arm. Tommy swung around and put his fist right between Dale's eyes. Dale stumbled backward and fell across the railing on the deck to the ground below.

The sight of Dale going over jarred Tommy back out of his anger. He went from the haze of rage to clarity of fear in a quarter second flat. He ran to the railing and looked over to see Dale lying about twelve feet below and not moving. He ran down the stairs to where Dale was lying. He dropped to his knees, placed two fingers on Dale's neck, and held his breath. There was an unmistakable pulse. Tommy was relieved. A fall like that could have easily snapped a man's neck if the landing was bad.

From up on the deck, Tommy could hear Norm as he was trying to talk Jim through his anxiety attack. But there were other voices. These voices came from somewhere other than the deck. He looked toward the ocean, and his fear escalated. There were four people in sight—four people who had, in all likelihood, seen what just happened; four people who now held Tommy's career in their hands. What concerned him most was that one of them held a camcorder in one hand. If the events from moments earlier had been recorded, he might as well turn in his resignation now.

When Dale opened his eyes and began to speak, Tommy encouraged him to lie still. Dale moved each leg, arm, finger, and toe. One by one, he moved them with thoughtfulness to assure that each was in working order. Then he raised his head and eventually stood to his feet. By the time the two sand-covered men reached the top of the stairs, Norm and Jim were standing and watching their arrival. Jim had pulled himself together and was leaning on the railing with his right hand pressed tightly over the spot on his chest that now held markings from the toe of Tommy's shoe. Norm had a look of disgust on his face as he leered at Tommy.

Tommy kept one hand on Dale's back to support him.

"Norm you keep an eye on things, and I am takin' Dale to the hospital."

"I don't think so," Dale said in a defiant tone. "I am fine." Looking at his sand-covered arms, he continued, "I need a shower, not a hospital."

"Dale, look over the edge here where you fell. You need to let a doctor check you over. A fall like that could really mess you up. Now, come on."

"Okay, I'll go. But, I will drive myself. You stay here in case another call comes in."

After Dale left, Norm took Tommy aside. "Listen Tommy, you need to apologize to Jim. From where we were sitting, we didn't see Jim do anything out of the way."

"You're right. I don't know what came over me." Inside, he did know. He knew that Jim knew about the rape. He also knew that his short fuse had once again been lit, and his lack of self-control kept him from putting it out.

Jim had walked back into the kitchen and poured him a glass of water when Tommy came in.

"Jim, I am sorry. I lost it, and that was uncalled for."

"You're right, Tommy. But, I was almost as ready to strike as you were. It kind of reminds me of our senior year basketball games. Ah, the good ole days."

Both men smiled as they shook hands.

"Norm, if you think you have this, I think I'm gonna take off."

Norm looked at the tape machine and said with a note of sarcasm, "You really think I can push that button all by myself?" Glancing up with a grin, "Take off, boss. I think Jim and I can handle it."

Jim sat back in his recliner and watched himself and Andrea Everson talk about Kristy and Susan on *7 News at Noon*. It was strange and unsettling to see himself on TV. Hearing himself speak and watching himself cry made the loss of his wife and kidnapping of his daughter become more real to him. Music played softly in the background. As he watched himself point to the place where he found his wife's body, he could see her in his mind's eye floating in the pinkish water. A picture of Susan in her winter jogging suit was put on the screen. He felt helpless. If Susan were able to talk to him, she would know what to do.

In the transition from the deck to Kristy's room, a picture of Susan two weeks before Kristy's birth was on the screen for a moment and then faded to be replaced by a picture of Kristy swinging just as she had been yesterday when he watched her from the window. He closed his eyes and watched his memory replay the scene. He kept them closed and listened to Andrea's voice.

"...a compelling story of loss and hope. If anyone has seen Kristy please call the Port Suni police or notify us here at News 7. The numbers and e-mail are on the bottom of the screen." The music faded to silence.

"We will be back with a short message from Police Chief, Tommy Sutton, after this short break..."

Jim picked up his remote and pressed the red power button. The TV became silent and blank. He continued to sit with his eyes closed thinking about times past. Susan's memory called him back to the week of their first anniversary. They had taken a vacation that was to include one day stops in Savanna, Myrtle Beach, and in Bluefield, West Virginia. In Bluefield, they went horseback riding at a state park. When they returned to the hotel room, Jim pulled out a map and spread it over the table, looking over the route home.

Susan walked over to the table and pointed her finger at Bluefield on the map. "What if we go there tomorrow?" A puzzled expression covered Jim's face. He looked back at the map and said, "That's where we are."

"So, why don't we stay?"

"Why?"

"I want to ride again. That was so much fun!"

The next morning they found a privately owned stable that offered rides along the banks of New River. He remembered watching her as she rode. She laughed and carried on like a kindergartener on a carousel.

He opened his eyes and looked around. Standing to his feet, his eyes drifted to the chair that Susan often sat in with Kristy on her lap. "I miss you," he said.

Norm raised his head from the game of solitaire he was involved in and replied, "You talkin' to me?"

"No. No, I was talking to my Susan and Kristy."

Jim walked to the dining room table and sat with Norm. They talked briefly, being careful not to mention the events of the day. After small talk had been exhausted, Jim finally asked the real question on his mind.

"Norm, do you think Kristy will be found?"

"I don't know. I hope so..." Norm trailed off and stopped. He realized that what he wanted to say was probably not what Jim needed to hear.

"You think she is dead, don't you?"

"Jim, I didn't say that. I just don't know."

Ring!

Norm put on his headphones and gave Jim the nod.

"Hello?"

"Jim, it's Inez. I just wanted to let you know we will be boarding the plane in just a few minutes."

"You guys doing okay?"

"Yeah. Alfred hasn't been himself, but I am sure it's just the shock."

In the background, he could hear the announcement for flight 147 to Atlanta boarding at gate eight.

"They're callin' for us now. See ya at about four thirty."

10

Tommy arrived back at his office at 11:47 a.m. He sat in his office and watched Andrea in her interview with Jim. After a commercial break, he watched in embarrassment as he babbled out a mouth full of nothingness for the world to see. He felt total humiliation when he heard the applause from his co-workers in the other offices.

After taking a moment to regain his composure, he pulled out some forms from his desk and began to fill in the blanks concerning an officer injury. On the lower part of the form where it asked for statement from eye witnesses, he wrote, "I was standing on the deck with Jim Fender when Officer Dale Abernathy came running out of the house. I assumed he had some news concerning the case. As he approached me, his foot caught on the leg of a lawn chair, and he tripped and fell over the edge. I tried to catch him, but he was just out of reach. When he went over, he struck his head on the railing and then landed the ground."

As Tommy filled out the papers, he didn't notice Larry standing in the hallway, looking in at him through the small window in his door. Tommy had always considered Larry a good friend and an excellent cop. Larry had helped on many occasions, coming up with the clue that everyone else missed. He seemed to have a knack at knowing how the criminal mind worked even when logic was tossed out the window.

Tommy pulled out a stamp and ink pad from the top drawer and stamped the top sheet, "Complete." He tore off the top sheet and put the rest in the second drawer of the filing cabinet in the back of the office. He took the top sheet to his secretary to be filed for insurance.

On his way to the secretary's desk, Tommy glanced over at the video tapes from the surveillance machine. August 1, 2, 3, and 4 were standing noticeably on the lower shelf by themselves. It wasn't until after he had dropped the forms with the secretary and was headed for the door that he realized the tape he had been looking for was right there on the end. Tommy picked up the August 4 tape and carried it with him.

After going out to the parking area and retrieving his sunglasses from over the visor of his squad car, he went into the garage to sign his car back in for the day. Alex met him at the door with a puzzled look on his face.

"What's up, boss?" he asked with a bit of confusion in his voice. "Are you sick or somethin'? I ain't never seen you leavin' this early."

"No, Alex. I just have a bunch of things on my mind that I need to sort out."

"Hey, boss. I saw you on the TV earlier. That was pretty cool. You's a TV star now, kinda like that ole show with Boss Hogg, only you're Boss Sutton."

Tommy really didn't like the comparison. After all, Boss Hogg always came out looking like an idiot. But he knew Alex didn't mean anything bad by it.

"Thanks, Alex. I'm going home now."

"Later, Boss Sutton." Alex broke out into a chuckle.

Tommy signed the log that Alex kept on his car and hung it back in its place on the wall. As he walked out to his own car, he looked at the tape and rubbed it thoughtfully, wondering what clue it might hold about the knife. As he reached his car, he was again struck with a feeling of stupidity and frustration when he thought about the possibility of fingerprints on the tape case. Any that had been there would have surely have been wiped off by now, and to take it in and ask to have it checked at this point would only show off his ignorance. Even if it did have someone else's prints on it, they would surely be someone who was on the force and nothing unusual.

Larry watched from the side window of his office as Tommy kicked his tire, and he chuckled. "Sutton, you're about as dumb as they come." He watched as Tommy got in his Crossfire and drove away. He watched as Alex walked out to Tommy's squad car, the one with the big 01 on the roof, and began his inspection and cleaning. "And there goes dummy number two."

11

Tommy arrived at his dad's house around 2:30. He sat in his car for another minute or so, listening to a CD he had ordered to help boost self-esteem and build confidence in leadership. So far, he had heard nothing that he didn't already know. In his mind, he could hear that all-too-familiar voice that told him what an idiot he was.

"One thing you've learned from this series of educational stuff is not to waste your money on educational stuff," he said as he stepped out of the car.

Tommy slammed the door to the car as he turned toward the front door. He was already playing out the scene he knew was coming up inside. He had never been good enough at anything to suit his dad. In school, even though he held an A-B average and played basketball on the number-one team in the division, it wasn't good enough. When he had first come to the force, Thomas had ridden him hard to make good choices and do his best. He excelled at it, and when his dad had retired, Tommy was a shoe-in for the open position. But his dad had said, "It's a good thing for you that everyone thinks I was a good cop or you'd be out of a job."

He had nothing to go on, and someone inside the force had to be helping the culprit. He was sure that his dad could offer some advice, but would he give it? How long of a "you're not worthy to hold the position" speech would he have to endure before he would finally get to the answer?

Tommy learned very shortly after his mother passed away not to come in his dad's house without knocking. He had gone over one evening to check up on his father after trying to call and getting no answer. He had opened the door and come rushing in. His dad instinctively pulled his revolver and pointed it at him. The look in his eyes said he'd been crying. Tommy had yelled out in fear. He realized it was just a reaction to the surprise, but he didn't want to be looking down the barrel of his dad's gun again.

Tommy knocked three hard raps. He heard the rustling of paper from the inside. The door opened.

"Boy, get in here. Have you lost your mind, or are you just a complete idiot?"

"Hi, Dad," Tommy said with his head hung low. "It's good to see you too."

"I am glad you came over but that thing on TV. Sheesh. That was the worst display of idiocy I have ever seen. Ain't I taught you nothing about how to talk to reporters? You gotta be strong and you have to make 'em believe you have it all together. Ya blew it, boy."

"I know, Dad, but I have a bunch of issues to deal with on this one, things I can't say, things that I wish weren't true."

Thomas looked carefully at his son. He wished in his heart that Tommy could have been a stronger, manlier man. He wished he hadn't been such a momma's boy. He wished that Tommy would have been more like him, willing to do what it takes to get what you want.

Thomas had never realized that Tommy wanted nothing more than to please him. Tommy had worked so hard to play basketball because he knew that his dad loved to watch it on TV. Tommy struggled through his schooling, staying up all hours of the night, trying to keep his name on the honor roll. Tommy had even raped his girlfriend just to please his dad.

What Thomas saw was his wife always making a big deal over everything the boy did. In his mind, it was all for her. And even though he had suggested the rape and had enjoyed getting a peek, retrospect had only turned that into just one more thing Tommy had to be bailed out of.

"Dad, I have a problem. I know I screwed up. I know you could be doing a better job pacifying the media. I know you would have never let this thing get out of control. I know a lot of things, but I need help."

"What's such a problem?"

"I wish it was just a problem. It is a pile of problems. It's a huge pile of unexplainable problems."

"Okay. Tell me."

"Dad, the murder weapon was stolen from the evidence room. The surveillance tape from yesterday was missing. Now it has turned up. The phone van we checked for prints showed nothing helpful. You saw the TV thing. Everything we have points to the department. If anyone in the department has a motive, it's me. What can I do? What am I missing?"

"I know you didn't do it, boy. It ain't in ya. But by now I thought you might have been doing something about it."

"Yeah. I did. I kicked Jim in the chest and knock one of the guys off the deck and he is at the hospital now. Yeah. I did something all right. I lost it."

"That ain't what I meant. I meant do something, something about the evidence, something about motives."

"What in the world are you talkin' about, Dad? I am not following you."

"You remember the case out in California where this guy killed his wife and took her out in a boat and threw her in?

She was preggers, so when he got caught, they charged him with both murders."

"Yeah. I remember."

"It really wouldn't take a lot to manipulate the evidence to make it look like Jim did it."

"What?"

"Think about it, boy. Who found the body? Had he called anyone for help before a passerby saw him holding her? Who had her blood on his hands and shirt when you got there? Has anyone else heard from this so-called kidnapper? Even when Jim was contacted, it was not when anyone else could verify it."

"Dad, do you have any idea what you're suggesting I do? That would be wrong."

"Boy, listen. Either you will go down for this or you need to get the spotlight off you for a while until you can sort this out. But I think your old buddy Fender ought to fry for it anyway. If he wouldn't have messed up your nose, Susan would've been yours anyway. Were there any fingerprints or blood on the knife?"

"No. Why?"

"Cause all they can prove about the knife is that it *may* have been the murder weapon. They cannot say for sure that it was."

"I don't know. That's askin me to send someone away for something they didn't do."

"Son, are you sure he didn't do it? Can you prove he didn't?"

"No, but when we get his little girl back, that will be a problem. She will tell whatever she knows."

"She ain't comin' back. You might as well know that now. She will die."

"What? How do you know that? We might find her and… Dad, what do you know that I don't?"

"There's more going on here than you need to know, son. Just take my advice and leave it alone. Pin it on Fender. You know you can. With a little funding in the right pockets, we can have all the witnesses we need. There might even be a girlfriend or two."

"Dad, I love ya, and I know you were a great cop, but you're scarin' me. Did you do this? Did you kill Susan?"

"No. Have you ever thought of me as stupid? No. Of course I didn't do it. I wouldn't take a chance at getting my hands in the middle of something like this. C'mon, boy. Give me a little credit."

Thomas walked into the kitchen and picked up the phone. "Boy, I tell ya what. Let's have some pizza, and I'll give you some heads-up. How 'bout it?"

"Whatever."

After Thomas had ordered the pizza, he took Tommy out in the backyard.

"Boy, look around. You see how nice this yard is, how nice the pool is, even how nice my house is?"

"Yeah, Dad. I see. I've seen it a lot of times."

"Have you ever wondered how I got all this and was able to travel so much on a cop's salary? Didn't you ever question that? Don't you find it odd that when you told me which house you were buying I had cash to pay for it for you? And that silly Crossfire you drive. How'd I have money to buy that?"

"I just thought you had done well in the stock market or in saving or something. I really hadn't given it much thought."

"Well now, boy, I think you should be askin' yourself if you could do this off of what you make. Interest that good or that kind of luck in the market, it ain't happenin' is it? So the obvious question oughta be, 'So how's a guy that makes the same money I make get so well off?' When ya ponder that one a few minutes, I am sure a few other questions will come to mind."

"So was the financial backing for the great Sutton empire built on inherited money?" Tommy asked with an exaggerated sarcasm in his voice. "Really, Dad. I don't get the point or how your *empire* will help me in the situation."

"Go in the kitchen and grab me a beer, and I will tell you a story that'll make a man out of ya."

When Tommy went into the kitchen and opened the fridge, he was surprised to find that the only thing there besides the condiments in the door was a leftover pizza and a case of dark beer with three missing.

When he returned to the patio, Thomas had made his way into the pool. As he rose out of the water, the fact that his hair was thinning became quite evident.

"Just put it in one of those can holder things, and I'll be out in a minute or two. Just coolin' off a bit and enjoyin' the water."

Tommy sat down in one of the lounge chairs and leaned back. He allowed his mind the freedom to drift back across the events of his childhood. He couldn't remember having any financially hard times at all; but often, kids are not aware of the struggles their parents go through. He did, however, remember taking a lot of trips during the summer. They would usually take at least two big trips a year, cruises to the Bahamas, flights to California, England, and even twice to Australia. Although he had never given it much thought, he had been to more places than anyone else he knew.

When he was sixteen, he drove a new Mustang. He got a second new Mustang when he graduated high school. His clothes were the best, and he always had the latest and the greatest when it came to any kind of technology. He realized now that it was foolish to think all this could have been afforded on his dad's salary.

His mom had never worked outside the home. He had heard her say that his dad had promised her that if she would marry him, he would make sure everything was good enough financially that she could stay home and raise the kids. She had been disappointed that they had only had one child, but she had loved Tommy enough for a dozen.

"Tommy, door. Go get the pizza and pay the man. Okay?"

Tommy jumped to his feet. He had no clue how long he had sat there and drifted in thought, but apparently, it was long enough for a pizza to get cooked and delivered. He rushed to the door and returned momentarily with the pizza in hand.

"Grab you a brew from the fridge, boy, and let's do some damage on this pepperoni pie."

Tommy went to the kitchen and got himself a glass of water. He really didn't like beer, and he felt like it would be best if he kept his mind clear. He returned to the lounge chair, grabbed a slice of pizza, and leaned back.

"What's wrong, boy? My beer ain't good enough for ya?"

"No, Dad. Your beer is fine. I just think it'll be better if I don't drink right now."

"Yeah. You're right. When you leave you might get pulled over." Thomas grinned at the thought of his own humor.

"So, Dad, what's the big secret to your success, and what does it have to do with this case?"

"Son, you sure you don't want a beer? What I have to say might be kind of hard to swallow without some alky to wash it down."

"I'll take my chances. Just tell me."

"You know I was chief for twenty-five years, most of your life. I was a good cop for the most part."

"Yeah. So I've heard you say, and I get reminded of it all the time. But you're not now, and I need help with now."

"Just hold on a second, and I'll get there. Patience is a virtue, boy. Anyway, one day, some idiot kid robbed the bank on Oak Street. I chased him in my car, and when I caught up with him, he stopped. He jumped out and pulled a gun. He left me no choice, so I killed him. He didn't have a mask or anything, so he was easy enough identified by the tellers. The money was never found. Well, actually, it was. Just not turned in. That made a nice bonus.

"It wasn't long till another yahoo tried to knock off the convenience store over on Babcock. He threw the bag of money out the window while I was chasing him. I spent some of the money in cash, but I started making little deposits. I never put in more than I made, but I had found a new source of income, and so we started doing things with it.

"I never told your mom where the money came from. I just said that it was perks of the job or a bonus or something. She was a good woman. She took good care of you, and I took good care of her."

"Yeah, but, Dad, it ain't supposed to be that way. Cops are supposed to be the good guys. You told me so yourself."

"Son, just listen. I kinda got used to changin' things on the reports, and it got easier. Actually, I got excited at the possibility of getting more when there was a robbery. After I had kept the money from four in a row, I got worried that someone would get wise to me, so I decided not to keep more than one in four.

When I had been chief about six years, one of my men lost his temper and shot an unarmed drunk, killed him right there on the side of the road in a sobriety test. Bill's wife had been cheating on him, and he was really stressed. The drunk was calling him some names he didn't like, so he shot him. He called me on the radio and said he needed some help. When I got there and saw what had happened, we took the body to the beach. We looked at his wounds and determined that the bullet had passed all the way through him. After we took everything off the body, we threw it in. We parked his car in the lot by the jetties. Two days later, when they found what was left of his body, it was determined that he had fallen on the rocks and into the water. It looked like a couple sharks had helped us with that one."

"Dad, please tell me you're lying."

"I ain't finished. Just wait. I've been waiting a long time to tell someone about all this. Now shut up and listen.

"I really felt bad for the guy's family, but they got a nice insurance check, and the woman was married again in less than two years. It all worked out okay.

"Bill committed suicide about six months after that. He never could get over it. I told him he just needed to toughen up and be a man. He just couldn't do it.

"Anyway, when you pulled that stunt on the beach with that Susan girl, I had already figured out how to make things look any way I wanted them to. I had even robbed a store myself and put some loudmouth jerk in jail for it. He spent eighteen months behind bars because he wanted to threaten me.

"I was set financially. My job was secure. My life was good. Then you got your nose busted and people started laughing at you. You lost your girlfriend. What made it worse was that the guy that messed up your nose had your girl. He married her, and you had to settle for second best, not what you wanted, but seconds. I watched you sit outside and cry I can't even count the times. I knew you were hurting. But if other people saw you out there being such a wuss, they'd be sayin' stuff like, 'Them Sutton boys can't handle anything.'

"I said then that I'd make all them Fenders pay, not just Jim, 'cause he was just an offshoot of the rest o' them scuzzies. When you joined the force and got married, I kind of lost sight of that vow until a couple years ago. You and Janet were having problems in your marriage. Remember that?"

"Yeah, Dad, but—"

"No buts. Listen. I started watching her. I followed her one Saturday night up to the Starlight in Daytona. She went in, and within five minutes, guess who else showed up?"

Tommy could hardly believe what he was hearing. But he had to ask the obvious. "Jim?"

"No. That other Fender boy, Jerome."

Tommy jumped to his feet. "No, Dad. Tell me it wasn't you who killed Jerome. Please, tell me—"

"Boy, shut up and sit down. This is hard enough without you goin' all bonkers on me.

"When they came out of the bar a little over two hours later, they were holding hands and kissin' right out there in public. Can you imagine what people would have said about you if they'd seen that? They'd said, 'Them Sutton boys don't know how to keep a woman happy, or she'd be home with him.'

"I couldn't let people be talkin' about you like that, so I followed him most of the way home. That was right after I bought the red Blazer. I really didn't know what I was gonna do. No real plan at all. I guess I was thinking a good scare would fix the problem.

I don't think it took him too awful long to realize that he was being followed 'cause he started makin' some weird turns and then started speeding up. We were runnin' better than a hundred when he lost control and ran off the road. I didn't stop because I didn't want him to know who was following him. The next morning, they found his car against a tree with him dead in it. Anyway, it served him right messin' with your wife like that."

"Dad, I really don't think I want to hear anything else."

"Boy, I'm gonna finish. I need to tell you just a few more things. Grab ya another slice and listen.

"I saw those goody-two-shoes Fender folks falling apart. They were really upset. That made me happy. I mean, it really felt good to me. So I thought, 'Your boys have caused me so much heartache, so let me show you some more.' I went out and hired me some people to console them and got some pictures. After sending a few now and then to each of them, boom. Divorce. You talk about a plan comin' together. That one did.

"Now I'm not gonna say I know anything for sure about what's goin' on now, but I won't say I don't either. You can figure it out if you want to. I just don't want to see that family or any part of it causing you any more problems."

"Tell me what you know about Kristy!"

"Son, I told you that I may not know anything. But, if I did, I couldn't consider telling you 'cause you would screw it up, just like you do everything else. Believe me, it's best this way."

Tommy sat dumbfounded for a few moments. When he finally was able to process a little of what he had been hearing, he wasn't sure if he wanted to talk. He sat and stared at the man he thought he knew, realizing that he did not.

"Dad, why did you tell me all that? You know I am going to have to investigate it, and you'll go to prison. I really don't want to do that, but I have to."

Thomas just looked at him and laughed, not just a gentle chuckle but a roar. He laughed so hard that tears streaked his face. His laughter scared Tommy.

"Dad, pull it together. I am serious. I will have to do something."

Thomas forced himself to stop laughing. "Boy, yeah, you gotta do something all right or you're going to jail. But you're smart. Let Jim fry, and you'll be fine. As for me, you and anyone else you might think is on your side ain't smart enough to prove anything. And as of right now, I deny ever saying any of it."

Tommy drove back to the station, silent and confused. He still could not believe his dad was capable of those things, but he also knew his dad was right about this case. He had to do something, or he would fry for this. He also knew that if his dad really were involved in this, his tracks would be well covered.

One of the biggest things that had Tommy puzzled was that Thomas had taken no responsibility for putting him up to "that stunt" with Susan.

He was also hurt knowing that his wife had been cheating on him. He felt, to some extent, numb. He loved Janet and wasn't sure how to deal with it. His knee-jerk reactions had gotten him in too much trouble, so he decided he would try to put this aside until a more opportune time when he had more time to think it through. "What a world," he said to himself. "Find out your dad's a loon and your wife has been cheating on you, all in one day."

He pulled back into the lot at the station. The clock on his dash read 3:54 p.m. He looked around and noticed that his squad car wasn't there. Just as he was walking into the garage, Alex pulled in. Tommy thought he looked a bit more cheerful than usual. He also hoped he wouldn't start calling him Boss Sutton.

Alex walked into the garage whistling "Yankee Doodle" and snapping his fingers. When he saw Tommy standing there, he stopped whistling, and the smile left his face.

"Ya gotta squeak I was tryin to figure out, boss. Had it long?"

Tommy had no idea what squeak Alex was talking about; but that was what made Alex such a good mechanic, his eye and ear for detail. There was no doubt in Tommy's mind that Alex would get it taken care of, whatever it was.

Back at the Sutton house, Thomas sat deep in thought about times past. Many of his memories were good, and many were not. As he reflected and drifted, his mind kept going to the night his older brother, Frank, died. It seemed that night was when all his trouble started.

Frank was seventeen and full of ideas, ideas about how to get away with anything and everything. He had his parents completely fooled. They would have never believed that it was him who had stolen the neighbors' car and set it on fire. They didn't believe he was guilty when the school had called and told them Frank was selling dried parsley rolled up in cigarette papers, calling it pot. No. Not Frank. He would never do anything wrong. He was the good child.

They didn't believe Thomas when he told them the party was Frank's idea and that Frank had even lined up getting booze for the evening. But everyone else believed it. They all knew the truth. They all knew that "them Sutton boys" could really have some fun and cause trouble, that is, if Frank was doing the planning. But if it wasn't for Frank being like he was, them Sutton boys would be worth absolutely nothing. Once, Thomas had asked Frank why he worked so hard at being sneaky. His reply was ingrained in his head like the grooves on a vinyl record and played over and over as if the groove had been scratched. Frank looked him in the eye, placed his hand on his shoulder, and said in as serious a tone, "Listen up, Tommy. I do it as much for you as for me. See, I don't want to hear them say that them Sutton boys can't do nothing right. As long as everything goes good, they say that them Sutton boys can do anything. You, my little brother, are one of them Sutton boys. You are, and you always will be. Even after I'm gone, you will be."

Frank talked one of his older friends in to bringing him some booze and collected five dollars from each guy who attended to pay for it. He told all the guys to tell their parents they were going to be surf fishing for the night. The three girls that came, Kathy Shaw, Karen Summers, and Mandy Harrington, had each told their parents that they were spending the night at one of the other girls' homes. The plan was as close to flawless as they could figure.

Thomas had asked Kathy to go steady with him two weeks earlier. This would be the first time they had had any time together without any adults around. Kathy had said no to the party several times before Thomas finally convinced her to come.

The party was at the beach, at the location the guys had told their parents they would be fishing. The fishing poles were standing in the holders to give the illusion that they were really fishing if any of the parents happened to ride by to check. There was a full moon, six guys, three girls, two fifths of Southern Comfort, and a case of Miller ponies.

One of the guys who had refused to come to the party was really fishing just out of sight, south of the party, with his father. Thomas had wanted Mark Fender to be there, but Mark had just made up some comment about not wanting to be around when Thomas, his temper, and alcohol got together. He also had said that he and his dad were planning on spending time together, loading up an ice chest or two with Blue fish. Mark and his dad always seemed to be doing things together.

Close to an hour had passed, and each of the guys had downed a few shots of Comfort and a beer or two when they started feeling the urge to prove their manhood. It started with arm wrestling and a couple rounds of uncle. At the end of the night, no one would remember who had won any of the challenges.

As natural progression dictated, it wasn't long before a swimming challenge was issued. The guys divided up into three teams of two. The girls would each throw an empty beer bottle into the ocean, and the guys would swim out after them. Each team would get one point for each bottle they brought in. Before they started, the agreement was that they would do it ten times, and the team with the most points at the end would be the winner. Frank added a rule that each of the guys had to drink one shot of Comfort between rounds. Frank drank three each time "just to make it fair." As Thomas recalled, the other kids called their team simply "Them Sutton Boys." After the rules were made and the team lines were drawn, they were ready for anything.

It was round six, and the bottles were thrown. When they hit the water, a school of mullet broke the surface. All of them knew they shouldn't swim in with the fish because of the probability of a shark coming in for a meal. The problem was that the team that chickened out would forfeit the game. So out they swam. The bottles were retrieved. When that round ended, Them Sutton Boys led the game by two points—not exactly a commanding lead, but good enough for Thomas to shout out a few brags and an insult or two.

Frank placed his hand on Thomas's shoulder, "Let's just quit. There's no way they can catch us, so why embarrass them anymore?"

The Blonde Boys contested, "We ain't giving up that easy!"

"I guess we'll just have to show 'em, huh, Frank."

Frank pulled Thomas to the side and called back to the others, "Excuse us, fellows, while we discuss some strategy."

"What's goin' on, Frank? You ain't wimpin' out on us are ya?"

Frank looked at the water and then back at Thomas. "No. I don't feel right for one, and for two, I saw something. I don't know what it was, but there was something in the water lookin' at me."

"Come on, Frank. I got Kathy over there, and I really don't want her to think that us Sutton boys are quitters. Can we go just one more round?"

"Even if we quit, everyone will know we would have won anyway."

"Please, Frank. Just one?"

"Okay, one, and that is it!"

"Cool beans. One it is."

Frank addressed the group. "Listen up. This round is for all the marbles. The winner of this round wins it all. Fair enough?"

An affirmative vote was taken.

Three shots later, Frank was in the water for round seven. Two bottles were directly in front of him, and Thomas was right behind him. He reached for the bottles and just stopped.

"Grab the stupid bottles!" Thomas yelled. Frank didn't move. Thomas swam as hard as he could, but just as he got around Frank, The Blonde Boys made off with them both. Thomas turned and headed back to the shore. As soon as he stood to his feet, he began the lecture.

"What was that? You just gave the whole thing away. If you were that dead set on loosing, why even agree to go another stupid round?"

"Cool off, Thomas. It ain't nothing but a game. We could tell everyone you won, but why lie when the truth is so much more fun?" one of the Blonde Boys offered.

Thomas looked around for Frank, realizing he hadn't seen him come out of the water.

"Frank?" Thomas said, trying to see him in the group.

"Frank!" he yelled.

Looking out at the water, he saw him still floating in about the same place he let the game slip away.

"Not funny, Frank! Get up here!"

No sign of movement.

Almost simultaneously, the five guys hit the water.

When they got Frank's body to the shore, there was no pulse and no sign of breathing. The girls began to scream, and all the guys tried to work together to do CPR as best as they knew how.

A couple of minutes later, the Fenders came running up. Mr. Fender checked for a pulse and then took Frank in his arms and rushed him to the hospital. Thomas's father told him later that Frank had died of alcohol poisoning and nothing was going to bring him back.

Mark stayed at the beach with the other kids to help keep Thomas under control. But Thomas knew that wasn't why. Thomas knew that Mark was only there to steal his girl, the girl that eventually became Mrs. Mark Fender, the girl whose son was now getting what all the Fenders had deserved all along.

Thomas was convinced that in some strange way, he was responsible for his brother's death. That night, when he got home, he made a promise that he would do everything he could to live up to the image Frank had set up for all them Sutton boys.

12

Kristy sat on the bed in the small room she had been locked in and petted the cats. There were three of them. One was calico. Her name was Missy. One was black with a white triangle on his chest. His name was Super Dude. The last one was black with a touch of white at the end of one foot. His name was Tippy.

The room she was in was a small bedroom with only a few furnishings. There was a window, but it had shutters closed over the outside so all she could see looking out was down at the grass. There was a bed, a nightstand, a dresser, and a little bookshelf. The bookshelf had several children's books on it, and the top shelf had a TV. Kristy had watched *Sesame Street* and *Barney* this morning.

On the wall were several pictures of different people she had never seen before and a couple of the bad man. On the dresser in the corner opposite the door sat some pictures of people she did know. Two of them were of the police officer who the kids at daycare had called Rudolph. Some were of her mommy, some were of her daddy, and a couple of them were of her. It looked as if the pictures of her and her parents had been taken at their home from the beach area.

She missed her mommy and daddy a great deal. She held tightly to her dad's watch every time the bad man came in because it made her feel safer. But she would rather have been holding his hand.

She had spent a lot of time alone since the bad man took her, a lot of time for a little girl to have to think. At first, she had spent most of her time curled up on the bed, crying; but then the bad man had taken her out and let her talk to her dad on the phone. He put tape on her wrists and ankles so she couldn't "do anything stupid." The bad man had told her that he had killed her mommy and if she didn't be good he would kill her too. He hadn't really done anything bad to her. He was actually kind of funny to watch. He did everything carefully. The house was very clean. When he came in, he wiped off everything. Even the ceiling fans had no dust on them. As soon as they finished eating, he washed all the dishes, wiped out the sink, cleaned off the stovetop, and swept the floor in both the kitchen and the dining room. He had given her a bucket to use if she needed to go to the bathroom and another bucket filled with ice and bottles of water in case she got thirsty when she was locked in. She tried really hard to not have to go; but after a while, she did. As soon as he had come in afterward, he just smiled and took it to the bathroom, emptied it, washed it out with Lysol, and brought it back. Even though Kristy was lonesome and scared, she was also excited. The bad man had told her before he left this morning that she could see her dad today and talk to him on the phone. She was happy. The bad man had let her draw a picture and put some letters on it to let her dad know she loved him. The picture was a big heart with a man holding hands with a girl inside of it. Across the top she wrote in her best penmanship, "Kristy loves Daddy."

She heard the car as it pulled into the carport. She heard the keys as they rattled at the door. She heard him as he walked across the room toward the room she was in. She could hear him moving things outside the room and then the rustling of his keys again. He had a lot of keys.

The door opened with a sudden jerk. He stepped in. "C'mon, girl. Don't just sit there. Let's go see what Mr. Fender might be up to today."

Kristy jumped off the bed and ran toward him. He jumped back, and a sudden cold look crossed his face that scared her. She stopped.

"Look at that bed. We can't leave a mess like that. Are you such a grub at home?"

"I'm sorry, mister. I just don't know how to fix it."

"Pay attention, and I will show you. From now on, as long as you are here, you will fix the bed."

"Yes, sir."

She watched as he made the bed. He was careful to get all the wrinkles out, and he took time to pick a few cat hairs off the covers.

"You see how easy that was?"

"Yes, sir."

"Okay. That is your job, okay?"

"Yes, sir." Kristy was afraid it wouldn't look as good when she did it, but she knew she had to try.

"C'mon already. I don't have much time."

Kristy held out her hands and asked, "Mister, are you gonna tape me again?"

"Are you gonna be good?"

"Yes, sir."

"Then no. For now, I will trust you. If you do something stupid, I will hurt you and tape you, okay?"

"Okay."

When they got to the kitchen, he stopped and pulled a canning jar out of the cabinet and the Windex out from under the sink. He sprayed the inside of the jar with the Windex and then dried it out, being careful that his bare fingers did not touch the inside of the jar. He then had Kristy fold and

EYES OF THE OCEAN

roll the picture and put it inside the jar. He wiped out the inside of the lid and carefully put it on and tightened it. Then he sprayed and wiped the outside. When he finished, the jar sat spotless on the counter.

He put on the hat and sunglasses that were usually kept on top of the microwave. Kristy thought he looked a lot like the guy all the kids called Rudolph when he had them on, except his nose wasn't red.

"Grab it, Grub, and let's go," he said as he pointed at the jar. He looked in the mirror, tipped his hat forward, and smiled. He pulled a large ring of keys from his pocket and twirled them around his finger. He picked up a small can of cooking spray and put it in his pocket.

Kristy picked up the jar and carried it. She had no idea why the man had been so careful to put it in a clean jar. In her mind, she just thought he was being too clean again. Whatever the reason, her dad was soon going to have a letter from her. She was happy.

They went out to the carport and got in the police car and drove for about twenty minutes. Kristy was sure they had driven past the ice cream store at least twice where, on hot days, her mommy used to take her. They stopped at a payphone just down from it. He told Kristy to sit still until he called her.

The bad man pulled out his wallet and two prepaid phone cards and a piece of scrap paper with a phone number written on it, with "Jimbo's cell" written over it. He dialed the 800 number to the first card, put in his pin number, and then repeated the process with the second card. After listening to the sales pitch, he dialed the number on the paper.

Kristy could hear the bad man talking. He was making his voice sound really mean, just like he had when he called her dad last time. After just a minute, he hung up the phone and got back in the car.

"Mister, you're not gonna let me talk to my daddy, are you?"

"Yes, I am, grubby. Just listen to me, and do like you're told. By the way, when you think about me when I ain't there, what do you call me?"

"I dunno."

"Yes you do. Please tell me."

"I call you the bad man."

"That's cool. I like that. Kinda. From now on, you call me 'bad guy,' okay? Or you can just call me 'guy' if you don't want to say 'bad guy,' okay?"

"Okay, Mr. Bad Guy."

"No. Don't call me mister. I didn't tell you to say mister, did I? Just call me bad guy."

"Okay, Bad Guy."

They were now stopping on the side of the road south of Kristy's house. Next to where they were parked was a path that went down through the palmettos and lead to the beach. Guy opened the trunk and got out a telescope. He took off his shirt and hat and put them in the spot vacated by the telescope. Guy rapidly opened the back door to let Kristy out. Kristy carried the letter-holding jar with her. He turned and walked down the path carrying the telescope, and she followed. Kristy thought the telescope was exactly like her daddy's.

The telescope was large and had a tripod attached. Guy sat it up and looked through it up the beach. He looked both directions and smiled.

"Look in here, Kristy, and you can see your daddy. That's your house up there, and that's your dad on the deck. You can't see him good unless you look in this."

Kristy had used her dad's telescope before to look at some of the planets and the stars. She had been so happy when her dad had taken time to sit with her and tell her about how God had put all those planets and stars up there just for us to see His power and to give us light at night.

Kristy looked in the eyepiece. She really could see her dad. He looked like he had been crying, and he was holding his cell phone in one hand and his side with the other. He was up against the railing on the deck and kept looking back and forth. Finally, he looked her way and squinted. He saw her. She could tell. He smiled and waved a big wave. She started jumping up and down and waving too. She was so happy. She forgot about Guy for a second and started running toward her dad. She only made it a few steps before Guy grabbed her.

"Listen up, grub. I told you to behave. Now I gotta hurt ya."

"Please, mister. Please don't hurt me. I forgot."

"What did you call me? I told you not to call me mister."

"I'm sorry. I'll call you Guy. I am sorry. Please don't hurt me."

"Just shut up and bury the jar here. Then we'll go, and you can talk to your old man on the telephone."

When the jar was buried, Kristy watched as Guy wrote something in the sand and drew an arrow pointing to where the jar was buried and a circle around where the jar was. They started back toward the car. Guy was dragging a large branch behind him to cover his footprints as they walked in the soft sand. When they reached the car, he opened the door, let Kristy in, and slammed it behind her. He retrieved his shirt and hat and put the telescope back in the trunk. He then slid in the driver's seat, started the car, pulled out onto the paved road, and stopped. He got out and the drug the branch back and forth over the tire tracks a few times to make sure they couldn't be seen. He got back in the car and drove back to the pay phone.

From the pay phone, he repeated the two-calling-card process and dialed Jim's cell. As soon as the phone rang, he heard Jim's voice come on the line.

"Hello."

"Jimbo, did you see your little grubby girl?"

"I saw. You didn't hurt her when you grabbed her, did you?"

"Nah. Not yet. But I told her I was going to if she did something stupid."

"She's only five. Please don't hurt her. She just got excited."

"It ain't nuttin' big. Anyways, I promised that she could talk to ya. Now ya'll be good and talk nice."

Guy had Kristy standing next to the car when he called. He signaled for Kristy to come to the phone. She walked carefully toward Guy and the phone he held extended her direction. She was looking around as she walked, hoping to see someone who would help her.

"Daddy, are you there?

"Yeah, sweetie. I'm here. Are you okay?"

"Yes, Daddy. I'm fine." Kristy changed her voice to a whisper. "Daddy, I can see the ice cream store."

Guy was looking around at everyone and everything that was moving. He was hoping that no one would recognize him or her. He kept his head tilted down a little so the brim of the hat kept his face shaded. He was beginning to feel panicked.

"Hurry up, grub. We gotta go."

"Bye, Daddy. I love you. I left you a letter in a jar buried on the beach."

Click!

Guy rushed Kristy back into the car. After going back to the phone and spraying it with an olive oil pan coating and wiping the phone off with his handkerchief, he ran around to the drivers' side and jumped in. Within a few minutes, they were safely back inside Guy's home. He felt safe again. He also felt very proud, proud because he was pulling off a crime and nobody had any idea he was involved. So proud, in fact, that he broke out in song. When Kristy heard him singing, she recognized the tune as "Yankee Doodle."

> Big Ole Bad Guy went to town,
> Driving a girl named Kristy.
> Everybody thinks I'm dumb,
> But that's just words that trash me.
>
> I'm the baddest criminal
> That anyone ever did see.
> I work with a bunch of cops,
> And they will never catch me.

Guy broke out in a roar of laughter. Then he turned to Kristy and glared. After a couple minutes, he went in the kitchen and grabbed a ham and cheese cracker pack and gave it to her. He locked her back in the room and slid the recliner back in front of the door to keep it blocked, just in case she found a way to unlock it. Afterward, he put the hat, glasses, and cooking spray back where they belonged and wiped off the counter. He looked at the clock. It was 3:33; and again, he broke out in laughter.

13

Jim walked outside to the play area in the side yard and sat on one of the swings. Life seemed to be so out of whack. Just yesterday, when he got out of bed, everything was good. Now everything was wrong. The biggest question on his mind was, *What have I done to bring this on?*

Jim's cell phone rang. He pulled it out and looked at the display, which read, "Caller ID unavailable."

"Hello?"

A familiar, gruff voice came over the receiver. "Jimbo."

"Is Kristy okay?"

"Yeah. The Grub is fine. As a matter of fact, I am gonna let her see you."

"You're what?"

"You gotta do me somethin' though, Jimbo. Ya gotta promise that you won't mention anything to anyone until after I call you back next time. Is that a deal?"

"How are you—?"

"Jimbo, is that a deal?"

"Anything. Just tell me what to do."

"In about five minutes, go out on your deck and look south. We will be there. Just know this. If anything looks out of line, I will kill her. You understand me, Jimbo?"

"I understand."

"Not a word."

EYES OF THE OCEAN

"I understand."

"Good."

Click!

Jim walked down to the water's edge and then back up to the house. He went in the kitchen and got a glass of water.

"Jim, are you okay?" Norm asked after seeing the distant look on Jim's face.

"Yeah. I'm fine."

"I saw you talking on your cell. I was wondering if it was the in-laws or what?"

"No. Just a business call."

"Well, if I can do anything…"

"Thanks, Norm."

"Your ribs all right?"

"Yeah. Just dented."

Both men chuckled a little, and Jim headed to the deck. Jim wished he had his telescope. He had left it out on the deck one night after he had been showing Kristy the stars; and the next morning, it was gone. He knew that sometimes those things happen. When you live on the beach, so many people walk across your backyard, you have to be careful not to leave stuff lying out.

Jim walked over to the railing and looked both directions. He knew the guy on the phone had said south; but just in case, he wanted to look both ways. After a few moments, he realized that way down the beach to the south were a shirtless man and a child. They had a telescope looking toward him. Could this be Kristy? He hoped with all that was in him that it was. He started waving. The child was looking in the telescope. Suddenly, she started running toward him. The man grabbed her. Jim knew it was them. He watched as they did something on the beach, but he really couldn't tell what. They picked up the telescope and left.

She was alive. He was so happy. Even though he hadn't been able to get close, he knew she was alive. There was still hope.

Now was time to wait for the next call so he could tell Norm about this. He wanted so badly to just run in and tell him everything now, but he also didn't want to do anything to jeopardize his daughter's well-being. Whoever had her was a killer, pure and simple. It wouldn't be worth it if somehow that guy found out he had done what he was told not to.

Jim walked down to the water's edge again and looked southward. The only people in view were a little farther on down the beach from where he had seen his daughter. It was a man and a woman walking a dog, and they were headed this way. Jim started walking south.

Ring!

When the conversation ended, Jim was already to the place where he had seen them earlier. Written in big letters in the sand were the words, "The Grub put it here."

Next to that was an arrow that pointed to a circle.

Jim dug up the jar and opened it. He pulled out the picture. He stood there and looked at it and cried. Within a couple of minutes, the couple with the dog had arrived.

"Hey, buddy. Something wrong?"

Jim didn't answer. He just looked up.

"Hey, John, that's the guy who was on TV, the guy whose girl got kidnapped," the woman said excitedly as one would if they had run into a celebrity.

The man looked at him closely. "I think it is. He's still got the same duds on. Buddy, you heard anything else?"

"No. Nothing." With this, Jim left the couple behind and ran back to the house. "Norm, I got a letter from Kristy."

"In the mail?"

"No. In a jar. Earlier, when I was outside, the guy called my cell phone and said he was going to bring her to where she could see me. He told me to go on the deck and she would be able to see. I did, and I saw her. They left this buried in the sand."

Norm looked at the jar. "Jim, put the jar down. If it has or had any prints on it, you're gonna mess them up."

Jim put the jar down on the table. He looked at the jar and realized he had rubbed his fingers all over it. If there had been prints, there probably weren't any now.

"You say he called your cell?"

"Yeah. He called it twice. Once before I saw them and once after. He told me not to tell anyone until after the second call."

Norm took the phone and checked the caller ID. He saw two calls listed as "ID unavailable." He pushed a few buttons and wrote down Jim's cell number from the display. He then took out the battery and wrote down the electronic serial number. He placed the battery back in the phone, put the back on, and turned it on.

"Who is your carrier?"

"Cellular Plus. Why?"

"We've got to get a trace started on those calls."

"If it will help anything, Kristy told me she could see the ice cream store when they called the second time. She was probably talking about Dipper Dan's over on Magnolia. I wanted to drive over there, but I was almost to the point where the jar was buried. I figured by the time I got there, they would be long gone. I even thought about calling you, but if he saw the police coming…"

Norm picked up the phone and began to dial. After pressing a few buttons, he stopped and placed the receiver back on the hook. Jim could tell he had something he wanted to say but was making sure it was going to come out right.

"Jim, there is something you need to know. In light of all the stuff on the news over the last few years, it won't be long until they start looking at you as a suspect. If you have any more con-tact from the perpetrator, you need to let us know right away. Regardless of what he tells you, we have to know. If we would have known this time, we might have been able to catch him and get your daughter back."

"I don't know. He said he would kill her if anything looked out of line."

"What would you expect him to say? Just tell us."

"Okay. I will."

"Has he given you any clue as to what he wants from you?"

"Not a word."

"It just don't seem right. There should have been some kind of clue. He has contacted you by phone three times and sent you a letter from her but no clue. Not a hint of what he wants? Do you owe someone a lot of money or something?"

"No. Absolutely not."

"It just seems that by now he would have told you or hinted as to what he wants."

"I don't know. I'm not the cop."

"Jim, some things just haven't fit from the beginning of this whole thing. I don't know what's going on. But some things don't fit the rest of the picture."

"I guess that's why you guys get paid the big bucks. All I know is my wife is gone forever and some weirdo has my daughter."

"Write down the names of everyone you know of who has your cell number. If you know their number or address, put those down too. I'll go ahead and get some folks over to Dipper Dan's."

14

Alfred and Inez picked up their luggage from the conveyer and walked out to the loading and unloading area. As promised, the rental car company had a shuttle waiting to take them to their car. They hopped on and sat back. To look at either one, you could see the stress, worry, and anxiety on their faces.

Finally, Inez broke the silence. "Do you think it will be best for us to stay at the house with Jim?"

"I'm really not sure, but that is what he is expecting. I don't think it would be right to back out and get a hotel now."

"I know. It's just that I don't think I can sleep in that house. It will be too scary."

"Inez, she was our daughter, and Jim needs us now. Anything we can do to help him, we should do it. Even if it means sleeping in a scary house. And when we get Kristy back, she will need comforting."

"I guess you're right."

They went into the rental office and paid for the Crown Victoria and left the credit card number. Alfred loaded all the luggage into the trunk and off they went, following the signs that pointed the way to I-4. After just a few moments, they found themselves eastbound, crossing the Lake Monroe section of the St. John's River. Once they had crossed the river, Alfred was looking off to the left of the interstate, thinking that it was just a few years ago that everything for the next several miles was nothing but cow pastures.

"Alfred, where you gonna stop to take dinner to Jim?"

"I was thinking about the Italian Grill there on A1A."

"Sounds good. I hope it's still open."

When they were nearing the first Deland exit, Alfred could no longer hold back the tears. Susan had been so proud when she had gotten her degree from Stetson University. He exited and drove by the school. The Crown Vic found its way into a parking space outside the campus chapel. Inez and Alfred both cried.

After about five minutes and a multitude of tears had come and gone, it was back on the road again, back out to I-4 and on toward Daytona. About six miles short of the I-95 exit, Alfred noticed a red Blazer in his rearview. The grill had a custom-made cover on it. It was chrome with the slits in the shape of a skull. Just the looks of it made Alfred nervous. He moved to the right lane to let him by, but it dropped in behind him. He backed off the gas, and the Blazer slowed down too. Alfred's heart pounded.

Inez looked at Alfred and saw the look of fear on his face. She noticed he kept looking in the mirror, so she turned to look at what he was seeing. The look of the grill so close behind her startled her, and she let out a yelp. The sound startled Alfred and made him jerk the wheel. The Blazer closed in to about eight feet behind them.

Alfred punched the gas, and the Blazer kept up. Several lane changes and dodged cars later and the Blazer was still on their tail. By this time, Alfred was soaked with sweat caused by fear. Inez was holding tight to the dash and was deep in prayer.

Suddenly, Alfred noticed the distance between the two vehicles diminishing. The horn on the Blazer let out a blast. It wasn't just a beep. It was an air horn like those on a tractor trailer. As Alfred stared into the mirror, the Blazer all but rear-ended them before swinging out to the left lane. The Blazer cruised up beside them. The driver, a young guy Alfred would have guessed to be in his early twenties, with his jet black hair, pierced lip, and upraised middle finger, laughed as he cruised on by.

Alfred found his way to Highway 92 and found another place to stop. He was in the parking lot of a large grocery store. After sitting silently for a few moments, he looked at Inez and started to laugh. He had no idea at what; he just laughed. Inez was frightened and all but in tears. Just yesterday, her daughter had been killed, and a couple of minutes ago, it looked like they were going to join her. And now her husband was laughing as though he had lost his mind.

He pulled himself together and said, "What some places won't do to push you into shopping with them. And since we're here, we might as well go in and pick up a few things."

They went in and walked around a while. As they perused each aisle, each picked up a few random items along the way. After they had walked around inside for about fifteen minutes, Alfred felt his hands quit shaking and his knees quit knocking enough for him to be safe to drive again. When they got to the register, they emptied the contents of the shopping cart onto the conveyer. Inez looked at the combination of items and smiled. They had a two-liter Pepsi, a bottle of steak sauce, a can of refried beans, a pack of burrito shells, and a can of air freshener.

After stopping at the Italian Grill and a few more minutes of driving, they arrived at what had been, up until yesterday, their daughter's home. Although they had done quite well at holding themselves together so far, the thought of going in and not seeing Susan or Kristy there to greet them was more than they were ready for. They got out of the car and headed for the house, Inez carrying the grocery bag and Alfred with the brown bag that held the take-out Italian. They walked around to the side door and rang the bell. Jim opened the door, and all three broke down into tears and cried with each other in a three way hug.

15

August 6

Susan's parents stayed up until the early morning hours talking with Jim and looking at pictures. Looking back on that evening, all three would find it surprising that they were actually able to laugh and even more so at how easily sleep came once they were in bed. They slept in until the phone woke them.

Jim ran downstairs to make sure the tape was set just in case. "Hello?"

"Hello. Mr. Fender?"

"This is he."

"Hi. This is Bob Birchfield at the coroner's office. I was calling to let you know that your wife's body is ready to be picked up. If you would just call the funeral home of your choice and have them come on down, we'll have her ready."

"Okay. Do I need to sign anything?"

"No. Just make the call."

"Thank you."

"Bye."

Jim called Johnson's Funeral Services and had them go pick up the body. They set up an appointment for that afternoon to make all the other arrangements. They recommended that Jim call East Port Suni Memorial Park to secure a couple of adjacent plots.

By the time he finished making the necessary calls, Inez had breakfast almost ready. She had taken a steak, sliced it into strips, and fried it in butter and onions. Then she scrambled some eggs with diced peppers, salt, and pepper and rolled it up in burrito shells with steak sauce, cheddar cheese, and sour cream. This was her special variety of breakfast foods.

"I hope you don't mind, Inez, but I have secured a couple of plots over at East Port Suni. It made the most sense to me of all the other places. I guess I should have asked you."

"No, Jimmy. She was your wife. Where she is buried is your choice. I just never imagined that I'd have to go to her funeral." Inez fought back the tears.

"It's okay. Cry if you need to. I know I have and will."

Norm and Dale had arrived to take over for the night shift, Dale sporting a large, purple circle in the center of his forehead and walking with the help of a crutch tucked under his right arm, both men wearing smiles as they walked and hobbled in the door.

"Sheesh, Dale. You sure you need to be here?" Jim asked. The tone of his voice and expression on his face radiated the genuineness of his concern.

"Yeah. I'm fine. Doc says there ain't nothin' broke. I just got some sprains and bruises. But if you get in trouble out there today, you're on your own."

The three men all burst into laughter, leaving Inez confused about the whole situation.

"I know I am a woman and this is probably man talk, but what in the world happened to you?"

Dale looked directly into Jim's eyes and shook his head. Jim knew that Dale was going to cover for Tommy as much as he could.

"Inez, this is Norm and Dale. They man the phones here at information central during the telethon. Norm tries to do the safe stuff like pushing buttons while Dale, being the daredevil he is, dives head first over the balcony out back."

The three men all burst out into laughter again.

Dale sat down and began to check all the equipment while Norm looked over the log from the previous night's activity. The two of them had settled in for what they hoped to be a day of boredom, each of them with books, cards, and games on their cell phones.

Inez brought each of them one of her breakfast burritos and a glass of orange juice. Norm and Dale accepted breakfast gladly. Jim and Inez went out to the deck to sit and eat. Jim carried his cordless phone out with him and set it on the table. Alfred joined them just a few minutes later.

The morning was a little cooler than it had been for the last couple of weeks. In fact, it was at least ten degrees cooler than the day before. Looking out across the water, a storm could be seen stretching across the horizon. Streaks of gray extended from the sky and connected the clouds with the ocean below, giving the appearance of the rain holding the clouds up. In closer, the water was rough for this time of day. Jim guessed the waves to be at least three to four feet. The gulls were cruising, looking for a free meal.

Just north a few hundred yards, a family of five was playing in the water, each enjoying the waves with their boogie boards. Another couple sat just to the south with their daughter. The mother and daughter, each with long, dirty blonde hair, were busy building a sand castle while the father was busy snapping pictures. From this vantage point, Jim thought they looked so much like he and his family had just a few days ago.

At first, he watched them, even smiled as if they were a great memory come to life. Soon, the reality of the impossibility of ever having those times again slipped in, bringing with it heartache and tears.

The Harwoods hadn't noticed the family on the beach until they noticed the tears beginning to crawl down Jim's face. They all sat silently and tearfully as they watched the three ghosts of good times past. The woman turned toward them, and Jim could see the face of the ghost. She was not as pretty as Susan but still held a beauty of her own. He tried to see the color of her eyes but could not.

Ring!

Jim jumped to his feet with a start and grabbed the phone. The combination of things again brought a yelp from Inez's mouth while Alfred slid his seat back and jumped to his feet. All the sudden commotion had gotten the attention of the ghosts on the beach, and the observers became the observed.

"Hello."

"Hey, Jim. Ben Jackson here."

"Hey. How's it going?"

"Great, man. I called to tell you how sorry I am about your wife and kid. I saw the thing on the news yesterday."

"Yeah. Well, did Mr. Hyatt call you to close the deal?"

"Sure did. Said you had told him to call me. Jim, I really appreciate the hard work you put into it."

"No prob."

"I also wanted to say thank you for letting me have all the commission."

"It's okay. I had to take care of things here, and someone needed to take care of it. You knew more about all that was going on than anyone else. You deserved it."

"I don't know about deserved, but thanks anyway."

"Listen, Ben. I really don't want to sound rude, but I need to keep the line clear, okay?"

"No prob. I'll try to stop by and see you soon."

After as much small talk as any of them felt they could handle, Alfred went into town for some groceries while Jim and

Inez picked out a dress and shoes for Susan. Jim wanted her to look as colorful as possible, and Inez wanted more of a somber look. They agreed on the Easter dress she had worn to church. Jim remembered how the dress had set off the depth of the blue in her eyes. A set of freshwater pearls for her neck and a set of matching earrings finished off the outfit. They also picked out a small, four-by-six picture of all of them taken last Christmas to put in her hand.

Tommy was noticeably absent from the Fender residence that day. Jim assumed he was embarrassed about his behavior and was trying to stay out of sight. He was kind of glad he wasn't there; but in a way, he wished he would come by. It would be nice to hear something of how the search for his daughter was going. Norm had just said that when they knew something, Tommy would let him know. Jim also wanted to tell him that he didn't have any hard feelings about the big, purplish place on his chest. Jim realized that they were all under a lot of stress. He decided that if Dale could be a good sport about it, so could he.

After Alfred got in from the store, Inez cooked lunch for everyone. She really enjoyed cooking, and it helped keep her mind off everything else.

Jim went with his in-laws to make the arrangements while Dale and Norm manned the phones that never rang, played cards, and told jokes. When the trip to the funeral home was over, all five played cards together. For the most part, it was an uneventful day in the Fender household.

16

Tommy had forgotten about the videotape until he got in his car to go to work and saw it lying in the passenger seat. As soon as he went in his office, he popped it in the VCR and started a search for anyone who might have gone in or out of the evidence room. He fast-forwarded through it three times only to find no sign of anyone.

Andrea Everson and a camera crew were at his office by 8:30. Tommy had rehearsed his answers several times. He needed to make a more positive impact on the community with this interview, or it might end up in the national limelight.

During the interview, Tommy held a relaxed appearance and spoke with confidence and purpose.

"I am here this morning in the office of Police Chief, Tommy Sutton. Chief Sutton, when we spoke yesterday, you said that you had some information that you were not at liberty to discuss. Can you give us a little more insight today?"

"Yes, I can. And thank you for giving me this opportunity to share this minute with the people. We are quite confident that we have obtained the murder weapon. We also have a videotape that may give us some insight to who may be behind this."

"On our news blog we received several comments that you seemed unsure of yourself and possibly distracted in our last interview. Would you like to comment on that?"

"Some of the residents of Port Suni are aware that the murder victim in this case was my high school sweetheart. I must admit, I have been struggling with this."

"So, it is more to you than just another case. It is personal. Do you think you are up to the challenge of remaining fair and objective?

"Absolutely. I am ready to do what needs to be done to solve this case, and with the help of the rest of the team here at P.S.P.D., all the evidence will be looked at thoroughly and objectively."

"I must say, Chief Sutton, you truly sound confident in your-self and your staff."

"I am. This case will be solved, and the perpetrator will be brought to justice."

"Thank you for your time…"

"Miss Everson, if you don't mind, I would like to have just a moment or two more of your time to speak to the community."

"Certainly."

The camera zoomed in on Tommy's face.

"Folks, I am being as honest with you as I can be. This case continues to have many unanswered questions, the most imme-diate being the whereabouts of Kristy Fender. We need your help. If you have seen Kristy, or even think you may have seen her, please give us a call. You don't have to give a name. Nobody has to know who called. It might be the information you have that leads us to her. Thank you."

"Thank you, Chief Sutton." Turning back to the camera, Andrea continued. "Again I will remind our viewers, the Port Suni Police Station number and e-mail is available on our Web site as well as on the bottom of the screen."

With a nod, the cameraman turned away and began the pro-cess of packing up. Tommy walked out to the news van with Andrea. She shook his hand then turned to get in the van. Stop-ping for a moment, she looked back at Tommy.

"That was truly powerful. Any doubts that may have been raised by yesterday's interview will surely be erased by today's."

"Thank you for giving me that chance," he said and then stuck one finger in the air. "Now on to looking over the paperwork again." With that, he started back to his office.

When Tommy started reviewing all the notes he had, he noticed the new entry that the coroner had faxed over. Nothing unexpected there. Because of the rapid cooling of the body by the ocean water, an exact time of death could not be established. An estimated time had been put in due to Jim's statements. An attached form showed that the wound would have definitely been consistent with the knife retrieved from the phone man.

The report on the note in the jar stated there were no readable prints anywhere on the jar except for Jim's. It also said the jar was a jar used for canning, and the lid was from a mayonnaise jar. Nothing on or about the picture gave any indication of what was going on.

The phone calls to Jim's cell were not traceable. The payphone near Dipper Dan's seemed to have been covered with cooking oil and rubbed down. No one remembered seeing anyone using the phone.

One problem with altering the paperwork was the tire marks in Jim's driveway. They were definitely not made by Jim's car.

The VCR display showed 11:04 a.m. Tommy hit the eject button, took the tape out, placed it in a yellow envelope, and dropped it in Norm's inbox with a note that read, "See if you can find anything wrong with this tape." Back in his office with the door closed, Tommy sat back in his chair and began thinking about everything his dad had told him. Deep down inside, he knew his dad must at least know who was behind this mess and why. He wanted more than anything to be able to forget the conversation from the day before and get on with life, but he couldn't. He knew that if he didn't take Jim down for this, he or his dad would surely take the fall. The conversation played over and over in his mind. The more it played, the more he realized he needed to start making some progress, or outside police agencies such as the SBI or FBI might want to step in. Help from the outside would almost assuredly bring blame on the department and ultimately on him. If that happened, as his father would say, "Them Sutton boys would be put away for a while."

One question began to inch its way from his subconscious mind to the forefront of his thoughts. Once there, the question only gave birth to more questions. Yet no answer could be found. Why had his father said, "Anyone else you might think is on your side?" Did that mean someone was not on his side? Did it mean someone else on the force was plotting against him? After a few minutes of reflection, the questions became not "If" but rather, "Who and why?" Tommy decided that even if Jim went down for this, he needed to know who was behind it. He pulled out a notepad from his desk drawer and started to write down all the people who worked in the station, from the custodians to the dispatcher.

Janet stood outside her husband's office, watching him as he mentally replayed everything. On her way in she had stopped by the water cooler and got a cup of water to bring to him. She knew that she hadn't been the best wife for at least the last two years. She was finally able to cope with Jerome's accident. The feeling of guilt kept her from showing Tommy any affection at times. Janet had never intended for the affair to happen. It just did.

Tommy had always treated her good for the most part. Sometimes when he was stressed, he would have an outburst of temper, but he would calm down within a minute or two. Even though he had put his fist through the wall a couple of times and broken a lamp once by kicking a chair into it, he had never directed his anger at her in a physical way.

She remembered when Thomas had told them he was going to be retiring soon and that he thought he could make sure Tommy got his job. Tommy really started pouring himself into his work. It was not unusual for him to spend twelve to fourteen hours a day at the station. Within a month of Thomas giving him that news, his mother found out she had cancer, and six weeks after that, she was dead. Thomas retired, and Tommy was the right man for the job. But the stress made things at home a little more heated. The pressure on Tommy had really begun to take its toll on Janet as well.

One evening about two years ago, Janet went for a walk on the beach to try to pull herself together. Feeling unloved and like she had taken second place a job, she found her way to a semi-secluded area and sat up close to the dunes to cry. Inside she wanted so badly to for Tommy to hold her like he used to. To smile and tell her everything would be all right. She didn't think anyone would notice her, but she was mistaken.

Jerome had seen her walking and had followed her from a distance. He could tell that she wasn't her normal cheerful self. She looked at the sand as she walked and kept her arms folded together. When he saw where she went to sit, he knew she must be upset.

He had never stopped loving her even though they had broken up right after her graduation eight years earlier. Jerome had always dreamed that somehow he and Janet would end up married and have a house full of kids. Seeing the sadness that radiated from her made him sad as well.

He went over and sat with her to see if he could cheer her up. Jerome had been blessed with the gift of gab. A few jokes and a couple of remember-when's was all it took before she was laughing. He walked her back up the beach to her car. For the first time in a long time, she felt a smile in her heart.

The next day, she went back to the same place only to find that Jerome was already there waiting on her. He said he was really hoping she would come, even though neither one had mentioned seeing each other again. Meeting on the beach became a habit, and before long, lunch did too. It was only natural progression that led them to start frequenting the Starlight. On a few occasions, they would drive out to the beach and make love afterward.

One night, they realized that both of them must have had some unresolved issues about their past. Janet decided she was too much in love with Tommy to continue with the affair. That same night, Jerome told her that he felt like could finally move on with his life. That night they walked out together, laughing and enjoying knowing that the hiding could end. That night, she had kissed his lips for the last time. That night, he died.

She had often wondered if they hadn't ended their relationship if he would still be alive, or if they had never had those times together, or if...

Tommy looked up from his desk and saw her standing outside his door. She looked as if her mind was a thousand miles away. Watching her as he walked to the door, concern rose up in him. When he opened the door, she jumped, slinging the cup of water on Larry, who was walking down to tell Tommy how good of a job he had done on his latest TV interview. Instead, the cold water in his face and down the front of his shirt took his breath, and it was all he could do to hold himself together. He had no idea what had happened to cause her to sling water all over him, just that it had happened.

"I am so sorry," she said as she reached forward to put her hand on his shoulder.

He glared at her for a second then turned and stormed off down the hall toward the men's restroom. Janet felt like a total klutz, and Tommy had no clue what had just happened.

Tommy was surprised to see his wife. It had been a couple of years—before he got his promotion—since she had shown up at the office without calling first.

"Is everything okay?" he asked.

"Everything is fine. I just wanted to come see my wonderful husband."

"I'm getting ready to watch the news. Come on in and watch with me."

"Don't you make the news here? Seems like that would be enough," she said with a grin.

He leaned in and gave her a little kiss. "Come on in and watch. I hear there will be a surprise on today."

Watching the interview, Janet was more proud of Tommy than she could remember ever being. He sounded so confident and sure of himself.

"That was good. I am so proud of you!"

"Yeah, I called it, 'A Minute With the People.'"

"I think you will do just fine with this case. In the end, you will be the town hero."

"I don't know about that. Not even sure that I want that title anymore." Just the thought of having the title that had been previously ascribed to his dad didn't have the same appeal as it did before.

"Tommy, I want you to know that I am so proud of you. I am proud when people call me Mrs. Sutton, and I am proud when I am seen in public with you."

Tommy wasn't sure how to respond. He felt like she was putting him up on a pedestal so that it could be kicked out from under him. She hadn't been that supportive of him in a long time. "I am not sure what you've been drinking, but I want to buy you some more."

"I want to have more, but I think we need to talk first."

Tommy began preparing his mind and his heart for the pedestal to be kicked as they walked to the car.

They went to the 22nd Street Bistro for lunch. After they had ordered, Janet began to talk.

"I need you to know up front that I love you. I have since before I said, 'I do.' After all we have been through, I would say, 'I do,' again."

Tommy's eyes filled with tears when Janet took his hands. His heart sank expecting the "Dear John" speech.

She leaned in and kissed his hand. "Do you remember Jerome Fender?"

"I do. Jim's brother."

"There is something I need to tell you." She swallowed hard. Her lips trembled as she fought to say the words. "A couple of years ago…"—the tears started—"I didn't mean to, but I ran into Jerome on the beach. You were overworked, and I was lonely."

"Janet, you don't have to say anything else." Tommy struggled with how to tell her how he knew about the affair. "I was talking to…I was talking to someone about the Fender case yesterday, and they told me that they had seen y'all together." He was fighting to hold himself together. He was in public, in uniform, and it was all he could do to keep from breaking into a full blubbering sob.

"We had an affair, Tommy. It went on for a while."

"I know."

"We met one night at the Starlight up in Daytona." She had to stop to regain her composure. "Before we left that night, we decided to call it off. We both thought it best. Tommy, I love you, and I am sorry."

Tommy wanted to say something, but he was afraid that if he opened his mouth, he would lose it. He nodded his head.

"I feel so bad. I have not..."

They sat and stared tearfully at each other, squeezing each other's hands for a few moments, and then Janet continued. "That night on the way home, Jerome wrecked. I often wondered if maybe he was really upset and..."

Tommy had already been made aware of part of it the day before by his dad; but when she told him that they had called it quits that very night, Tommy had a very hard time holding back his anger, not at her, but at his father.

"No, sweetheart. No, you can't blame yourself for that. It wasn't your fault."

She held her head down, "I am sorry. I didn't mean for any of it to happen. I didn't..."

Tommy stood up and helped Janet to her feet. He signaled for the waiter. He had them put their lunches in to go boxes.

Once they arrived at Janet's car, they held to each other and kissed.

"Janet, I love you. Affair or not, I still love you. Nothing will change that."

They held each other a few minutes longer before Tommy had to return to work. Janet was relieved because she no longer had to bear that awful secret alone. Now that she had confessed, Tommy could deal with it better. He was certainly glad that he wouldn't have to confront her with it later.

When Tommy arrived back at the office, it was 4:30. Norm was sitting at his desk with the video tape in his hand.

"Tommy, where did you get this tape?"

"From off the shelf with the rest of them. Why?"

"Because this tape is not one of our tapes."

"It came from right over there, and it has our surveillance pictures on it. I took it off the shelf myself."

"All well and good my friend, but this tape is not one of ours."

Tommy just stood there, trying to figure what Norm was talking about. How could he know so quickly when he himself had looked it over several times?

"So tell me, Norm. Why is that not our tape?"

"Because all of our tapes are Sony, and this one is JVC."

"That's weird. I expected something on the tape to be wrong but not the tape itself."

"I'll take it home and check it out," Norm said.

17

August 8

Jim had made it through setting up for the funeral and the time of receiving friends without falling apart too badly. The funeral home had done a great job at fixing her up. She was beautiful and looked very much at peace.

Alfred had driven down to the funeral home with Inez in the front next to him and Jim in the back. As they pulled into the parking lot Alfred looked at his watch.

"It'll be twenty minutes until the service starts."

"We'll have time to look at her..." Inez's face became drawn and streaked with tears. "She's my baby. I can't believe she's gone."

Jim and Alfred tried hard to be strong to no avail. The three tear-streaked faces remained in the car for a couple of minutes before forcing themselves to go in.

There were a lot of vehicles there, including two vans from television stations and one from the *Daytona Sun*. There were a lot of people there that Jim knew and twice as many that he didn't. The cameras were manned, and the reporters were talking. Jim was surprised to see that Andrea had shown up without her camera crew. She said she was there only as a friend, not as a reporter.

When they walked into the chapel, the casket was open down front. There was a line of people going by one at a time, saying good-bye. Many of them were crying. Many were not.

One of the funeral directors came down and escorted the threesome to the front. Jim walked over to the casket and looked at the love of his life. Tears began to creep in from under his eyes and find their way out. He reached in and placed his hand on hers. He had, for some reason, always believed he would be the one to go first; but time had proven him wrong. He looked at the dress she was wearing. It accented her hair so well. He noticed some of the pictures that were placed inside the casket with her. One particular picture stood out. It was a picture of Susan pushing Kristy on the swing, and it looked very recent. It had been taken from the beach side of the house, but Jim did not remember ever seeing the picture before. He picked it up and looked at the back; and written in black ink was a note that said, "Jimbo, the Grub wanted her mom to have this and the other."

A rush of faintness filled his body. Whoever had Kristy had left this note. They had been here, or they were here now. And what other? He looked closer and saw a folded piece of paper in Susan's hand. He pulled it out and opened it. It was simple a note in a child's writing that said: "I love you, Mommy. Have fun in heaven. I miss you. Love, Kristy."

Jim just stood there and stared for a moment in disbelief. Anger began to swell up in him. He saw Tommy standing in the back of the chapel and asked one of the funeral directors to go get him and Andrea and bring them down. He looked anxiously around the room, and all he could see was a sea of faces. Not one of them seemed any more likely to be the kidnapper than any other. It looked like half of Volusia County was there, and they all seemed to be friendly people. His anger quickly turned to frustration when he realized the impossibility of finding the person who had put the note and the picture in the casket.

Tommy came down front as quickly as he could get there, with Andrea right behind him. Jim showed them the picture and the note. Tommy carefully took the picture by the edges and looked it over. Andrea looked at the note from Kristy.

Jim was so stunned that he didn't hear any of the message that Dr. Eller brought. He sat quietly in thought as they rode in the family limo to the graveside. As they pulled into the gates, the sign announced that they were entering East Port Suni Memorial Park. The grass was all green and neatly trimmed. He didn't mention anything to the Harwoods about the note or the picture. He felt like it would be better to wait until the service was over and they were back home.

Jim did pay a little more attention to the graveside service. When "Amazing Grace" was sung, it was all he could do to keep from crying; but for the most part, he was numb. He looked around occasionally to see if he could figure who might have left the picture and note and how they could have gotten it there.

When the service was over, no less than fifty people came up to him and tried to encourage him. A lot of people were snapping pictures of the flowers and the family. Many of them shook his hand or hugged his neck and offered a few words of hope and comfort. Even people who Jim had never seen before were there offering their support. One young lady named Kathy Prevatt had spent a bit of time talking to Jim and holding both of his hands. She smiled as she talked, and Jim forced a smile in return. Kathy leaned in and gave Jim a big hug and whispered in his ear something about he could cry on her shoulder if he wanted to. Jim returned the hug, and when he did, she kissed his check. Before she left, she took both of his hands again, looked into his eyes, and said, "I love you, Jim. Always have."

Jim tried hard to remember Kathy. He didn't remember ever seeing her before, but he must have known her in school or something. After a few moments' deliberation, it was forgotten.

The ride back to the funeral home and then back to the house was silent. Jim had noticed several cameras filming and snapping pictures but didn't give them much thought. He was beginning to get used to the attention. Even when he was home, having people out on the beach looking and taking pictures was becoming commonplace. Since Tommy's lunchtime speech two days earlier, more and more people were following their curiosity to the beach behind his house.

When Jim arrived home, his front porch was covered with assorted plants, dish gardens, and flower arrangements that had been delivered and placed neatly around the walls. He and the Harwoods walked around, looking at them and trying to identify the names on each of the cards. Most were from people they had never heard of. There was one card that stood out—one that simply said, "Kristy."

Jim reached over and took the card and carefully opened it. Inside was a small brown envelope. The envelope had a note typed on it: "For you." Inside the brown envelope was a small zipper storage bag with a lock of dirty-blonde hair closed up inside. Jim was very careful to not touch it too much, and he immediately went in and gave it to Norm. He didn't want to mess up this time like he had before.

After a short discussion, Norm made some calls: one to the station to let Tommy know about the lock of hair, one to have a pizza delivered, and one to Pretty Petals Florist. Jim was hoping they could find some information on the person who had sent the flowers with the little gift attached.

The shop owner came on the line, "This is Sarah. How may I help you?"

"This is Officer Norman Nichols, Port Suni Police Department. Your shop delivered some flowers for the Fender funeral today."

"Actually we delivered a lot of flowers. Something wrong?"

"Not wrong. I was just hoping to get some information about a person that had ordered one in particular."

"Wow, that may be a bit difficult. Most of the people that ordered flowers were new customers."

"This particular customer had something special to put in the envelope with the card…"

"I do remember. I was a small brownish envelope, right?"

"That would be the one. What can you tell me about that customer?"

"It was a tall man. I'd say about six-foot-two. I didn't get his name. Kinda medium build."

"Did you notice what he drove when he pulled up?"

"No, sorry. But, he was wearing a printed T-shirt. I can't remember what it said. Kind of one of those generic things I think. Blue jeans and tennis shoes I think."

"Anything else?"

"Not that I can recall."

"If you happen to think of anything else, call the station if you would…"

"Actually he had dark hair and brown eyes?"

"That's great. Anything at all about him comes to mind, mannerisms anything. Call me. If he comes in again, don't wait, call."

When Norm got off the phone, he tried to sort out the notes he had made. He called Tommy and informed him of the new development.

Tommy just laughed. "Why not? Nothing else makes sense. I'll just add this to the book of nothing and see what I get."

―――――――――――

Jim went up to his room to change clothes. While he was upstairs, he looked in Susan's closet. He tried to remember a time when she wore each of the dresses or outfits hanging in it. When he came back down, he was wearing jeans, a printed T-shirt, and a pair of running shoes. As soon as Norm looked at him, he stood to his feet with a determined abruptness. He looked Jim from top to bottom with the eye of a critic.

"Jim, weren't you wearing something like that yesterday when you ran out to the store?" he asked with a puzzled concern in his voice.

"Yeah, but it's not so bad to wear the same kind of clothes two days in a row, now is it?"

"No, it's not, but…" His voice trailed off to silence.

"But what?"

"But dressed like you are right now, you…Never mind. I don't know. Just looked kind of interesting."

Jim laughed, went to the living room, and sat down. It seemed rather humorous that the police would find it interesting that he wore similar clothing two days in a row. "Don't most people wear similar clothing most days? Is it really unusual to wear jeans and a printed tee shirt?" he asked himself.

He picked up a business card from the end table next to his chair. He looked at the name printed on the top: Andrea Everson. He was so glad she had been there without her camera crew. She could have joined the media circus and exploited Susan's funeral as several other journalists had done. *Thanks are in order,* he thought. He took his cell phone from his pocket and dialed the number listed as her cell.

18

Jim walked along the beach. The sky was gray. The waves were high, and they crashed one after the other. It seemed that each one was crashing in closer. The waves seemed to be angry, almost as if they were after him. He wanted to walk away from the water, but Susan was calling to him to come closer—no, not her voice, but he could feel her presence beckoning him. He couldn't put his finger on how, but he knew she was.

Suddenly, he saw Tommy running out from the saw grass that decorated the sand dunes. He was running hard and fast. He was looking directly at him. He looked so much younger, like he did in high school, and he was wearing his basketball uniform. Dale started running out of the saw grass after him, yelling for Tommy to stop. Tommy began to laugh hard, and he stopped dead in his tracks. He turned and raised his hand. He was holding a gun in his hand now and began pulling the trigger. He shot five times in rapid succession. Dale kept running toward him even though his chest had been ripped out by the impact of the bullets. Tommy waited until Dale was right next to him and fired one more time, taking the top of Dale's head off in a pinkish red spray that formed a small cloud and floated away.

Dale, now lying on the ground at his feet, looked up at Jim and said, "Man, they're gonna fry you. They're gonna put you in the pan and fry you." It then appeared as if he started dissolving and melted into the sand, leaving an arrow pointing to a circle in the sand. Jim recognized it as the same arrow and circle where he had found the letter from his daughter.

He dropped down and tried to dig, but the ground was too hard. He raked his fingers harder only to feel the same kind of pain one would feel if he tried to dig through bricks with his bare hands. He could feel the flesh being torn from his fingertips. He began to pound on the ground but made no dent. His hands were throbbing with pain. He looked at them only to see them heal before his eyes.

Tommy laughed again and said, "That's where I raped her. That's where it happened, and I have tried and tried but I cannot make the marks of it go away. Now that grub dug a hole, but I can't do anything with it. Dale was going to tell everyone what I did, so I had to fix him."

Jim stood back to his feet and looked very carefully into Tommy's eyes. They were blood red and focused. He was no longer holding the gun but now held a long knife in its place. The knife was raised slowly and stopped. Jim wanted to run, but his feet would not allow it. He wanted to scream, but his voice would not come. He tried to swing his fist, but his arm had become as stone, stiff and unable to move. He was petrified with fear. He was about to die, and he could do nothing to prevent it.

Jim noticed a big, floor model TV sitting on the ground behind Tommy. The news was on, and Andrea was the anchor for the hour. She was speaking of a murdered woman when she looked up and, with a look of horror on her face cried out, "Don't do it." Tommy turned and shot the TV; and it went up in a cloud of smoke, leaving only Andrea lying on the ground, dying. Looking at Jim, she said, "You let this happen." Within a few seconds, she too was absorbed by the ground.

In the distance, he heard the sound of laughter. He looked up and saw the three ghosts that he had seen from the back deck a few days ago now dressed in swimming attire and walking toward him. They were laughing and playing together. The man took the little girl up in his arms and swung her around. She laughed, and the sound was so sweet to Jim's ears. She changed form right before his eyes and became Kristy. The woman became Susan, and the man was absorbed into the ground. Jim struggled and finally squeezed out the word, "Help." It was so weak that he didn't think anyone could have possibly heard it.

He looked at Susan. She was so beautiful. He was caught momentarily by the beauty of her eyes. He shook his head to refocus and realized that she was now wearing the dress she had been buried in. Blood started running down the front of her body where she had been stabbed. Her lips, now with a bluish hue, mouthed the words, "You let this happen, Jim. You let him hurt me again. You promised that you wouldn't let anything happen, and now look at me. You could have stopped him." She slowly lay down and seeped into the ground.

He looked back at Kristy only to see that a large spot on her head had been shaved. She said, "Daddy, see what the bad guy did to my hair? See how bad he was? You were supposed to stop him, but he got me. You and the angels all let him get me. Why didn't you stop him, Daddy?"

He looked at her closer to see that she was now wearing a dress just like her mother's. Suddenly, blood began to pour from the same place as it had on her mom. She cried and lay down, and the ground soaked her up as well.

Jim was afraid, angry, and confused all at the same time. Tommy stepped closer. He was now wearing his police uniform and was holding his pistol again. He raised the pistol and pulled the trigger. Jim felt the bullet as it passed through his hair. Jim stepped backward as Tommy again pulled the trigger, this time taking off just a small piece of Jim's ear.

"Step into the water, Jimbo." The voice that came from Tommy's mouth was the same as he had heard from the phone receiver. "Go ahead. You know she wants you to. She is calling for you. Step in, or I will shoot you and the ground will suck you up. It won't hurt much. Just go."

Jim turned back toward the water, and the look of it took his breath. The waves were at least twelve feet high, and they were pinkish in color. Rising and falling with each wave, sitting at the crest, sat a row of stuffed animals, each with dark, batlike wings. As each wave rose up, he could see a pair of eyes staring out at him. He stepped closer, and in the waves, a large mouth opened just below the eyes. The mouth was full of row after row of teeth that crashed shut just as the wave fell. The eyes of each stuffed animal grew larger and redder as each wave rose and fell.

As the final wave rose up, it rushed forward and engulfed him. He felt himself being turned every direction and slammed over and over against the floor of the ocean. Jim tried to reach the surface, but he could not. Through the water, he saw Tommy standing there laughing. The tumbling stopped, and he stood to his feet. He was unable to breathe. His mind began asking the question, "Is this what it feels like to die?"

Darkness overwhelmed him and drew him away. He could feel himself being gently lifted from the water by two strong arms. He felt himself being carried higher and higher and then being set gently on soft grass. He was still trying to take a breath but could not. He forced his eyes open; and right in front of him was a face, big, red, and ugly. The face resembled Tommy, but he knew it was not. He seemed to be someone that could be trusted but he knew could not. The gruff voice yelled out, "Now you're mine, Jimbo." He raised a pitchfork over his head and plunged it toward Jim.

Jim screamed and sat upright in his bed. He was soaked with sweat. His hands were shaking. When the Harwoods came running in, he was holding his head in his hands, crying.

Inez placed her hand on the back of Jim's head, "It's okay, son. I've been crying a lot myself."

When Jim spoke, his voice was shaky. "It was just a bad dream. Scared me." Raising his head, he could see the concern in both of the Harwoods' faces. "I'm sorry. I didn't mean to…"

"No, Jimmy, it's okay. Let's go downstairs and talk."

The three went down to the kitchen and got a cup of hot chocolate each and went to sit out on the back deck. As they opened the door to step out, a gull that had landed on the deck took to flight. The sound and sudden movement scared Jim so bad that he slammed the door back closed and knocked his hot chocolate out of his hand onto his foot. It wasn't so hot as to burn him, just to make him jump and yell.

Jim was actually glad that the bird had been there because within just a few minutes, all three were standing there, laughing. It was so good to laugh. Jim had been so stressed for so long that nothing outside of having Susan and Kristy back could have been as good for him as laughter. The laughter then led to a more pleasant conversation.

Alfred recounted the events of the evening Jim and Susan announced their engagement. "…and you sat in that glider."

Jim laughed out loud. "How was I to know the cat was there? You just stood there with your mouth open."

"Inez had propped the broom up by the door, and when that squalling cat came out from under you, he hit the broom and sent it falling."

Inez joined in, "When that broom hit me in the back and that cat ran by…"

"You could have taken it out on the broom instead of the lamp," Alfred interrupted.

"I was just trying to get out of the way of whatever it was that was after me."

They continued to talk about the funny things that had happened over the years. Most of the night passed them by. It was 3:30 a.m. when they headed back to bed. They were all tired, and Jim actually felt like he could sleep. But as soon as he closed his eyes, the images of the earlier dream came back in full force. Jim did not find sleep that night.

19

Tommy sat in his office, reading through the reports. Everything still looked as if it could actually be Jim that was the perpetrator. The only contact had been made with Jim could not be verified by anyone.

The tire tracks in Jim's driveway were not really an issue. Those may have been made by the perpetrator, or they may have been there for a few days. That would be hard to prove. It was Jim's word that they were new. That could be used to say he was trying to cover his guilt. Norm had checked the tape carefully and found that, along with it being a copy, the time stamp actually showed a period of close to ten minutes that had been edited out. That just left the issue of the knife. None of these were actually public knowledge, and those details never had to be disclosed.

If anyone ever did find out where the knife came from, there was no way to prove beyond a shadow of a doubt that this was the murder weapon, only that it could have been. The knife had been meticulously cleaned before being left with the phone guy, and there was no trace of blood on it. The phone guy, Jay, had been in and out of the station many times working on various communication issues. Who is to say that he wasn't the one who stole the knife and made up part of the story to cover his own guilt?

Some of the pressure would soon be lightened because today, he would notify Jim that he was a suspect. Today, he would go on public record as having some leads that might implicate Mr. Fender. Today, a woman would come forward and confess that she and Jim were having an affair and that she had told Jim that she didn't believe she could ever raise anyone else's children. Today would be the beginning of the end of Jim Fender and Tommy's big problem.

As he made sure all the *I*'s were dotted and the *t*'s were crossed, Thomas called.

"Son, Miss Prevatt will be coming over around noon. You need to be ready to react with shock and surprise."

"I will, Dad. Are you sure she will be able to hold up to the pressure?"

"No doubt about it, boy. She wants to be famous and is willing to do anything to get there. And on top of that, she is a talented actress."

"Famous? How could this work into being famous?"

"Had you ever heard of that Frye girl before that murder out in California?"

"No, Dad. I guess you're right. I just hope I can hold up my part."

"In a very real sense, boy, it is do or die for you."

"I still think there has to be a way that I could find out what is really going on without doing this to an innocent man. I mean, Jim really is not a bad guy and—"

"Boy, let me tell you something. He is a bad guy, him and his whole family. They deserve to go down 'cause of what they have done to us. You ain't gonna go getting soft now, are ya? Just be a man, and get it done. You don't want people to be talking bad about us Sutton boys, now do ya?"

"I just don't understand the big deal about what people say."

"Listen to me. People start saying bad things about the Suttons and then the next thing you know, they replace you. You do like your job, don't you?"

"Yeah, Dad, I do, but...okay. I guess you're right. And anyway, as of now, Jim is really the only one we can even begin to point a finger at."

"So don't show any mercy or weakness. You show everyone what us Sutton boys are made of. Don't bend. Don't back up. Just go after him like a shark after a school of bait fish, and don't let one of 'em swim away."

"Okay, Dad. I'll do it. I just want the real guy caught."

"Boy, listen up. You don't know it ain't him. Just deal with it, and take him down."

"I will. Bye, Dad."

Tommy reflected on all the evidence he had compiled. He wanted to make sure all of his ducks were in a row. There was no way he wanted to make a mistake that would embarrass the Sutton name; nor did he want to cause the suspicion to turn toward him. If Ms. Prevatt turned out to be as good of an actress as Mr. Sutton had claimed, there would be nothing to worry about.

Tommy walked to the garage to get the vehicle sign-out sheet. He picked up the clipboard marked "Boss's Car" and started to write in the time and date. He signed it in the out column, thought for a moment, and scratched a line through his signature and hung it back up.

Alex came running over. He had a look of excitement on his face that said he had something important to say. After he looked at the sheet, he looked at Tommy, puzzled.

"No, Alex. I won't be takin' that car today. I think I'll use my Crossfire. I feel a bit sporty."

"Okay, Boss Sutton. Keep a record of your miles so I can sign your mileage log for you."

"No. I think I'll pay for this myself."

"Boss, if only people know what a good guy you are, they'd have a parade for you. Hey, since you won't be using your car today, can I take it for while and put a good wax job on it?"

"Sure. That would be really nice. When you came up, you looked like you had something to say. I really didn't mean to interrupt you."

"It ain't nothing, Boss. I just had a poem I made up about you."

"Cool. Let me hear it."

"Naw. It's dumb anyway."

"No. Please do it for me."

"Okay. It goes like this: 'Ole Boss Sutton was a really good cop/ but then one day he had to stop/ So new Boss Sutton took his place/ That was good for the human race/ But even though policing ain't art/ new Boss Sutton is way too smart/ Guy who keeps that little girl/ new Boss Sutton will give a twirl.' Well, what'cha think, boss?"

"That was really good, Alex," Tommy said out of kindness. The truth was, he really hadn't been paying attention to what he had said. "Well, I'm gonna go now. I'll be back in a while."

Tommy got in his Crossfire and cranked up the volume on the CD player. He took out the self-esteem self-help CD and put in the twenty greatest hits from the nineties. He lowered the top and chirped his tires as he pulled out of the lot. He was feeling good.

Alex watched as Tommy pulled out of the lot and went over to the car with the big 01 on top. After a moment's reflection, he looked side to side and pulled out his keys and opened the door. He took a moment to enjoy the aroma of the pineapple air freshener he had put in yesterday. As he slid into the seat, he smiled and thought to himself, *I'm gonna have some fun today.*

Larry watched intently as Alex drove away. He was about to walk back toward his desk when the phone rang.

A female voice came from the receiver, "Hello, I need to speak with Chief Sutton, please."

"He isn't in his office at the moment. Is there something I can do to help you?"

"I am not sure. I think I need to speak with the chief about some information on the Fender case."

"I can set you an appointment if you would like. I am sure he would be excited to meet with you if you could shed any light on this case. Can I get your name please?"

"Kathy, with a *K*, Prevatt."

"Is there an 'e' on the end?"

"No."

"When would you like to speak to him? The sooner the better, I am sure."

"Could I come in during my lunch break? Maybe around 12:15?"

"Hold on, and I will radio him to verify the time."

Larry radioed Tommy and set the appointment.

The call ended, and Larry sat back in his chair and placed his hands with his fingers woven together behind his head and a smile on his face.

20

Kristy really had learned to hate Guy. He was no longer funny to watch. When he had cut her hair and put it in that little plastic bag, he was very rough with her. He also made her take a bath while he watched. He didn't try to touch her, but she didn't like it. He said he couldn't trust her not to do something stupid and that even little grubs had to get clean sometimes. He said he would make it up to her and let her write a letter that her mommy could take to heaven with her. But when he took it, he said something about it really making her daddy hurt more.

Guy left her there that morning just like he had every morning so far. He gave her some breakfast and put plenty of snacks in the room for her. She was surprised to hear him come back in the house as early as he did. She actually got excited when the keys began to rattle in the door. When Guy stepped in, he looked really happy. Kristy was glad he didn't have the mean look on his face that he did when he cut her hair or when he made her bathe. She jumped to her feet and straightened out the wrinkles in the bedspread.

"C'mon, Grub. We're gonna go somewhere and play."

"Are you gonna really let me play outside?"

"If you come on and don't make me wait all day."

Guy walked over and inspected the bed while Kristy slid her shoes on. He checked for dust on the dresser and wiped off the collected dust from the front of the TV. He looked at Kristy, and a smile crossed his lips.

"You really are a pretty girl, Grub. Too bad you can't be grown up."

"Guy, are we ready to go yet?"

"Yes, we are ready."

Guy picked up his hat and glasses from by the microwave and headed out the door. They got in the police car and backed out of the driveway. As they traveled, she looked out the window, trying to see anything that looked familiar. She saw the ice cream place. As they passed her home, she looked, hoping to see her dad. Instead, she saw a woman whom she thought looked like her Grandma Inez. Within ten minutes of leaving Guy's house, they were parked in a private area that was no more than one hundred yards from A1A. The trees and palmetto bushes had them fairly well hidden. It was a large, open sandy area.

Once they were parked, Guy got out, looked around, and smiled. He took off his shirt and glasses and put them in the front seat. He looked around one more time before opening the door for Kristy.

"All right, Grub, you can get out and run around," he said trying to sound mean. "But, if I say for you to do something, you better do it! Do you understand?"

"Okay. I will," she said. "I promise."

When they got out of the car, Kristy could occasionally see glimpses of cars as they passed by and could hear many more than she could see. Guy pulled out a blanket, a McDonald's bag, two apples, and two drinks. He said they should have a picnic. When he handed Kristy her double cheeseburger, he decided that it was too big for her to handle; so he pulled out his pocket knife and cut it in half. He also took one of the apples and stuck his knife into it and sat it on the blanket.

After they had eaten, Kristy got up and began to run around, playing and jumping. It was so good to be out in the sun again. She loved it because it reminded her of being home. She wished she had monkey bars or a swing to play on. She had been used to spending time outside every day. Since she had been with Guy, she had hardly seen outside.

"So, Grub, tell me, if I kick back a little, you ain't gonna do something stupid and try to run off, are you?"

"No, Guy. I promise. I will just play here. Thanks for bringing me outside."

"Yeah. Well, don't get to likin' it too much 'cause it ain't gonna happen every day."

Kristy played, running back and forth. She sat down and began making a sand castle. After a few minutes, she looked over at Guy and saw that he was asleep. The knife was sticking in the apple next to him. She had seen a lot of people on TV get stuck with knives, and they always stopped whatever they were doing. She looked to see how far it was to the highway. If she could get the knife and stick him, she was sure she could get to the road before he could catch her.

She walked quietly over to him and picked up the apple and the knife. When she pulled the knife out, the apple fell to the ground; and that was just enough to cause Guy to open his eyes. He saw her standing there with the knife and jumped to his feet. Kristy rushed in toward him and stuck the knife in the top of his left leg as deeply as she could, and turned to run. Guy pulled out the knife and threw it as far away as he could. Kristy had hit an artery, and blood was gushing out quickly and running down his leg. He chased Kristy down, grabbed her, and threw her into the backseat of the car and slammed the door behind her.

Guy opened the driver's door to get in but staggered backward. He looked down and saw that his pant leg was soaked with blood. He was afraid to drive. Looking around, he thought if he could just get to the road, someone would surely stop and help him.

He leaned over and looked in the back seat and said, "You hurt my leg bad, Grub. I'm gonna get you when I get back!" He hit the lock button and slammed the door." He was feeling really faint, and it was all he could do to stay upright. It seemed that the short distance to the highway had become an endurance event with everything on the line. At one point, Guy fell against a tree, hitting his head hard and nearly losing consciousness. He stumbled past the last of the palmettos and mustered a few more steps. As he reached the edge of A1A, he collapsed, and his life continued spilling out onto the highway.

Kristy watched him walk away, and she was glad he was gone. He disappeared beyond the palmettos. She sat back and cried. She had almost made it. She was so close to getting away, but now she was in a car that she could not get out of. It was so hot inside that her clothes soon became wet with sweat.

Out on the road, she heard the sounds of a horn blowing and a man's voice. She could not make out what he was saying, but the sound of the voice made her feel less worried.

Kristy tried with all that was in her to kick out the window, but it would not give. She tried to kick out the wire guard plate that separated the front and the rear, but she could not. She was just too weak, too hot, and too sleepy. Maybe if she just took a small nap.

She looked at her dad's watch on her arm and smiled. It always made her feel good to know that she had something of his. Both hands were pointing at the eleven. She took the watch off and held it in her hand as she lay down and drifted off to sleep.

21

Jim was depressed. Even though he had a nice talk with Alfred and Inez during the night and they had a few laughs together, he just could not shake the dream he had. He walked into Kristy's room, and the animals reminded him of his dream. He went out on the deck, and the ocean pricked the point of recall. Walking back into the kitchen, his eyes filled with tears when he saw Kristy's recent artwork displayed on the refrigerator. He was filled with emptiness.

Susan's morning jog would have been over by now. His mind played an internal video of her sitting at the table with Kristy. He watched as she carefully guided Kristy's hand as she worked on her penmanship. Susan stood to her feet, looked at him, and spoke, "I love you, Jim Fender." He reached out as if to touch her.

Norm and Dale had finished testing the equipment and checking over last night's call log when they noticed Jim with his tear-streaked face raising his hand toward them.

"Something I can do for you, Jim?" Dale asked.

"What?" Jim replied halfway between memory and reality. "I was lost in thought."

"Can I get something for you?"

"No, I'll be okay."

He walked over to the window that overlooked the side yard at the monkey bars and swing set. One of the swings rocked back and forth, cuing a new mental video. This time Kristy sat in the swing. She looked so happy. Susan was pushing her and singing "Swing low sweet Kristy Fender."

He forced himself away from the window and went to his room. He knelt by his bed to pray, and when he closed his eyes, he could see the eyes in the waves. After he showered, the condensation on the mirror caused the reflection of his own eyes to look like those in his dream.

Jim ate a late breakfast with the Harwoods and told them about the dream again. This time, he included a little more detail. He thought that if he talked about it, it might quit haunting him.

" ...I could hear Susan calling me into the water."

"I can see where you missing her would cause you to dream that," Alfred said as he lifted his glass of orange juice to take a sip.

"Okay, but why was Tommy the bad guy? He is trying to do all he can to find out who is behind this mess. I know he has a short temper and overreacts to sudden movements..."

Laughing and rubbing his forehead, Dale groaned out, "Amen to that!"

"Yeah, but that doesn't make him a bad guy. And that TV thing with Andrea. I know I see her on TV, but why did she have to die? I know it's just a dream, and I know that dreams can get weird..."

"That part with the waves having eyes and teeth...scary. No wonder you woke up in a sweat. And no wonder that bird scared you so bad! I'd probably still be running," Inez interjected.

"Well, whatever the meaning of it all, I am glad it is over, and I hope I don't ever have a dream like that again," Jim said as he carried his plate to the sink.

Norm and Dale helped Inez with the table, then brought out a box of dominoes and a score sheet. Alfred and Inez took a place at the table and signaled for Jim to join them.

"Nah, I think I'll go for a ride. I think it'll do me good to get out of the house for a few minutes."

"Will you be stopping by a grocery store?" Inez asked.

"Not really planning on it, but I may. I don't have any idea where I might go."

"If you do, call me. I'm trying to decide what to do for dinner."

"I'll do it. I think I'll head toward the inlet. Maybe watch the boats for a while."

He lowered himself into the driver seat of his Lincoln Town Car, a car that was not his choice of cars; but it helped make the impression of success on his clients. He did like the sound system though. He cranked up the motor, the Beach Boys on the radio, and went cruising. The time on his display read 10:36 a.m.

Jim was going at least thirty-five by the time he hit the end of his driveway, and he didn't slow down or even look as he turned right onto A1A. He pulled in to the Quick Stop and went inside to buy a Pepsi. It didn't take long until he noticed people looking and pointing. He wanted so badly just to scream out at the top of his lungs, "Leave me alone!" But it was not in him to actually do it. When he left the store, he decided that there might be a little more privacy if he went south. He turned left out of the parking lot, and soon, he passed back by his home.

Just as he passed his driveway, his cell phone began to ring. He pulled it out of his pocket and looked at the display. He did not recognize the number, but he answered it anyway. He stopped at the parking area just past his home, a place where occasionally people would park and walk the path down to the beach so they could have some privacy.

"Hello."

A female voice came from the receiver, "Jim?"

"Yes, and this is?"

"Kathy Prevatt. You remember, from the funeral?"

"Yes, I remember. Do I know you from anywhere else?"

"Not yet, but you will. I need to tell you some things. Do you have a minute?"

"Sure. I have all the time I need and then some."

"Good. Jim, I really think you are a good guy. I don't know a lot about you, but what I know is good. I just want you to know that everything that I say to other people about you is not about you. It is about making a better life for me."

"Kathy, I am sorry. I don't understand."

"It's okay. You will know soon enough. Just know that I am sorry I have to do this."

"Okay. Can you tell me one thing?"

"I don't know. Try me."

"How did you get my cell number?"

"Sorry, Jim. I can't tell you. Bye."

Click!

Jim pulled back out on the highway and had driven about three miles when he noticed something lying in the road. At first, he thought that some tourist had lost their clothes, but these still had a person in them. Jim came to a stop, and the piled-up body did not move. He blew his horn and nothing happened. He rolled down his window and called out, but the body still did not move.

Jim got out of his car and walked over to the body to get a closer look. He recognized Alex Carver right away. His pant leg was soaked with blood. Jim reached down and felt for a pulse. It was there, faint, but there. Jim grabbed his cell phone from his pocket and dialed 911. The conversation lasted a little over a minute when Jim decided that the best thing for him to do was to put Alex in his car and take him to North Suni Hospital in Daytona. He told the 911 operator what he was doing and told them to make sure someone was ready to take care of him when they got there.

Jim opened the back door of his car, picked Alex up, and put him in. Alex did not appear to be a heavy person, but in dead weight, it was all Jim could do to lift him in. He ran around to the other side of his car, and off to Daytona they went. While he was turning around, he saw what appeared to be the sun reflecting off some glass in the wooded area on the west side of the highway where he found Alex. Jim blew through town doing seventy in a thirty-five. Fourteen minutes later, Alex was being taken from the backseat of Jim's car and rolled into the hospital on a gurney.

Jim, when they were taking Alex in, thought that he had never seen that much blood in one place before. He found himself getting a bit shaky—his knees, his hands, and even his voice.

"Sir," one of the nurses said as she put one hand on his elbow, "why don't you come over here and have a seat?"

"I'll be okay," Jim said as he walked with her. "I'm just a little shaky."

"All the more reason to sit. I have some papers for you to fill out for me, and I want to be able to read them. If you sit, you might be steady enough to write," she said with a smile.

As soon as he sat, he realized how shaky he really was. Soon he pulled himself together enough to fill out all of the paperwork. Once he finished, he carried it to the receptionist.

He went in the bathroom, and when he looked in the mirror, he saw that he had blood all down the left side of his shirt. "No wonder everyone keeps staring at me," he thought.

Larry arrived at the hospital about fifteen minutes later.

"I got here a quick as I could," he said as they shook hands.

"I just finished the paperwork they gave me a couple of minutes ago."

"Wow, your shirt ... so what happened?"

Jim told him as much as he could remember.

"So, there was no one else around?" Larry asked anxiously.

"Nope. No one."

"No car?"

"No. Just him in the road."

"I wonder how he got way down there without a car?"

"I really don't know. His car may have been further down the road. I turned around and headed back this way as soon as I put him in my car."

Larry walked over to the receptionist and spoke to her for a moment then returned to his seat.

"You didn't see any footprints or hear anyone?"

"If I think of anything I forgot, Officer Phillips, I will tell you. I did not see or hear anyone or anything else."

"I'm sorry. It just seems odd that he would be way down there by himself without a car."

"No prob. I guess y'all have to ask a lot of questions."

"That area is wooded on both sides right?"

"Yeah, most of the way to the inlet."

"You think maybe anyone that may have been with him could have been in the woods?"

Jim shrugged his shoulders, getting slightly irritated with the questions that seemed to be repeated. "Seriously. I don't know. I found him and didn't see anyone else. No one on the road or in the woods. I really think I would have noticed a car."

Larry was very fidgety. Every couple of minutes he was at the desk, asking if there was any news. You would think it was a dad worried about his baby by the way he was acting. After his third trip to the desk, a nurse came out to give an update.

"The cut in the upper part of Mr. Carver's leg severed an artery. He is in surgery right now."

"Do you believe he is going to make it?" Larry asked.

"The doctors have indicated that they think he will. He lost a lot of blood before he got here. He has an IV and a unit of blood being administered right now and will have to have more."

"He hasn't been able to talk yet, has he?"

"No. He has not been conscious and probably won't be for a while."

"As soon as he is, I need to speak to him," Larry insisted.

"Don't get your hopes up. He will probably make it. The question remains about brain damage. Mr. Carver did not get enough blood to his brain for a while. It is quite possible he may have sustained significant damage from that. He may not remember anything. In the worst case, he may in fact spend the remainder of his life in a vegetative state. Not saying that he will have any noticeable brain damage at all, just saying to be prepared."

"When can you let me know?"

"Only time will tell. What I can tell you now is that if he had been five minutes later getting here, he would be dead. Mr. Fender most certainly saved his life by bringing him rather than waiting for an ambulance."

After speaking with the nurse, Larry handed Jim a clipboard with a form on it to fill out a written statement. At that point, he began filling out his forms from the information Jim had already given him. He was most of the way finished when Tommy called in on Larry's radio.

"I will come up there as soon as I can, but I have that appointment I need to take care of first."

"No rush. I have this end covered."

"Have you had a chance to talk with Alex?"

Larry gave as much of an update as he felt he should before re-holstering his walkie-talkie.

Jim stopped at a sub shop and got a meatball sub with provolone and Parmesan on a honey wheat bun. That had been one of Susan's favorites. He drove down to a picnic area on the beach and parked and ate his sandwich. He missed his wife and daughter so much. It was only when he finished eating and started wiping his mouth that he remembered how much blood he had on his shirt. The sauce on the napkin looked like blood, and the thoughts started to settle in and cause his stomach to churn.

On the way home, he stopped at an auto detailing shop and had them clean the blood from the backseat before it had time to set or begin to smell too much.

The young man behind the counter looked up when Jim walked in. His eyes, glued to Jim's shirt, followed every move.

"Can I help you?" he said, still looking at his shirt.

"I need my car detailed."

"It will be a few minutes before we can get started on it."

"Well, I am sure it will take a while. The back seat has a lot of blood on it."

"Is that what's on your shirt?" His nose wrinkled as he spoke.

"Yeah. Long story. How long do you think it will take?"

"Blood is hard to get out. A few hours at best, I'd say."

"Dumb question, I know, but do you have a loaner?"

"No. Sorry. How far do you need to go?

After giving the address, he agreed to take him home.

22

The dominoes game was going in Alfred's favor for a change. They were only on the fourth round, and he was already in the lead by 107 points. They were working on double nines, and his was the only train not up. All of his dominoes were lined out. Barring something horrific happening, he was about to make the lead even greater.

Ring!

Everyone rushed to the appropriate place, Norm with the headphones, Dale at the tape deck, Inez watching, and Alfred answering.

"Hello."

A female voice from the receiver asks, "Is Jim there?"

"No. He went out for a ride. May I ask who's calling please?"

"How long ago did he leave?"

"I don't know, half an hour, maybe forty-five minutes or so. Who did you say was calling?"

"He's had plenty of time to get here. Just tell him when he comes in that Kathy called and I can't hide us any longer. I didn't mean this way when I said I couldn't raise someone else's child."

"What? I don't think I understood you."

"Well, I understand the wife but not the child. I am sorry. Just forget I called."

Click!

No one could believe what they had just heard, and no one would repeat it regardless of how many times Inez begged. Dale rewound and listened to the conversation at least a dozen times, every time with the same confused look on his face. Norm pulled out his log book and started writing down the important information. The call was logged in at 11:41 a.m.

After a few minutes of reflection, Dale suggested that Alfred take Inez for a walk on the beach while he and Norm took care of a few calls. They suggested that Alfred sit her down and tell her what was said. Dale told Alfred to realize that this case had received a bit of air time so this could just be some kind of practical joke.

Alfred had a problem believing the joke part. He had heard a girl named Kathy tell Jim that she loved him yesterday at the funeral. The way that she had held his hands and looked at him said so much more than, "I am sorry." She had even kissed him. Now this. As the Harwoods walked out the door to head down the beach, Norm was dialing the phone to call Tommy.

"This is Norm. I need to speak with Tommy if he is in, please."

"Actually he is out of the office right at the moment, but I can relay a message for you."

"Just have him call me as soon as he can."

"No problem. I will contact him and let him know. Hey, Norm. We got a call a few minutes ago about Alex. Have you heard anything?"

"No. What happened?"

"Not sure. He was in some kind of an accident. Larry is on the way to the hospital to see him now. I thought you might have heard something because Jim Fender was involved in some way. He was the one who called it in."

"No. Haven't heard a thing. Jim left to go for a ride earlier, and I haven't heard anything since."

Within five minutes, Tommy rang in. Dale answered the call.

"What ya got for me?"

"A phone call came in, and I am not sure what to think of it."

"Got it on tape, right?"

"Yeah. It would be good if you could come by and listen to the conversation as soon as you can, or I can bring it to you."

"I have an appointment with some woman named Kathy. Says she has some information for me."

"By the way, what happened to Alex?"

"Wow, news really does travel fast. Good or bad. I'll tell you about it later when I come by there."

―――――――――――――――――――――

Out on the beach, Alfred tried hard to tell Inez what had transpired on the phone. He tried to tell the truth, but instead, he just told her part of the truth.

"Honey, that was some woman on the phone. The way she talked, I think she has some kind of feelings for Jim."

"Jim is a nice guy. I am not really surprised that other women would like him."

"No, not like that. Like she likes him, and he likes her."

"No way! I don't believe it for one second. Jim could never…"

"Inez, look at me. I don't know what is going to come of this, but I think it would be best if we go home."

"What are you talking about? When they find Kristy, she will need us. Jim will need us."

"We can come back then."

Alfred took her in his arms and held her. He knew that she wanted to stay. He also knew that phone call had lit a fuse and an explosion of some kind was imminent. Already grieving the loss of her daughter, Inez did not need to be around during the fallout.

Inez whispered, "I don't want to go. Losing Susan is the hardest thing I have ever had to face. Everything inside of me is torn into pieces. Being here with Jim is like still having a part of her."

"I know. You are a strong woman." He felt the warmth of her tears as they soaked through his shirt. "We need to go. At least for a few days."

She turned to face the house. "You can make some phone calls and arrange a flight home."

Inside, Norm and Dale had begun to have a discussion of their own.

"Dale, do you think that chick was for real?"

"I don't know, but she sounded like it. If not, she is one sick cookie."

"If not, then why would she have called?"

"Possibly to get attention, to stir up trouble or to be in the spotlight? Who knows?"

"And if she is for real, then what does that say about Kristy?"

"Either she is dead and the body is hidden somewhere...or if she is alive, he knows where she is."

"And what about the phone call on his cell?"

"It wasn't traceable. It could be that he had someone call it. Could be that maybe that phone guy was in on it too. He claims he saw Kristy, but outside of that and other than what Jim says, there is no proof of any kind that she has actually been alive for days now. The picture in the jar, the hair in the bag, the photo in the casket was all found by him."

"So, if you had to take what we have now and go with it, what would you do?"

"Norm, you know Tommy will have to be the one to decide, but I think I would have to arrest Jim and charge him with the murder of his wife. I would have him interrogated to see if we could find the girl. If she is alive, she needs to be found. If she is not, everyone else needs some closure."

"So you think we ought to be ready to arrest him and take him in for questioning as soon as he gets in?"

"No. I think Tommy should tell him he is a suspect and give him a day or so to see what he does. I think if he is guilty, he will try to run. If the girl is alive, he will lead us to her. If the girl is dead, he will show us where her body is. If he is not guilty, then he will just hang around and be depressed."

"And as far as us?"

"I think we should pack up and get out, tap the phone externally so he doesn't know, then see what happens."

The Harwoods returned from their walk. Inez went straight to the kitchen and started cooking. Alfred went to the phone and started the process of booking a flight out for the next day. Neither one had much to say outside of the necessary.

When lunch was finished, Alfred and Inez excused themselves to go pack. Even though they had only been here for just a few days, it seemed so long. So much had happened, and they were tired. After they packed their bags, they sat on the side of the bed together.

"Alfred, you don't think Jim was having an affair with that woman on the phone, do you?"

"Sometimes it's better not to ask what someone thinks unless you want to know the answer."

"If I didn't want to know, I wouldn't ask. I only want your opinion."

"Inez, sweetheart, as much as I love Jim like a son, that woman on the phone was very convincing. If Jim was having some kind of relationship with her...I don't know. Yes, I think they were."

"Apparently, from the way Dale and Norm are acting and the way you're acting, some of the suspicion for the murder now falls on Jim. Do you think he had anything to do with it?"

"I should hope he didn't, Inez. I just don't think it is wise for us to be here while the police try to sort this whole thing out. Whether or not he did it, I think that call will help them figure out who did. It might help them find Kristy."

23

When Jim walked in, Tommy was in the recliner. Alfred and Inez were upstairs taking a nap, and Dale and Norm were packing up the equipment. Everything was almost ready to go. The tape deck was still up and functioning with a tape in and rewound to the appropriate place. The first glimpse of Jim in his bloody shirt brought all the attention on him.

"Sorry. I found Alex down in the road, so I took him to the hospital."

"Yeah. I know," Tommy said. "It took you quite a while to get home from the hospital, didn't it?"

"I guess. I stopped for a bite of lunch and dropped my car off to get it cleaned up."

"Jim, I really don't want to have to do this, but I guess I'll have to. Have you ever heard of a Kathy Prevatt?"

"Yeah. As a matter of fact, I met her yesterday at the funeral. Why?"

"So you have never heard of her before that?"

"I don't recall ever meeting her before then. Maybe I had, but why?"

"Play the tape, Norm."

Norm apologized to Jim before he pressed the button. Jim was totally taken back by what he heard coming from the tape. He could not think to say anything. His mind rejected what he was hearing. His whole body refused to believe it. He sat down with his mouth wide open.

"Well, Jimbo, I know you're surprised to hear that she called you here, but she did. She also came in my office and gave me a statement about the affair you two have been having for the last few months. She said she had told you that she could deal with being with you if you would divorce Susan, but she wouldn't be able to deal with raising someone else's child. Now, I need to ask you again, do you know this woman?"

"Before yesterday, I had never heard of her."

"A minute ago, maybe you had. Now definitely you hadn't. Let me see your cell phone a minute."

Jim handed the phone over. A few seconds later, a phone number was on the display under the heading, "Received Calls." Tommy held out the phone and asked Jim who the number belonged to. It was the number from when Kathy had called him. Tommy pulled out a small notebook from his pocket and opened to a page that was dog-eared about halfway back and compared the phone number he had written under the name Kathy Prevatt with that on the display.

The Harwoods heard Jim's voice and came down to see what was going on. They could hardly believe what they were hearing.

"Kind of ironic that her number should be on your phone and that you talked for almost three minutes. Not like a major conversation, but not a wrong number either." Tommy smiled as he spoke.

"She called me. I don't know why, but she called me."

"Okay. So you're telling me that this woman you've never met before your wife's funeral just out of the blue calls here and says something like this to your dead wife's father and then calls your cell phone?"

"Yeah. That's what I am saying."

"So why did you give her your phone number?"

"It's in the book."

"Not your cell. Her name isn't listed on the sheet of names you gave us the other day of everyone who knew your cell number. She either is a very lucky guesser or someone gave it to her."

"I don't know how she got it. I really don't, but I didn't give it to her."

"Are you sure she doesn't call you on occasion with her caller ID blocked?"

"What are you talking about?"

"Is that who called your phone twice that you said was the kidnapper?"

"No, it wasn't."

"Were you going to meet her when you left this morning and just didn't make it because of finding Alex?"

"No. That's ridiculous."

"Has anyone told you that the person who sent those flowers with the hair attached to them looked like you and was dressed like you were that same day?"

"What? No. C'mon. What are you doin'?"

"Jimbo, it don't look good. I am giving you notice that as of now, you are suspect in the murder of your wife and abduction of your daughter."

"But I...what?"

"Jim, do you know where your daughter is? Is she alive?"

"I can't believe this. I don't know who this woman is. I didn't kill my wife, and I wish to God that I knew where my daughter was. Inez, Alfred, tell them I didn't do it."

The Harwoods sat silently. They both wanted to speak, but they couldn't. Both wanted so badly to believe Jim, but there were too many questions. Finally, after a few moments of silence, Inez began to cry.

"Alfred, Inez, I didn't do it. I swear I could have never done anything to Susan! I loved her so much. Kristy...I just didn't do it."

Tommy looked at Jim carefully. He really didn't want to do this, but his dad was right; something had to be done. Possibly, this would get enough pressure off him that he might actually be able to do some kind of investigation. He had a feeling that if he did, he wouldn't want to know who was actually behind it. He really hoped it wasn't his dad. And if it was, then what? Would he be able to charge the great Mr. Sutton with this and make it stick? Would he be able to watch his own father go to prison? He didn't want to do this, but he had to.

"Jim, stick close by. Don't get any ideas about taking any trips anytime soon. I am not saying I think you did anything. I am just saying that all the evidence points toward you."

"Tommy, you know me and have for a long time. Do I seem like the kind of person who would be capable of such a thing?"

"Under the right conditions, stranger things have happened. Jim, I don't know what to think. I just have to do my job."

By the time Tommy, Dale, and Norm got packed up and out, it was almost five. Jim couldn't believe how tired he was, but he didn't want to go to bed, so he called Andrea. She came out with a camera crew, and they shot a live segment for the seven-o'clock report. Jim had showered and was in fresh, clean clothes when the interview hit the air. He felt like he would feel better if he was the one on the news talking about being a suspect rather than waiting for Tommy to do it in the morning. Andrea told Jim that she believed in him and would do everything she could to make sure that the truth was kept up front. The portion of the interview where they talked about Jim taking Alex to the hospital had given a bit of the local hero motif to the whole broadcast. Jim closed the interview by tearfully asking the public to please call the TV station if they had any information on the where-abouts of Kristy and showing a few more pictures.

It had been no more than ten minutes when Andrea's cell phone rang. It was the studio calling. They said that a man had called in and said he had seen Kristy riding in the back seat of Tommy Sutton's police car just this morning, and Tommy had been driving at the time. The caller said he had called in to talk to someone at the station about it and talked to an Officer Phillips. The caller said it sounded like Tommy was trying to do a number on Jim.

As she hung up the phone, she looked at Jim and smiled. "Let's step outside for a minute. I need a breath of fresh air."

Jim agreed, and they stepped out onto the deck. Andrea pushed the door closed behind them.

"We may have a little good news for a change. Someone thinks they saw Kristy just this morning," she said in a near whisper.

Jim was so excited he had to force himself to stand still. "Wow! Who was it? Where was she?"

"Shush. Keep it down. It could be just someone looking for a minute in the limelight. Let me check it out a little closer before we get too excited."

"I'm going to call Tommy!"

Andrea grabbed his shoulder and gave him a stern, "No!"

"Jim, I know this doesn't make a lot of sense, but you need to trust me. You cannot say anything to anyone about this. Give me a chance to do a little looking around."

"But I don't understand. Why not tell the police? They are the ones who can do something about it."

"Jim, please trust me. I can't say anything more. Just please."

"I do. I know you will do what's right, but I just don't understand."

She took Jim's hand and looked at it. She turned his wedding ring and said, "You owe it to her. Let me help you find out who did this."

She helped load the last of the equipment in the van just as the rain began.

That night, Jim slept.

24

August 10

Larry was almost ready to walk out the door to head to the office when the phone rang. It was a nurse at the hospital.

"Mr. Phillips?"

"Yes."

"One of our patients, Alex Carver, asked me to call you."

"He's awake!"

"Yes. He woke up about an hour ago and has been asking for you."

"Tell him I am on my way."

Larry called the office and left a message for Tommy that he was going to Daytona to check on Alex.

Larry went as quickly as he felt safe to go.

At the nurse's station, he was greeted by name.

Larry looked around for a second, "Oh, I guess you saw my name on my uniform."

"Actually, no. Mr. Carver has not stopped asking for you."

"Is he okay?"

"He seems to be agitated over something he left in his car. I'm not sure what he is talking about, but he keeps saying someone needs to get the Grub out of the car."

"Did he say where the car is?"

"No. I have tried to assure him that we will make sure he gets plenty to eat. He says that he isn't hungry."

"Can I go in to see him?

"Down the hall, fourth door on the right."

As soon as Larry walked into room 429, Alex started trying to push off the nebulizer mask where they were trying to keep his lungs clear. Since he was only a little over halfway finished with his albuterol cocktail, the respiratory therapist was quite insistent that he keep it on.

"Alex, just relax and finish. We can talk when you finish this."

"But you don't understand. The Grub—"

"Trust me. It was well over ninety yesterday. The sky was clear. If the Grub was in the car, it can't be saved."

"No. I didn't mean to—"

Larry interrupted him, "Alex, let's just wait until this nice gentleman finishes, and then we can talk."

Alex closed his eyes and started to cry. He really hadn't wanted any part of this whole mess, but Larry had told him that a case like this would help Tommy get a big raise. He also said that Jim had caused Tommy a lot of problems and when he had gone into Tommy's desk and found his yearbook and the pictures in it, he had believed him. Alex didn't want to kill anyone. He had refused to even consider it when Larry had suggested it. Instead, he had agreed to take the girl and keep her out of sight. He had tried hard to play the tough guy to keep Kristy in line, but he could have never really hurt her. But now he had probably killed her.

As soon as they were alone, Larry started asking questions.

"Alex, I need to ask you some questions. If you can't answer now, I will come back later, but I need to know."

"I will tell you what I can."

"What happened to your leg?"

"I closed my eyes for a couple of minutes, and the Grub got my knife."

"So, that little girl cut your leg with your knife?"

"Yeah, I am stupid just like everyone says."

"No, Alex, you are not stupid. You made a mistake. So, if she cut you, where is she?"

"I put her in the car and locked the doors." He started crying again. "Somebody needs to go get her."

"I can go check on her soon. Can you tell me exactly where you parked the car?"

"I went down A1A to that place where I go when I want to be alone outside. You have to pass the Grub's house to get there. It ain't on the side with the ocean."

"What were you driving? Your car is at the station?"

"Tommy's car. That's why you have to hurry. She can't open the door or open a window or nothin'. She's stuck."

Larry sat back quietly and thought. He saw an open door here for him not just to take Jim down but also to take Tommy along with him. When Thomas had retired, he felt that he should have gotten the promotion, not Tommy. Way back then, he had determined that one way or another he would someday get that job. He knew that Thomas had ways of making bad things happen to people who stood against him, so Larry had agreed to help take care of Jim. Now if he could work it out to where Thomas thought he was still trying to get Jim and take Tommy down too.

"Alex, that is perfect," he said with a smile on his face. "Yes. This could be the thing that does it."

"I don't understand, Larry. How can this be good for Tommy?"

"Just tell anyone who asks that Jim put that knot on your head and that he cut your leg trying to get Tommy's car from you, that he put the girl in it and that you collapsed and don't know anything else. Got it?"

Alex just nodded. From the best that he could figure from all he had been told, Jim had actually saved his life. The doctors had said that if Jim would have waited for the ambulance, he would not have made it. Now he was being told to make everyone think that he had killed his daughter. Was all of this really to help Tommy?

Alex was not a good communicator. He liked to play around with trying to write poems, but he knew they weren't ever going to be publishable. Since he couldn't always articulate everything the way he wanted to, most people thought of him as mentally slow. He had been picked on and used most of his life, and no one ever seemed to have any regard for him at all until Tommy. Tommy had befriended him and given him a chance to be with the police every day. Even if he could not be one of them, he could at least pretend. Tommy had done so much for him—not just to save him from a fire, but he had given him a life.

Alex was now faced with a big problem. He had to choose which way to go. As best as he could see it, his choices were:

1. Say nothing. Tommy takes the fall, and Jim is a hero.

2. Tell Larry's story. Jim takes the fall, and Tommy is the hero.

3. Tell the truth. Then he, Thomas, and Larry take the fall, and there is no hero.

4. Tell Tommy, and let him decide what to do.

No option sounded good at this point.

How could he have ever allowed this to happen? When he left Michigan after high school, he was so full of dreams. He was going to come to the most famous beach in the world, build some muscles, get a tan, and have all the girls. Instead, no matter how hard he tried, the muscles wouldn't come. And when he wasn't working or taking classes at the community college, it was dark; so a tan was out of the question. After the accident, the burn scar across his chest kept him from even wanting to go to any public beach. And girls. That was a joke. When a girl was near, he just didn't know what to say. He would trip all over his words when he tried to use some smooth line.

"Alex, you are gonna be able to do this, aren't you?"Larry asked with definite concern in his voice.

"I guess I have to. I just really didn't want to hurt the Grub. She really was a nice one."

"I know, but you need to be careful. We don't want Tommy to have any problems with this, do we?"

"No. I will do it. I wanna be alone for a while if I can."

"It's okay. I understand. I'll come back later and get my report."

"If it's okay with you and if Tommy has time, I would rather have him do it."

"Okay. If that's what you want. Just be careful what you say."

Larry walked out the door, wondering if Alex would really be able to stand up to the pressure. Of all the people who thought of Alex as slow, Larry was top of the list. He had once made the comment that the only thing slower than a snail trying to cross a sidewalk on a hot day was Alex trying to say something deep, like hello.

As Larry drove to the station, his mind wandered. He wondered if anyone had found Tommy's car yet, if Kristy was still alive, if Alex was going to be able to convince Tommy, if he had thought of everything, and mostly how long until he could have his position as chief.

Alex picked up the phone and dialed his mother's phone number for the first time in six years. He was so scared and confused. He needed to hear his mother's voice, and everything would be all right. What he heard was a recording that announced that the number was not in service.

He knew that the sun was already up in full force and that the temperature inside the car he had locked Kristy in would have already have reached the one-hundred-degree mark. He couldn't believe he had been so foolish to get involved in this whole mess. Why could he not have just said no and told Tommy before it was too late? He could ask himself the same questions, and the answers only confirmed what he had been told a thousand times. He was just plain stupid, and he had proven it again.

Alex pressed the morphine button and drifted off to sleep.

25

Tommy arrived at the office around seven. When he first walked in, he was greeted by a message on his answering machine that Larry was going to see Alex at the hospital. Tommy was feeling pretty good about the way everything had gone the day before. All of the pieces were falling into place, and it wasn't going to take much to close the case. The only loose end was the girl. If she showed up alive, then what? Would she tell everything and cause his case to be exposed as a fraud? Was his dad right about saying that she would be killed? So many questions.

As he did his morning routine, he made a mental note that he needed to go see Alex as soon as possible. He was his friend, slow or not. He would have gone yesterday, but it had been a busy day, and Larry said that he was on morphine and probably would not be up to a visit anyway. Larry also told him that Alex didn't remember much of what had happened.

He checked all the paperwork, calls, and other notes from the previous night. There was nothing out of the norm. He signed off on the log book, showing that he had looked it over. He was almost ready to go out for the day when he decided to look at his yearbook again. He opened the drawer and reached way in the back and...no book.

Who could have gotten his yearbook and why? He kept his office and his desk locked. As far as he knew, the only one who had a key to his office besides him was the janitor, and he didn't have a key to the desk. He wasn't too concerned at first until he remembered the drawing he had done in it. In light of all that was going on now, that would not be a good thing for people to see.

He walked around the station, just glancing here and there, trying not to be too obvious. He really wanted to know who had his book. He wanted to know why whoever had it had taken it, but he saw nothing that would give him a clue.

When he went out to the garage to sign out his car for the day, he picked up the clipboard and signed in and then hung it back on the wall. He turned and started toward the lot and noticed that his car wasn't there. Whatever had happened to Alex had happened before he returned from waxing his car. When Tommy went back over to scratch off the sign out, he thought that maybe he would check Alex's desk for his book. He didn't think it would be there, but he did think that Alex was obsessed with him; and obsessions can make you do weird things. After all, he had been exalted to the position of Boss Sutton.

Tommy looked carefully in each drawer, trying not to mess anything up. Alex was a neat freak, and anything not just like he had left it would be noticed. There were lots of folders labeled for this or that and several handbooks outlining the best way to do this or that. Everything you would expect to find in the drawer of the head mechanic. The only thing that looked remotely out of place was a five-pack of JVC videotapes with one missing. Tommy closed the desk and went back to his own office.

He was already running behind schedule, and it was only 8:30. He had hoped to be on the road before now. He really wanted to drive his number 01 today, but since he couldn't find it, he would take his Crossfire again. He called Janet and talked with her while he drove. They really seemed to be getting their relationship together. For the first time in a couple of years, they were talking, laughing, and spending time with each other.

Even if this case never was truly solved, it had made him a hero again in her eyes.

By 9:00 a.m., he was in Alex's driveway. The carport was empty except for the fishing poles that hung neatly on the wall next to the door. They were so clean and well kept that Tommy thought they were probably never used. The yard was neatly trimmed, and the driveway and sidewalk were neatly edged. Everything made the house the best-kept house on the block and possibly in the whole town. He considered driving to Daytona to ask Alex, but if he was out, drifting on a morphine nap, he wouldn't get an answer. If he was alert, Larry said he didn't remember much anyway. Even so, if he didn't find it soon, he would wait and ask when he went for his visit later.

By 9:15 a.m., Tommy was at the carwash that Alex sometimes used when he wanted to wax one of the cars. There were several cars there, but not his. He got out and walked around, looking for anything that might say whether Alex had been there or not. After checking the trash cans by the vacuums, he found no clue. There was a small office there that sometimes held the owner long enough to get the money and make out deposit slips. Tommy got lucky, and Johnny was in.

"Mornin', Johnny."

"Hey, what's up, my friend?"

"Were you around here much yesterday?"

"No. I didn't even stop in at all. Why? Am I in trouble?"

"Maybe," Tommy said with a grin. "I was just checking to see if Alex had brought my car in yesterday. He is in the hospital, and I am trying to find out what happened to him and my car."

"Well, wonder no more. Remember that video monitoring system I had put in when I was having problems with vandals? Just so happens I keep it running all the time now."

"So, you have a tape of everything that happened yesterday?"

"More or less. It stores one frame every two seconds. That is good enough to catch most everything that happens and allows me to run the tape on a forty-eight-hour loop. As long as I get here every other morning and check on everything…anyway let's take a peek."

They fast-forwarded through, revealing no Alex and no number 01.

As Tommy rode around, he went past Dipper Dan's and the oily payphone. Andrea was getting into a white Ford Focus with a cone of ice cream as he drove by. Just past the phone was Jack's Barber Shop. Tommy decided to go in to get a trim and to see if anyone had seen his car. Surely someone had seen it or something that would help him find it. On his way in, he keyed the mic on his walkie-talkie.

"All units, has anyone seen number one this morning? It seems that Alex must have had it."

Several men broke in with a negative response.

"Okay, keep your eyes open. It may give us a clue as to what happened with Alex. Not to mention, I want my car back."

"How did the check on the area where Jim found Alex go?"

"No luck. We rode back and forth on that stretch of road a half a dozen times and didn't see anything unusual."

"My car is out there somewhere. Just let me know as soon as you find it."

Larry keyed in, "Tommy, be advised that Alex is ready to give a report but will only give it to you."

"That's good. It seems he is doing better. I just walked in the barber shop. I will head that way as soon as I leave here."

Tommy was the only customer in this morning. Jack didn't seem quite as friendly or as happy as usual when he signaled for Tommy to take a seat. There was a feeling of oppression that seemed to fill the room. The TV rattled off the latest sports statistics just before Jack hit the red button on the remote that zapped it dark and silent.

"So, Jack, how ya been?"

"Don't matter, does it, Tommy? I don't think it matters to you a bit."

"What in the world are you talking about? Of course it matters."

"I gotta know somethin', Tommy. You an' me have been friends for some time now. I never would have thought you'd do this. Never in my life would I have expected this."

"Do what?"

"You put on a pretty convincing act on TV about that little girl. You know, that little call-me-if-you-know-something thing you did."

"I really do wanna know. If anyone has seen her or has any information, I really want to know."

"Yeah. I bet you do."

"Okay, Jack. Tell me what's goin' on."

"Well, you act so innocent like you know nothing, and you plead for information…and the whole time you know where she is."

"What? What in the name of all that's good are you talkin' about?"

"I saw you stop out here the other day and let that girl use the phone, and I saw you ride by yesterday in your cop car with her in the backseat."

Tommy was so shocked that he just sat there and tried to understand what he was saying. He had driven by with her? He had let her use the phone? He was confused.

"There ain't no way. I didn't even drive my patrol car yesterday. There is no way you could have seen me."

"No. I saw you and her ride by in your car. And with that big number one on top, it is hard to confuse it with any other car."

"Jack, I didn't even get in that car all day yesterday, not at all."

"Tommy, you are my friend, and I won't volunteer any information; but if anyone asks, I won't lie either."

"My car is missing, and Alex had my car yesterday. Now he is in the hospital. Maybe it was him and someone?"

"Tommy, it was you, and it was the girl. I saw you with your hat and glasses. I know you when I see you. Now, let's drop it before someone comes in."

"But it wasn't me. I swear."

"Okay. That can be your story. I won't tell different."

Jack did his usual good job on Tommy's hair while Tommy sat silently, trying to understand the previous conversation. It made no sense. How could Jack have seen him driving a car with Kristy in it when he wasn't even in that car? How could he have been seen with someone he hadn't been around? If it had been a stranger, he could have said it was just that they saw the car and they assumed him to be the driver.

He tried to pay Jack for the hair cut, and like always, Jack refused. They exchanged a few pleasantries, and Tommy walked out. Once in his car, he headed toward North Suni Hospital in Daytona. Maybe Alex could shed some light on the situation.

26

Jim couldn't remember seeing a more beautiful sunrise. Stars that decorated the night sky were overtaken one by one as the canopy transitioned from black to purple and on to blue. The sun, as it rose, painted the bottoms of the clouds red; and the surface of the ocean, which was not too rough, shone with a rippled, red reflection. The rain that began as Andrea and her crew were leaving the night before had dropped a couple of inches before moving on out to sea. A small amount of foam was constantly being rearranged near the water's edge by the waves that were breaking in at about two feet. The beauty of the scene, and the freshness in the air that followed the rain, had a calming effect on Jim.

The Harwoods had flown out from Sanford, and Jim was at home alone. The house was quiet. Silence filled every room. There had been virtually no time since Susan's death that the house was not filled with busyness. Finally he could take time in his home to mourn his loss. Jim had never realized how nice it could be to be alone—no one to listen to every call; no one watching his comings and goings; no one to cast a critical eye.

He was hurt that in his in-laws had left. That phone call seemed to push Alfred across the line into doubt. He used protecting Inez as an excuse, but Jim was convinced that it was himself that Alfred was protecting.

He went into Kristy's room and spent some time in prayer.

"Oh, God, I am here before you. Broken and beaten by this life. Lord, forgive me for failing you. I am a sinner. In my heart I hate the person who killed my wife and has taken my daughter. I want to know who he is so that I can take revenge. Your Word tells us that vengeance is Yours to impose, not mine. Your Word says we should love our enemies, yet I can't even love. In the Psalms, David cried out for you to wipe out those who raised their heads against him. Lord, forgive me for not trusting You to do the same for me.

"Who am I that you should hear my prayer? Why should I even ask you to do anything for me? I would ask as James says, 'amiss.' You took Paul and Moses, murderers, and changed them. You brought glory to Yourself through them.

"When Job faced the loss of everything, he did not cry out for the death of those who had taken it. He instead said, 'The Lord gives and the Lord takes away. Blessed be the name of the Lord.' Why can't I do that? He mourned his loss, but he didn't seek retribution. Lord, give me peace. Lord, help my unbelief.

"Lord, I miss my wife, and I miss my daughter. Susan is with You. Shelter her under Your wings. I don't know where Kristy is, but You do. Keep her, and let her remember that I love her.

"Andrea is looking for some information. Bless her efforts. Guide her steps. Give her wisdom.

"Thank You for your Son, Jesus. It is only in Him and in His name that I can come to You. Amen."

After he prayed, Jim walked to his own room and opened the closet. On the top shelf was a large, pink, stuffed teddy bear that he had won for Susan several years ago at the Central Florida Fair in Orlando. He and Susan had agreed that one day they would give it to Kristy.

When the dust had been vacuumed off Teddy to the best of Jim's ability, he was placed carefully on Kristy's bed. Jim pulled back the covers and tucked him in. He walked to the door and looked back. He walked back and lay down with one arm around Teddy. Sleep overtook him. He dreamed of days on the beach with Susan and Kristy. A smile made itself at home on Jim's face as he slept.

The doorbell rang around 11:15 a.m. Jim forced his eyes open and sat up. The bell rang again. Jim sprang to his feet and down the steps. When he opened the door, Andrea was already halfway back to her car.

"Andrea?"

Andrea turned quickly and started walking back toward the door.

"Jim, we have to talk. Something is going on, and I don't know how to explain it. But we have to talk."

"Come in. I'll grab us Pepsis, and we can talk out on the deck."

"I don't know, Jim. I think it would be better if you come with me. We'll get a sub or something and find a quiet place to sit."

"Okay. Just give me a sec, and I'll grab some flip flops or something for my feet."

Andrea smiled. "I woke you up, didn't I?"

"Is it that obvious?"

"Not really, but you might wanna run a comb across your head before we go."

Jim laughed and ran in to get his shoes and fix his hair. When he went into the bathroom and looked at himself in the mirror, he couldn't help but laugh. His hair was standing up in the middle of his head like some type of shaggy Mohawk. He hadn't shaved, and he looked like he'd been beaten with an ugly stick.

While he worked on making himself presentable, his mind pondered the reasoning behind going. What *could be so important that they couldn't talk here?* he asked himself. *Is this a good idea, or one that will once again bring even more suspicion my way?* She seemed genuine and concerned. Surely she could be trusted.

He re-emerged from the house about ten minutes later looking somewhat human. His hair was wet and settled, he had sandals on his feet, and his face was clean and shaven. He had changed into a new shirt and put on some deodorant and some cologne. He was ready to go. He had enjoyed the time alone this morning, but now having company was good too.

Once they settled in and buckled up they were on their way.

"I must say, Jim, it is amazing what a few minutes, a comb, and a razor can make," Andrea said in jest.

"Well, good company brings out the best in me."

One of Jim's strongest traits that helped him in his ability to buy and sell at a profit was being quick with a compliment. He had a way with people that drew them to him. That same *gift* often seemed more like a *curse* in that his compliments were on occasion perceived as flirting.

Looking out in front of the car at the road, the heat rolling up off the pavement gave the illusion of water puddles on the road that would disappear as the neared them.

"You guys got loaded up just in time last night. Five minutes longer and it would have been loading in a downpour."

"I know. When we got back to the station, I was so glad we had a covered area to unload in."

Jim wondered what it was that Andrea had to say. Whatever it was, he was sure it wasn't going to be good. He anticipated the speech, *"... and when I got there, the good news was just a joke."* The way things had been going recently, surely the good had separated itself from the news.

Getting out of the car, Andrea pulled out a credit card and held it up.

"This one is on me—or at least on my expense account."

He put on a look of surprise. "Wow, it's been a long time since a good-looking TV star offered to buy my lunch. I think

I'll take you up on that. Wouldn't you know it'd be a sub shop and not a steak house."

Andrea ordered a tuna sub on oat bread. His mind had drifted to the times that he and Susan had been here; so when he was asked for his order, he just said, "Make it two of those."

She followed his directions to the same table where he had eaten lunch the day before. During the ride, he reflected on the morning. The sun rise, the nap, and his time so far had all been good. Maybe Andrea had good news for him as well. *Don't get your hopes up*, he thought as they pulled into the parking space.

Andrea took several napkins and spread them out over the table, wetting the corners of each to keep them from blowing away.

"One for you and one for me, "he said as he placed the sand-wiches on the table.

"I was really surprised that you ordered tuna. I would have guessed a hot sub of some type."

Puzzled, Jim opened his sandwich and looked at it. "Tuna? I ordered a meatball on wheat."

"Hmm. Well, sounded like to me you said, 'Two of those,' and I had ordered tuna."

After a moment of reflection, they were both laughing.

"I guess if I ordered tuna, I'll eat tuna."

"Come on now. Tuna isn't that bad, is it?"

"I don't know. For sure not my first choice," he said as he raised the sandwich to brave his first bite.

Andrea watched as he chewed slowly as if he expected it to have bones in it. "Well. Not so bad, is it?"

He finished chewing and swallowed and then took another bite. This time he chewed faster. He swallowed again. "Okay, so sometimes goof-ups work out. I would have missed out on a great sandwich if I would have been paying attention."

When they finished eating and clearing the table, they went for a walk up the beach. Jim really enjoyed the time he had to spend with Andrea. He knew deep inside that he was using her company as a coping mechanism to anesthetize the pain of losing his wife and daughter, but for now, he was willing to use her. Before they got very far, the question-and-answer session started.

"Tell me, Jim, how much contact have you had with Tommy since high school?"

"Up until all this…hmmm…let me think…none."

"None at all?"

"No. None at all. Okay. Possibly a nod when we passed on the street or something like that. We were fairly good friends up until the accident. But since we don't play on the basketball team anymore, we have had no reason to talk."

"No phone calls outside the casual passing on the street? Nothing?"

"None that I can recall. Why?"

"We will get there in a minute. First, I just need to try to find some information that might help shed some light. You said, 'Accident.' Are you talking about the nose thing?"

"Yeah. That would be the one."

"I also understand that everyone was shocked when Susan and Tommy broke up. It was like they were expected to get married and then all of the sudden they weren't together and you were right behind that on the rebound."

"I guess that's the way love is."

"Some people seem to think that you had something to do with the break-up. Is that true?"

"No. I was just the lucky guy who happened to be in the right place at the right time."

"Do you know what happened between them?"

"Andrea, is it really necessary for me to answer all this? It was so long ago, and I don't see what difference it will make."

"It might not. But if there is something you can tell me about it, it might help me to understand some things."

"Okay. If you say so, but I just don't know. Susan never told anyone but me."

"Okay. I understand. Did Susan still see Tommy...ever?"

"No! She did not. Nor would she." Jim felt the hate for Tommy swell up inside him that he hadn't felt since he first found out about the rape.

"No. I didn't mean like that. I just thought that maybe they talked."

"I don't think so. Really, I am sure of it. She wouldn't talk to him."

"Okay, Jim. Here is the thing. The call last night would lead me to think that there are reasons not to trust Tommy. It is quite possible that he knows more than he is sharing."

"I would hope he knows something more because he isn't sharing anything."

"It might be possible that he is involved."

"Andrea, Tommy might be a lot of things but...well, I just can't believe he would have anything to do with this. He really isn't that bad of a guy."

"Are you sure you don't want to tell me what happened? Even if I tell you that at least three people have seen Kristy riding around with him as recently as yesterday?"

"He what? No way. I don't believe it. Someone is messing with you."

"Jim, I want you to know that he had me fooled too. I even helped him get past that mess-up he made the first day on the air, but the truth is I have personally talked with three people who *unofficially and off the record* have told me that they saw her with him at different times and places."

They had come to a stop and were not paying much attention to anyone else around—not the dozens of other folks that were running, walking, swimming, and playing within plain sight. Neither did they notice the glimmer of light as it reflected off the binoculars at the top of the dunes. Neither were they aware that Officer Larry Phillips was at that moment not just watching them but scheming. He had watched as they enjoyed the meal together. He had even gotten a few pictures. The walking down the beach from Larry's vantage point looked like romance, but how could all this be used to destroy Tommy? He wasn't sure yet, but there had to be a way. If he could get rid of Tommy, he could be chief, just as it should have been before. When he did decide how to use this against Tommy, he also needed to make it look like he was trying to use it against Jim so that Thomas would be satisfied that he was doing right. After all, Thomas could destroy him in a flash if he wanted to bring out the file and pictures he had on him. He had so much information and a very short time to decide how to use it to his own advantage. So far, everything was working out just perfectly. Kristy would soon be found, and all eyes would be on Tommy.

Down on the beach, Jim had finally agreed to tell Andrea about the rape and the way Mr. Sutton had treated her.

Andrea had tears in her eyes as she thought of the hurt Susan must have endured. "That is a secret that I wouldn't want to have. I don't think I could have done it."

"Thomas had her over a barrel of sorts. If she told, she and her parents would be ruined. Her love for her mom and dad was enough to keep her from talking."

"I still think we need to find out as much as we can before we go to anyone."

Jim agreed.

As they walked back up the beach together, neither had much to say. In Jim's mind, there was a question that had to be answered, one that made the whole idea of Tommy being the bad guy seem a bit farfetched. If Tommy really did have Kristy, where would he be keeping her? If at his home, Janet would know. If at work, everyone would know. It's not like he could be anywhere for any length of time without someone noticing him being gone. But even so, the dream was adding some validity to the idea, even though it was only a dream.

27

Larry got back into his patrol car and headed south. He had determined to find Tommy's car before anyone else did. Maybe Kristy had survived. Maybe she had gotten out and was wandering around. Chances of either were slim to none; but just in case, he did have a little something he wanted to add to the scene.

One evening, when Thomas was still Chief, he had given Larry his keys to get him some papers from his office. It was during that time that Larry had made copies of all the keys: door keys, desk keys, filing cabinet keys, everything. The locks on the filing cabinets had been changed, but the rest had remained unchanged. After Tommy had become chief, the keys had allowed him to be privy to some very interesting stuff, stuff like personal notes Tommy had made to himself about his wife, stuff like the little note he received from the mayor of New Smyrna asking him to consider dropping a ticket he had written to one of their officers, stuff like this yearbook with all the nice drawings in it.

Larry drove on past the Fender residence a couple of miles and then slowed down and started looking carefully for any sign of a car off in the wooded area on the west side of the highway. After about another mile, he saw a glimpse of light as it reflected off the glass. Just a short way past that, he saw where cars had used this area, on occasion, to pull off. There probably had been a few fishermen looking for a way to get to the Intracoastal

Waterway. There had probably been a few lovers looking for a quiet place to be alone who found this to be the perfect place.

Larry parked across the entrance and got out to take a closer look. The first thing he noticed was that there hadn't been any tires go across the sand in the entrance since the rain. Just a few steps in and he could see number 01 sitting there. He walked over to peek in the window, and there was Kristy. In her hand was her father's watch. Larry tried to open the doors, but they were all locked. A short distance away was a blanket that had been blown about a little with an apple lying on the ground next to it. He got the book he had taken from Tommy's desk and laid it on the blanket and folded the corner up over it.

Larry tried to replay the story that Alex had told him. He tried to reenact the panic so as to figure out where he had thrown the knife. In less than ten minutes, the knife was in his pocket, and he was in his patrol car headed north. Just before reaching the Fender home, Larry pulled off on the shoulder and took a stroll through the palmettos to the beach. He walked out to the edge of the water and was about to give the knife a toss into the waves, when a thought crossed his mind that filled his heart with joy. He carried the knife back to the car, got out a small zipper bag, and slid the knife down in it.

Jim was waving good-bye to Andrea when Larry passed by. Jim looked as if they had enjoyed their time together.

Larry drove all the way to the Italian Grill for lunch. It was nearly 1:30 p.m. by the time he had finished eating. When he went back out to his car, he checked in on his radio. When the proper back to work chitchat was over, he asked if anyone had seen number 01. He really wasn't surprised to hear that no one had.

"Just for an update, I saw Alex's doctor when I was at the hospital. He says that Alex is getting along very well and will probably get to come home in a couple of days," Tommy explained.

"Did Alex have anything to help in his statement?" Larry asked.

"I didn't get it. I looked in at him, but he was asleep. The doctor asked me not to wake him. I'll go back and get it tomorrow."

A quick drive over to the beach and Larry was ready to check in with some news.

"Hey, Tommy, are you still by your radio?"

"Yeah, I'm here. Whatcha got?"

"Some guy just stopped me and said he saw a police car off in the woods on South A1A."

"Hasn't everyone already been down that way to look?"

"I haven't, but I'd love to. Norm can listen to the phone as easy as I can," Dale offered. It was just a matter of a few minutes when Dale pulled into the entrance to the open area that surrounded number 01. He didn't pull in very far before he decided to get out and walk. He didn't know why, but he had a strange feeling about this whole mess. Something just wasn't right. Why would Alex bring the car out here? Or if someone had taken it from him, why not drive it off or even strip it and sell it?

After he got out of the car, he noticed that he had not been the only one here today. There were footprints in the sand that had been made since last night's rain. Dale was careful not to step in them. Dale had discovered over the years that sometimes it is the most unlikely things that will lead you to the person or the place you need to see. He pulled his gun as he approached the car and eased up carefully.

When he got close enough to the car to see in the window, the first thing he saw was some blonde hair. He ducked down and called out, "Police. Raise your hands and step out of the car." He watched for the car to move to indicate some kind of movement inside the car.

Dale keyed his radio. "Send some backup. My car is next to the road, so it can be easily seen."

Tommy responded, "What's going on, Dale?"

"I found the car. I think someone is in it."

"Don't be a hero. I'll be there in a few minutes."

"Norm, if you're there, come on down here. The tape will catch anything you miss."

"On my way, Bud. Be careful."

"I will," Dale whispered.

Several officers keyed in to ask questions, but Dale didn't answer. He had decided to ease around to the other side of the car for a look.

He rose up just enough to see Kristy's shoes and ducked back down. He called out again. No answer came. He slammed his fist against the side of the car, which aroused no movement or sound other than that he had caused. He jumped to his feet, pointing the gun at the window. When he saw her body curled up in there, she looked as though she was sleeping peacefully.

He grabbed the door handle only to find it locked. He took his night stick from his belt and smashed the window. He reached through and touched her. He knew immediately that she was dead.

Dale decided to wait for Norm before touching or doing anything else. He walked back over to his car and began making observations. He pulled out his notepad and began to write. As he was writing, he realized this was the area where Alex had been found. There was blood on the highway to prove it. He looked from there back toward number 01. The footprints where Alex had walked out were still visible though distorted by the rain.

As Dale was making notes on his observations, Norm pulled in behind him and blew the horn. Dale's reaction looked like something out of an old Western. He threw his papers and pen into the air, pulled his gun, and hit the ground rolling. Norm laughed hard until tears filled his eyes.

Dale got back to his feet and re-holstered his gun. After staring at Norm for a few seconds through the windshield, he said, "You are an idiot, plain and simple. No two ways about it. I could have just killed you."

Norm pulled the rest of the way off the road and got out of his car, still trying to regain his composure. "So you're the hero who gets to claim the rights to finding the prize egg, huh?"

Dale had his notepad and pen back in hand, and he was busy writing. He looked at Norm and said, "This egg had a surprise inside, not a pleasant one, but a surprise just the same."

"What kind of surprise?"

"The girl is in there. It looks like she cooked a bit in the hot sun since yesterday."

"And you haven't called to get a wagon out yet?"

"Norm, I don't know what it is, but something isn't right. Take a look around. There are just some things that strike me as odd. You and I have both agreed that somethings have not fit together in this case from the beginning."

"Yeah. Okay. I understand that. But the body?"

"It won't make a whole lot of difference to anyone if we can have about thirty minutes to look first. Let me show you some stuff I've noticed so far. This is where Alex was picked up. See the blood?"

He pointed down toward number 01. "You see where he walked out from the woods? He was injured in there."

They walked over to Dale's car, and he pointed out the fresh footprints, both his and the others. He pointed to the edge of the open area.

"Whoever the other prints belonged to walked around the side of the area, kicking up places in the sand here and there as if looking for something. He moved the blanket a little. You can tell by the sand that was knocked up on it by the rain. They have also been all the way around the car. I don't know anything more, but I am sure that if we take a few minutes, we can find some answers."

"What seems strange to me is that Jim is the one who found Alex, and his daughter who was missing turns up here at the same place. After that call from that Prevatt woman, this really doesn't look good for Jim at all."

"That's true, but do you really think he would have told us right where he had picked up Alex if he was involved?"

"I don't know. Sometimes criminals do the dumbest things. That is why they get caught most of the time."

Norm got out the camera, and Dale started with taking fingerprints from the car. Both men were working hard and fast, trying to make sure they didn't miss anything. Lying in the front seat of the car was a hat, shirt, and sunglasses like the ones Tommy always wore. The glasses had been neatly placed on top of the hat with the shirt folded next to them.

On the ground, next to blanket, was an apple that had been picked apart by some bird. Norm took a couple pictures of the blanket. When he unfolded it, he found the yearbook. He used his pencil to open the front cover. Just inside were several places where it had been signed by teachers and students. Almost all of them started with, "Tommy." On the top right corner of the inside front cover, signed in familiar handwriting, was "Tommy Sutton."

"Dale, check this out."

Dale walked around and looked for a few seconds in unbelief. Had Tommy been out here? Had he done this?

Norm looked up at Dale and said, "You know what this means, don't you?"

"I can't believe that Tommy would do this."

"Look, Dale. You missed something here. Look closely at the book."

"Okay. I have seen Tommy sit at his desk and look at that book before. What am I missing?"

"The book isn't wet. It wasn't out here last night when it rained. Whoever put the book here wanted it to look like Tommy did this. Tommy's car, his book, and the man who married his high school sweetheart."

"Wow. Then that means that maybe…never mind."

"What? I want to know what you were thinking."

"Well, with everything looking like it does, I was beginning to think Alex was behind this. He left with Tommy's car; he gets injured and gets rushed to the hospital; and the next time the car is seen, it has the girl in it. But if someone was here this morning and left that book, they have been all around the car. Maybe the body was placed in there this morning. Then Alex couldn't have done it because he is in the hospital."

"Yeah. That's all true, but I think the girl has been in the car all night. We will know when they get her out. If someone brought this book here this morning and left it, they knew that the car was here and most likely that she was in there."

"Jim?"

"Could be."

It was about that time that Tommy called out from by the road, "So how's ole number one?"

Dale answered back, "Oh, she's got a busted window, but she'll be fine. But we have to have a talk before you get too excited. And watch where you step. We're trying to figure out those footprints."

"I'll be sure to walk easy. Why not get excited? I miss my car."

"You probably can't drive it for a while."

"A busted window don't take that long to fix."

"Well, that may be true," Dale said with a touch of sarcasm, "but dead body's put a kink in the whole thing."

"A body?"

"Yep, that Fender girl I believe."

Norm spoke up. "There is something else we need to discuss before you say much. Look there on that blanket. Recognize that book?"

Tommy didn't answer. He just stood with his mouth open.

"Okay, now here is the scoop so far. Jim picked up Alex from the road right out there. His daughter was found here. The book looks like someone is trying to set you up. Question: Do you think it could be Jim?"

Tommy thought for a second before answering. "It can't be. There is no way Jim could have gotten my book."

"Then tell us, Tommy," Norm said in his analytical tone, "if it's not Jim, then who?"

"I don't know. There has to be an answer. But who? Why would anyone do this to me?"

"'Cause you're a cop, and you have put a lot of bad people away. Because you hold a position of authority, so certain people would love to see you go down. Maybe 'cause your dad put the wrong guy away a long time ago. It really doesn't matter why so much as *who*."

Dale had to ask the question that had been on his mind. "If the book was in your desk, who could have gotten it?"

"That is the whole problem. When I noticed the book gone this morning, I tried to figure that out then. Who could get into my desk? And now I guess I have to ask the deeper question about…" Tommy tapered off into silence. A thought had just crossed his mind. He was so dumbfounded by the first thought that he had to stay silent for a minute.

"Tommy, I don't know what you're thinking, but you need to share," Norm said. "That way we can all ponder it."

"What if for some reason Jim decided he wanted out of his present life? What if he still holds a grudge against me over the…break-up thing with Susan back in high school? What if there really is another woman?"

"Possibly like that Prevatt woman from the phone?" Dale asked.

"Or someone else. But what if he convinced Alex to help him out? What if something went wrong yesterday and Alex got hurt and Jim had to rush him to the hospital? What if they really didn't plan for Kristy to die like this but it just happened to work out that way?"

Dale jumped in. "What if something went wrong, Kristy died in the car waiting for Jim to show up, and when he got here, he was so mad that he cut Alex? Maybe he was aiming to make him less of a man and hit lower than he had intended. Maybe Alex made it to the road and Jim decided he had better do something before anyone saw him. Maybe he didn't think he would live anyway with all that blood pouring out. Maybe Alex had already given him the book so Jim came back this morning and placed the book here."

Tommy keyed the mic and called to get some other folks to help and for the coroner's office to have a wagon sent out. He went to his car and started rolling out the crime scene tape. As he walked the parameter, he couldn't stop thinking about all that had happened. One thought that seemed funny and still yet filled him with anger was this: *What if the whole time he was trying to build a case to make Jim look guilty, Jim was trying to turn it all on him?*

28

Jim had really enjoyed himself with Andrea at lunch. She was probably the nicest person he had ever met other than Susan. He was still having a hard time swallowing the idea that Tommy had any part in the death of his wife, and to think that he could have Kristy was almost absurd. Yet, he knew that sometimes, for no reason, people do strange things.

Maybe Janet was giving him a hard time. Maybe he was afraid that Susan would eventually tell on him. A million maybes and a few thousand possibilities piled on top wouldn't change what Jim remembered of Tommy. He had his share of problems, but this seemed to be just a few steps beyond him.

Jim walked through the house, dusting a little here and there. He stopped off in the kitchen long enough to make sure the kitchen was clean. He went to his bedroom and looked into the closet he had opened earlier. All the clothes on the left side, the open side, were Susan's. He looked at it all and pictured her in each one. He had loved her so much. He missed her now as much as he loved her then.

He wanted so badly just to have one more day with her, share one more meal, watch her try on one more new dress. He wanted to hear her voice, feel her touch, watch her walk. Maybe if they could bring Kristy back that would help. He missed her too.

He sat at the table for about ten minutes and wrote down the things that Andrea had told him. He wrote down some of the possible scenarios that could have lead to all this, but none really seemed to make sense.

He sat out on the deck and watched the people walk by. He listened to the waves as they rolled in. He watched the gulls fly over. He thought about times past. But mostly, he cried.

When Tommy came to the door, it was close to 5:00. Jim was still sitting on the deck, crying, when the door bell rang. He stood to his feet and walked slowly toward the door, trying to pull himself together as he went. When he looked through the window by the door and saw who was standing there, he was filled with anger. Everything that Andrea had said came back like a flood. When he opened the door, he was so full of emotions that he didn't know what to say. He was angry because of the possibility that Tommy did have Kristy. He was hurting because of missing his wife. He was anxious because Tommy might have news about Kristy.

Jim focused on Tommy's eyes, and he knew it wasn't going to be good.

"She's dead, isn't she?"

Tommy hung his head. "Yes, she is. We found her body just a short time ago."

Jim's face drew tight, and tears filled his eyes. He held his head down whispering, "No, God! No." After a minute or so, he pulled himself together enough to ask, "Had she been hurt bad before—?"

"No. She didn't look as if she had been abused in any way."

"How did he do it?"

"We are not sure just who did what or how the whole thing came to be, but she probably didn't hurt much, just laid down and went to sleep."

"Was she poisoned?"

"Don't think so. At this point, the coroner is doing an autopsy. It looks like she was locked in a hot car too long and just overheated."

Jim broke into tears again. After a couple of minutes, he pulled himself together. He had seen stories on TV about children being locked in cars and dying of heat and had thought on many occasions that only a real idiot would allow that to happen to his child. Now those words came back to haunt him.

"Whose car was she in? Do you know?"

Tommy had to look away as he spoke. "It's under investigation right now. When we have enough information, we will let you know."

"Is there anything I can do to help?"

"Not that I know of except don't leave town. I am not telling you that I am going to charge you with the murder of your wife and daughter, but I am saying that it could come to that."

"Tommy, you know better than that."

"She was in your patrol car, wasn't she?"

"How did you know that?"

"I didn't, but you aren't drivin' it. You are drivin' your Crossfire. The way you looked away when you told me it was under investigation. How did she get there?"

"Jim, we really don't know. Maybe you could tell us."

"Come on. How would I know?"

Jim wanted to tell Tommy that he knew that he had been seen with her. He wanted to pay him back for every ounce of pain he had gone through over the last week. He wanted to re-break his red nose. He wanted to do a lot of things, but Andrea had warned him not to say anything.

"I really don't have a clue."

"You have any good conversations with Alex recently?"

"No. He wasn't up to a conversation the only time I have seen him recently."

"Did he have something for you, like maybe a book or something?"

"What in the world are you talkin' about?"

"Nothin'. Just don't go too far. I might need you."

"Tommy, is there any way I can see her?"

"Not right now. The coroner will be calling you."

"Can't you tell them that I need to identify the body or something?"

"Trust me, Jim. This case has a high priority. They are rushing the autopsy. You really don't want to walk in during that. It may not be too bad, but on the other hand…If it were my child and knowing what I know, I would wait."

"Can you at least tell where the car was? I would like to go there for a few minutes."

Tommy considered telling him, but he knew Jim would put things together and soon be on his way to see Alex. "I can't release that information just yet. I will let you know as soon as I can."

Jim went back in his house and closed the door. What a day this had been. From the beautiful sunrise, to the nap with the teddy bear, lunch with Andrea, the news that Tommy had been seen with his daughter…and now to find that she was dead and he might get charged for it. Almost every emotion he knew how to muster had been there today.

Jim climbed the stairs and stepped into Kristy's room. He would give anything to see her in there again. Teddy lay still and quiet. The row of stuffed animals kept watch from the overlooking shelf. He knelt next to the bed and picked up Teddy. "She won't be comin' back to play with you. She went to her other home to be with her mother." He squeezed Teddy to his chest and the tears began falling.

"Why didn't they just kill me? God, why not me?" He started to sob uncontrollably. He sat Teddy back on the bed. Within a couple of minutes, his breathing became deep and rapid. His hands began to tingle, as did his lips. He tried to stand, but his legs were weak. He was hyperventilating. He had heard of it many times, but other than breathing in a bag, he had no idea what to do. The emptiness of the house added to the anxiety.

He remembered hearing something about the drop in carbon dioxide possibly causing a heart attack. He wanted to go where someone could see him. Without going down the steps, which he could not do, being seen was not possible. His anxiety was drifting toward fear. The words he spoke just a few minutes ago echoed in his mind, *Why not me?* Was God going to take him too?

His vision started to fade to black. He was sure he was going to pass out. He climbed onto the bed and curled up on his side. He pursed his lips and attempted to force his breathing to slow. Frustration started to set in within a few seconds. He let out a growl followed by a loud, "Stop it!" He closed his eyes, clinched his teeth, and tried again.

He rolled to the other side, and Teddy stared him in the face. He put his arm around Teddy and pulled him in close. He began to relax. His breathing began to slow. A sense of relief flowed through him.

Jim soon stood back to his feet and put Teddy back in his place. He maneuvered the stares and got a bottle of water from the fridge. His mouth was dry and his body was tired. He walked to his recliner and turned on the TV. The seven o'clock news was going off.

The phone rang.

"Hello?"

"Jim? Is that you?"

"Yeah. At least I think it is."

"Are you okay?"

"I don't know that you could call it okay. They found Kristy."

"I know. I am so sorry."

"Why would anyone do that?"

"I don't know. We got a small bit of information a few minutes before we aired. No details. Just that she was found. And that she was…that was about it."

"Did you know she was in a car?"

"No. The byte we got said that the police were not releasing anything more."

"She was locked in a car."

"Jim, can I come by for a few minutes?"

"Thanks, but that's not necessary. I will be alright."

"It isn't a problem. I know you are hurting. I just wanted to lend a sympathetic ear. If you would rather be by yourself, I fully understand."

"If you don't mind. I really would like to talk through what Tommy said."

"It may be an hour or so. Is that okay?"

When he went into the bathroom to fix his hair, the man in the mirror looked horrid. His eyes were bloodshot, his hair was a mess, and he had the overall appearance of a man who had just taken a beating. "A shower and some eye drops are in order," he said as he turned away.

Twenty minutes later, Jim was looking at that same man, only now his eyes were clear and his hair was in place. He was wearing a pair of khakis and a navy polo shirt. His face still looked tired. "At least now you only look half beat." He nodded at the mirror and went to sit on the deck.

He leaned on the railing and looked up and down the all but deserted beach. One couple walked hand in hand. He looked out at the water hoping to see a shark or maybe a school of mullet. Instead he saw a diver surface for a minute and then re-submerge. Watching the ocean in the fading light had a soothing affect. He was soon lulled into a dream.

The doorbell rang, and Andrea stood waiting while Jim slept. After a third ring, she walked around back and saw him on the deck. She carefully, quietly, climbed the stairs and sat down in one of the other chairs on the deck. She sat just watching him sleep for close to ten minutes before she decided to try to wake him. She moved her chair close, placed her hand on his, and whispered his name. He never moved. She spoke his name again, this time a little louder. He opened his eyes. It took a minute to cross back from the land of dreams.

Andrea spoke again, "Jim, are you awake now?"

"Yeah, sorry."

"It's fine. By the way, I still have a couple of bucks left on my expense account. Want to help me spend it?"

"What do you have in mind?"

"Dinner?"

"I'm seriously not hungry. But, I will go sit with you while you eat."

"That's okay with me, but if you change your mind…"

Andrea drove them to Captain Mark's. This was her favorite seafood restaurant. She ordered the house specialty Coconut Shrimp salad. It was a bed of spring salad with a Pina-Colada dressing topped with six coconut shrimp. Jim ordered a Romaine salad with Ranch dressing.

"You sure that is all you want? I will cover whatever you order."

"I don't have much of an appetite this evening."

"So, what did Tommy have to say?"

"He reminded me a couple of times that he may charge me with Susan's death and added Kristy's to it."

"That was what I expected. Anything else?"

"He asked me if I had talked with Alex much recently. That was kind of odd. I don't know him that well."

"Did he give any indication as to what you may have talked about?"

"No. But the really weird thing was he asked me if he had given me some book or something."

Jim left half of his salad in the bowl. The ride home was quiet.

29

After helping file all the necessary paperwork to complete his day, Larry headed home for a few minutes. While there, he grabbed his scuba gear and put it in his car, grabbed a cold slice of pizza out of the fridge, and went for a ride. A few minutes later, he found himself at the pull off just south of Jim's home. Before walking down to the water, he put on all of his gear except his flippers. He slid a plastic zipper bag with a knife inside into his pocket and headed out to the water. He slipped on his flippers, and off into the deep blue. He went out about a hundred yards and north about a quarter mile and then in a bit to take a look.

In his carrying case strapped around his waist was a camera with a 50x zoom lens. He pulled it out and watched Jim as he came out on the deck to sit. As Jim watched the lovers walk by, he was being watched. Larry realized that Jim had spotted him, so he ducked under for a couple of minutes. When he looked back up, it appeared as if Jim was sleeping or reading. Larry really couldn't tell which. He watched patiently. He had watched from out here many times. From here is where he had taken the pictures that he had given Alex to put in the room with Kristy. On one occasion, he watched Jim and Kristy watching the sky with a telescope. He watched and waited until everyone was asleep and stole the telescope. He had let Alex use it so Kristy could see her dad. His plan was to plant the stolen telescope in Tommy's car, but Jim never reported it.

Larry also watched many mornings from out here to make sure he could get the timing right on killing Susan and taking Kristy. He was glad Alex had agreed to help him figure out the timing. Alex wasn't good for much, but he had helped him work out a couple of the kinks.

He had waited out here until Susan had swum up that morning. As soon as she was almost done with her swim, he swam up under her and thrust his divers' knife into her chest. He had played it through in his mind a thousand times before, but he never expected that much blood. He was sure that the water made it look like more than there was, but it was a lot. The idea that it was his knife was what made him think of the knife from the evidence room.

Larry watched Andrea as she knocked on the door. He snapped a couple of photos as she walked around to the deck. He snapped a couple more while she was waking Jim.

He watched them as they walked back down the steps and around the house. They got into the car and drove away. As the taillights disappeared into the distance, Larry appeared from the water. He took off his flippers and tank and carried them as he walked up to the deck. He rubbed the zipper bag across the contents a few times to make sure there would be no readable prints and then dropped the knife in the sand. He started to walk away, but knowing that Jim had left down the steps instead of through the house left a question. Is it locked? A few seconds of investigation, and Larry was in the house.

In the kitchen, on the table, he found the note that Jim had written earlier. Looking at the note, he wasn't sure what Andrea knew, but she obviously knew more than she should. Somehow, she had found out that Kristy had been riding in number 01. What else did she know?

He went upstairs and looked in the bedrooms. Jim's room was nicely kept, and the bed was made. It just had a couple of Susan's dresses lying on the bed and a couple pairs of shoes in the floor.

When he walked into Kristy's room, he saw the teddy bear there, all covered up. His first thought was that it was a person, so he jumped back; then when he realized what it was, he broke into a chuckle. He went over and uncovered the bear. He pulled out his divers' knife, the same one that had taken Susan's life, and stabbed the bear in the chest.

On his way back out, he took the note from the table and threw it in the trash. He didn't try to hide the fact that someone had been there. He left the water that had dripped. He left the door open. He was sure that Jim would know someone had been in his house and just as sure that it would not be reported. When he stepped out on the deck, the moon was just coming up over the horizon.

Larry loved the ocean—the look, the smell, and being in it. The moon looked so big, and the reflection on the water was almost hypnotizing. He walked to the edge of the deck and just stood there, enjoying the beauty. Looking both directions, there were no other houses and very few people on the beach. Larry pulled one of the chairs up next to the railing and kicked back. He really enjoyed the view from up here. He thought that maybe after Tommy got put away for the Fender murders and Jim realized that he was alone and the house was too much for him, maybe the new police chief could convince him to sell it at a reasonable price.

When he felt like he had sat there as long as it was safe, he stood to leave. He remembered the report on Dale accidentally falling over the railing. He looked over the edge and said, "It's a wonder the fool didn't die."

After walking back down to the water's edge, he put his tank and flippers on and started out into the water. He heard one of the waves crash. He looked and watched as the next one crashed. The sound of it made him think of a giant set of teeth crashing together. He took another step out, and the moonlight shining through the next wave gave it the appearance that there were a set of eyes in the water watching him. He tried to shake it, but the sound of the crash and the next wave rising with the eyes in it was more than he could take. He turned to walk out, but the sound of the next wave crashing seemed even louder and closer than any before it. He stepped out as quickly as possible and turned back toward the water. He couldn't figure it out. He had been in and out of water like this most of his life but had never had such a feeling of fear overcome him. It was as if the ocean was watching him and was ready to eat him up.

Larry walked south with his flippers in his hand. As he walked, the sound of the crashing waves caused him to walk farther and farther away from the water. He walked faster until he was almost to a jog. His heart was racing.

30

Andrea dropped Jim off around eleven. He walked to the door and unlocked it and waved as she began backing out the driveway. He walked on in, wondering why he had left so many lights on. The open door to the deck caught his attention immediately. He assumed he had left it open when he went out on the deck earlier. The water on the floor answered the question of the open door.

His thoughts raced, *Someone had come in. Someone may still be in.* He felt the hair rising up on his neck and arms. He slowly, quietly followed the trail of wet footprints to the stairs that went up to the bedrooms. He could see that whoever had gone up had also come back down.

He walked to the bedrooms and looked. His room seemed to be just like he left it. The footprints seemed to go to the doorway and stop. He went to Kristy's room and looked in. The bed had been turned down, and Teddy was lying on his back. He went to the bed with the intention of just rolling him back on his side and covering him up. He started to roll him when he saw the large cut with stuffing falling out. Jim came to a sudden halt. His mind superimposed the image of Susan with the hole in her chest over that of Teddy. It was like reliving the moment he found her. He could hear Kristy calling to him just as she had when he found Susan. His hands began to tremble. He turned his eyes toward one of Kristy's pictures and whispered, "It will be okay." He looked back at Teddy and said, "I will make it right."

Anger began to replace the hurt as Jim sat looking at the evidence that once again proved his failure to protect. Nothing or no one was safe when entrusted to his keeping. Drawing his hands into clinched fists, Jim looked around the room hoping for something to hit. His teeth ground against each other. He became aware that his breathing had begun to accelerate again. Rage was taking all control from him. Again, Dr. Eller's words came to him. In a sermon on the fruit of the spirit, Dr. Eller had said, "When anger is taking control, call on the fruit. Remember that *peace* and *self-control* are part of it." He forced himself to calm down.

Jim carefully took Teddy in his arms and walked him down the hall. He opened the top dresser drawer and pulled out a box of safety pins. Jim carefully pulled Teddy's chest together and pinned it closed.

"I'm sorry. I guess I failed you too."

Jim walked Teddy back to Kristy's room and pulled out a shirt. "Let me slip this on to cover the scar."

He was laying Teddy back in the bed when he heard a *pop* from down stairs. He listened carefully.

Nothing.

Jim yelled out, "Hey! Is anybody there?"

Silence.

Each step was deliberate, making sure his movement was not heard. He listened to the quiet for another moment before forcing out another call, "Answer me! Who's there?"

Just as he started to put his foot on the top step, *pop!* He jumped back into Kristy's room. "Who's there?" he demanded.

Silence.

"I can't do this," he whispered to himself and then yelled as loud as he could, "Answer me!"

Nothing.

In the back of Jim's mind, he actually hoped the killer was in the house and that he would jump out any second and grab him. He hoped that he could see his face just once before he died. And then if the knife plunged into his heart, he would know, and he wouldn't have to live with the pain any longer.

Jim pulled all of the strength and courage he could muster. He moved back out into the hall and then slowly down the steps. "Who's there?" He walked into the living room and looked around. Nothing unusual. He walked into the kitchen. *Pop.*

Jim wheeled around, looking for the killer, but saw nothing. Almost in a panic, he squeezed out, "Where are you?"

Pop.

It was coming from the deck. Jim eased toward the door. He could see no one through the window. He reached for the handle.

Pop.

He looked again at nothing.

Pop, pop.

He started to slide the door when he saw the seagull peck once again at its reflection in the glass. *Pop, pop.*

Jim grabbed the door and yelled, "Get outta here you stupid bird!" And then he slid the door closed, hard.

His hands started to shake and his knees to knock. He found his way to the recliner and sat. Jim allowed himself to laugh and then to cry.

Once he pulled himself together, he walked out on the deck. No sign of the bird. The moon was a good way up in the sky, yet it made such an alluring reflection on the water. He could see a dolphin a short distance out as it played in the water. He knew that he wasn't really just playing but he was tearing up a school of bait fish and enjoying the meal. It made him think of how so many things in life are not as they seem.

Just a week ago, life was good. On the surface, there was nothing but fun and games, but just below the surface lurked a monster. The monster had sat, idly waiting for the right moment to strike. When he did, he had taken almost everything. Jim was reminded of Job in the Bible, how when the devil had come into the picture, everything that Job loved was taken away. His living was taken away when his livestock and servants were taken; and then his family, his friends, and finally his health were taken, yet Job kept his faith.

But Jim was not Job. He did not stand firm when Susan was killed. He had not considered that God was in control when he lost the big sale. He had not thought, *Nevertheless, not my will, but thine,* when the news of Kristy's death had come. And he was too numb to even think when he found Teddy with a hole in his chest. Jim had his home, his health, and plenty in the bank to fall back on. He had received an insurance check for Susan that more than compensated for the financial loss. He knew that there would be one more coming, but no check of any amount could replace those people he had lost.

As Jim thought about all the events that had transpired, he thought about Alex and all that blood that had been spilled on the highway. He wondered if the same person who had killed Susan had done that to him. If so, how did it all tie in? He couldn't understand any of it. Too much of the truth was hidden.

Jim considered calling the police, but what good would it do? It would probably just mean that he would have to face Tommy one more time. After all that Andrea had said, and with the logical conclusions that he would have to draw from that, Tommy was not who he wanted to see. The only thing he could see happening out of a call to the police would be a sleepless night, and tomorrow was looking bad enough already.

After closing up the doors and locking them, he wiped up what little bit of water was left. He washed the fork and bowl he had used earlier and put them away. When he opened the drawer to put the fork in, the knives that laid on the left of the tray caught his attention. He picked one up and placed it against his wrist.

The thought that he could really do this was strong. He put a little pressure on the knife, and he could feel the sharpness pressing into his skin. He pressed harder until he could feel it cutting into his skin. Small beads of red rose up in two spots. If he just jerked suddenly, it would be a done deal. Nothing would stop the inevitable. But what if it didn't work? What if he cut tendons and lost the use of his hand and did not die? Maybe he should raise the knife up high as he could and then bring it down as hard as he could. Surely that would do it.

He raised the knife up and closed his eyes. With all that was in him, he mustered the strength and the nerve to do it. He thought, *If I only had the strength of Job, I could stop myself.*

The sound of the phone ringing burst through the room and startled Jim so badly that he slung the knife across the room. It stuck in the wall over the microwave. He just stood there and let it ring while he thanked God for interrupting him. As the phone rang, he headed toward his bedroom. He was almost to the top of the stairs before his cell phone began to ring. He pulled it out and looked at the display, which read, "Andrea."

"Hello."

"Jim, you had me worried when you didn't answer your phone. Are you okay?"

"I don't know if I am or not. I am so confused about everything."

"I just called to let you know that all the local stations aired the story about Kristy this evening. Jim, I am sure they are going to try to make it look like you killed her. I don't know how, but I am sure that is what is going on. It seems that every station was called by someone at the police department except ours."

"It doesn't matter anyway. Just let them fry me, and it will be over. I don't think I can do this anyway."

"Jim, please don't talk like that. I know you are not guilty of this, and I know you want the person responsible for this put away. Don't even think about goin' down without a fight."

"Your call just a minute ago was the only thing that stopped me from slitting my wrist. I don't know what to do. I can't even trust myself anymore. Maybe I did do it and just don't remember."

"What? You were in such a good mood when I dropped you off. Is it being in the house or maybe being alone? I can get you into a hotel or find you some company."

"No. Someone came in my house while we were gone and stabbed Teddy."

"Stabbed who?"

"Teddy. You know, a stuffed animal."

"Stabbed a teddy bear? Why would anyone do that?"

"If only I knew. I just don't know anything, Andrea. Nothing makes any sense at all. It's like the devil himself has been turned loose on me, and I am not big enough to fight him."

"Jim, you have to promise me somethin', okay?"

"What's that?"

"If you get to feeling like doin' that again, call me. Please. It's really not worth it."

"I promise. I don't know what came over me. I am really not the kind of person to give into something like that. I guess I'm losing my mind."

"No. You have been through more trauma in the last week than anyone should ever have to go through in a lifetime. You are quite a man, Jim Fender. And even if no one else cares what happens to you, I do."

"Okay. If you say so. I promise."

"Get some rest, Jim. Tomorrow we can talk."

Jim went to Kristy's room and lay down next to Teddy. He put his arm around him and held him close. The small cuts on his wrist placed a few spots on Teddy's chest. All the other animals on the shelf watched as Jim cried himself to sleep.

31

August 11

Tommy arrived at the hospital at about 8:15. Alex was just finishing his breakfast. Tommy wasn't really sure what to say or how to say it. He wanted to come out and ask all the obvious questions, but Alex was his biggest fan. He couldn't just start pouring questions all over him. He looked so pale and weak.

As soon as Alex saw him standing there, his eyes lit up, and a smile crossed his face. He pushed the tray and table back and struggled to sit up.

"Hey. Calm down, my friend. No need to get so excited."

"Hey, boss. I was really hopin' you'd come by to see me this mornin'. I wanted to talk to you yesterday, but they told me I was snoozin'."

"It's okay, Alex. I wouldn't leave you here too long without comin' to check on you."

"Boss, I need to tell you what happened. You got your papers and stuff, right?"

"I got 'em, but you don't have to say anything till you are ready."

"I gotta say it so I can quit thinking on it so much."

"Fire when ready," Tommy said as he pulled up a chair and opened his clipboard.

"Well, I know you ain't gonna believe it, but I got a hole in my leg to prove it."

"I trust you, Alex. Just tell me, and I will write it down."

"Okay, boss. I really like it 'cause you believe me when I say stuff. But here goes. I was takin' your car over to the car wash, but I decided to go home first. I went in and grabbed a little bite and decided I was gonna take it to a secret place I have and kinda do a picnic thing. Well, I got my stuff together and took your car. I'm sorry, boss. I shoulda took mine, but I didn't know."

"It's okay, Alex. Just tell me what happened."

"Okay. Well, then I went over by the car wash and put a few pieces of trash in the thing there by their cheap vacuum. Ours works a lot better, you know. And then when I was pullin' out, I saw that car pull out behind me."

"What car was that, Alex?"

"You know, that Lincoln that the Fender guy drives."

"Could you see who was driving it?"

"Sure could. It was that Fender guy. Anyway, I'll tell you about that in a minute. He had that girl of his with him, ya' know."

"Are you sure about all this, Alex?"

"C'mon, boss. You don't think I'm crazy too, do ya?"

"No. Sorry, Alex. Just go ahead and tell me what happened."

"Okay. I drove on down to that secret spot and pulled in. At first, I didn't worry about him following me 'cause I went right past his house. But when he pulled in behind me, he said he had a surprise. He showed me the girl, and I was so happy that he had found her. I was almost jumpin' I was so happy."

"So he said he had found her?"

"I'm tryin' to tell ya, boss. Just hold on till I get there. Anyway, then he started tryin' to talk me into takin' her and hidin' her until he could figure out what to do. I think he has had her hid the whole entire time. Anyways, I told him I couldn't do that 'cause it ain't right to hide a person like that even if it is a grub and all. So he took his knife out and said he was gonna cut up the seats in your car and get me in trouble if I didn't do it. So I said okay. I was gonna just get her and bring her to you, but he took her outta his car, and she kicked him and ran to me hollerin' help and stuff. He come runnin' with his knife still out. And when he tried to grab her, he poked the knife in my leg, and it started bleedin' real bad. He grabbed the Grub and put her in your car and slammed the door. I tried to let her out, and he smacked me on the head right here. You see that big ole place he made?"

Alex pointed at the place where he had run into the tree and hit his head.

"I see that. So you're saying that Jim had the kid the whole time and that he wanted you to help him hide her?"

"Yep. He was thinkin' 'cause I work with you cops that no one would ever think it was me. He was right, wasn't he, boss? Nobody thinks I did anything wrong, do they?"

"No, Alex. Nobody would ever suspect you of doing anything wrong. I need to ask you a couple of questions just to clarify some stuff, if that's okay."

"No prob, boss."

"Did you say that you went to the car wash in number one?"

"Yeah. Had some trash to get rid of."

"Did you or Jim have a high school yearbook there?"

"Why would I have that?"

"I don't know. I was just askin'."

"No. I am sure we didn't have your yearbook."

After a few more questions and a couple of pleasantries were shared, Tommy left. He had what he needed to officially charge Jim with the murder of his daughter. The biggest problem was that he knew that Alex was lying. He knew that number 01 had not been at the car wash. And he never told Alex which year-book, but Alex had said "your book." Something wasn't right. He thought about the possibility that Alex was responsible for any of this, and he just couldn't see it. There was no way Alex was smart enough to do all this and not be caught yet.

He got in his car and drove back to the station. When he went in, he was stopped by Larry.

"Hey, Tommy. Did you get by and see Alex this morning?"

"Yeah. I did. He seems to be doing quite a bit better. They might let him come home tomorrow."

"Did you get a statement from him?"

"Yes, I did. It's kind of interesting too. But I am not sure about it. It could be that some of the details are off because of the blood loss or something."

"Who did he say cut his leg?"

"He says Jim did it."

"And how did he say the girl got there?"

"He said Jim put her in the car."

"And the yearbook?"

"That is the one thing that troubles me. I didn't tell him it was mine, but he knew."

"Everyone knows you keep that thing in your drawer."

"Everyone don't matter. Just don't seem right that he would know that it was the one I was talking about."

"I talked to him this morning. Maybe I let it slip."

"It don't matter. I am getting on the phone with the DA and gonna get a warrant to search Jim's place, and I am gonna arrest him this afternoon."

"Good. Finally we can move forward a little."

Tommy started toward his office and looked over at the videos on the shelf. He stopped in his tracks and just stared for a minute. He walked over to talk to Dale and Norm about the tapes for a minute. After a little discussion, they all three found their way to Alex's desk. There they stood, looking at the pack of video tapes with one missing, the one that had been made to replace the missing tape from the surveillance machine. It was carefully removed and dusted for prints. The yield was good. There were several good prints there.

"Looks like things are gonna start fallin' into place. I was beginin' to wonder if we were ever gonna get even one real break," Tommy said with a big grin on his face. "I just didn't expect to find anything in Alex's desk. I actually hope that someone just stuck those in there and that he had nothing to do with it. Maybe someone just gave them to him."

"We'll have some answers soon enough," Norm said as he began to upload the prints into the computer system.

32

Jim didn't wake up until almost 11:00 a.m. He went straight to the bathroom and got cleaned up. The cuts on his wrist stung when he washed them. "That was not the brightest idea you have ever had," he said to himself. "Better put some ointment on that." He dressed and went out to walk on the beach. Today was going to be hard, and he knew it. At some point, the coroner's office would be calling to have him get his daughter's body to the funeral home. He would have to go down and make arrangements.

Jim walked southward for a few minutes until he reached the area where he had found the jar and the note in the sand. This was the last place he had seen Kristy. He hoped that in his mind, he would be able to replay the images he had seen from his deck well enough to try to get an idea of what the killer looked like.

While he was walking around, looking back toward the house, a man and a woman came out from the path that led out to the highway, carrying some scuba equipment. Jim had seen people come here to go out to the beach many times. It was easy access, and there were no parking fees. They talked a little small talk, and Jim watched as they suited up and went in the water.

A couple of minutes after they had gone under, Jim saw one of the divers resurface a short ways out. He could see the goggles just above the water, and it reminded him of the dream he had, only the eyes were on the water instead of in it. He watched as the eyes disappeared back into the water again.

He hoped that the walk would reveal something about the killer. Jim walked back toward his house with disappointment rising up within him. Instead of a revelation was a revisiting of the nightmare. As clear as could be, he could see the animals rising and falling with the waves. He could see the eyes in the waves and the teeth as they crashed. He could see Tommy in his rage. But what bothered him the most was that he could see the images of his wife and daughter as the blood flowed and the ground soaked them up.

When he reached the top of the steps that led to the deck, he caught a glimpse of something shiny, almost metallic looking, in the sand up close as if it had fallen off the railing. Jim walked back down to where it was and picked up a pocket knife. It was a little dirty, but it really didn't look like it had been there long. He thought that it had probably fallen out of Dale's pocket when he went over the rail. When he reached the top of the steps, the phone began to ring, and the knife went into Jim's pocket.

It was Bob Birchfield from the coroner's office again. They had done all they needed to do with Kristy's body. A couple of phone calls later and the deed that had been placed before him was done. The Harwoods were notified, and the funeral home had dispatched a car.

After a few minutes of searching, a bowl of fruity rice krisps sat talking to him. This had been one of Kristy's favorite cereals. Susan had said that it wasn't the taste but the cartoon characters who advertised them that made them so appealing to children. After a few bites, Jim had to agree. He ate them slowly, trying to pick out individual colors. Just as he rinsed his bowl in the sink, a knock came at the door.

He rushed to open it, hoping it would be Andrea. When he opened the door, he was surprised to see Tommy, Larry, and Norm all standing there. They first served the search warrant for the house, and then Tommy arrested Jim. Norm began looking inside the house while Larry checked outside.

As he began looking along the ground by the deck, a troubled look dominated Larry's facial features. He searched back and forth for the knife he had placed there the night before. He was sure where he had put it, but it was gone. Looking from the deck and raking his fingers through the sand, he searched frantically, refusing to believe it wasn't there.

When Tommy was checking Jim's pockets, he found almost nothing, just a wallet, a set of keys, and a pocket knife. Jim didn't put up too big of a struggle or argument. After all, Andrea had already told him that she was sure they were going to try to blame it on him. All the contents of his pockets were placed in a plastic zipper bag and labeled with a permanent marker. With the bag in the trunk and Jim in the backseat, Tommy drove away in number 04.

Inside the house, Norm was making some very interesting finds. A knife stabbed in the wall in the kitchen; a teddy bear with some blood on his shirt, which covered a pinned-together slit in his chest in the bed; and a note in the trash. Kristy's bed was the only one that appeared to have been slept in. On Jim's bed were a couple of Susan's dresses laid out as if to decide which would look better.

Norm noticed Larry outside, looking over and over along the same area of ground. He was on his knees, raking his fingers in the sand, digging little holes, and looking stressed. He would stop briefly now and then and look toward the ocean. He would walk up to the deck and then back down again and go back again to looking in the sand.

Andrea pulled into the drive about twenty minutes after Tommy had pulled out. She really wasn't surprised to see the police car sitting there. When she parked, she walked toward the door but decided to walk out toward the beach. Larry was on his knees, running his fingers through the sand. Andrea watched silently as he became more frantic. It wasn't long before Norm appeared on the deck.

"Larry, what in the world are you doing? There is more of the yard to search than just that one area."

Larry stood to his feet and just stared for a second. He looked out at the ocean and then back at Norm. When he was finally able to speak, he said, "I don't know. I just felt like there should be something here. Have you found anything?"

"Yeah. Nothing concrete, but yeah."

Andrea stepped on around the corner and asked, "Something? Like what?"

Larry pulled his revolver, and Andrea jumped back. Her heel caught on edge of the driveway, and she went down hard on her bottom. Norm ran down the steps for the second time to help a fallen person. After asking a dozen questions about how she felt, Norm helped Andrea back to her feet. They walked in the house, and Andrea headed for the couch to sit. She noticed that Larry had walked up to the deck and was now looking over the edge, down at the same area of ground he had been looking at before.

"So what have you found?"

"You know I am not supposed to tell you anything. On top of that, like I said, it's nothing concrete."

"I have to ask you, do you believe Jim is guilty?"

"I don't know. Nothing has added up to anything on this case. Some things point toward Jim, and others point away. Ms. Prevatt's testimony is the clincher. In the light of what she had to say, the 'what ifs' turn to 'why thens'."

"Okay, so do you think Jim is guilty?"

"I think he is in with someone else," Larry said as he walked in the back door. "I don't think he could have done it himself, but I think he at least knows who has done this."

Norm stood to his feet and asked Andrea, "Do you think he is guilty?"

"No. Absolutely not. I can't say who did, but I know it wasn't Jim."

"He has you fooled. He has been in the middle of this from the start, trying to get freed up for that Prevatt woman," Larry said as he rinsed the sand from his hands in the kitchen sink.

"He has not. He doesn't even know that woman. We have talked about it, and he hasn't a clue where she came from. Someone is going through a lot of trouble to indicate that he has done this, but he has not."

"Then why did he attack Alex and put him in the hospital?"

"What? How could you say that? Jim found him and took him to the hospital. If it wasn't for Jim, Alex would be dead."

"That's not the story Alex told us this morning."

"I don't know what you are talking about, but Jim saved his life."

Norm stepped between Larry and Andrea and said, "Listen. I don't know what the truth is, and I don't know what or who to believe about anything at this point, but what I do know is that we have an investigation underway. The truth will come out, but for now, we need to focus on what we have, not what might be."

"So back to my original question," Andrea said, looking at Norm. "What things have you found?"

Larry stepped around Norm and said, "Ms. Everson, we have a crime scene here to investigate. I must ask you to leave."

Andrea reached into her purse, pulled out a business card, and handed it to Norm.

"Listen, guys. I don't know what is going on. I don't know why Jim is being put through this. What I do know is this: Jim is not involved. He is a victim. If you want to let me know something or are willing to possibly look at some other options, call me."

33

As Andrea backed out of the drive, she called Brock Bell, an attorney friend, and asked him to go to the station and take care of Jim. They had helped each other on a few occasions over the years. She was sure that if anyone could make sure Jim got off, it would be Brock.

As she drove north toward Daytona, the question running through her mind was, *What had Alex told the police?* She was convinced that Jim was innocent. She knew in her heart that he couldn't have done this to Alex. But if she was right, why would Alex say otherwise?

When Andrea walked into room 429 of the North Suni Hospital, she did a double-take. Alex was sitting in a chair and was wearing his hospital gown looking at a newspaper. At first glance, she thought it was Tommy sitting there. She assumed that she had seen him before, but she was sure she had not noticed how much like Tommy he looked. He looked as though he had been crying, and his eyes were red; but so was his nose, and that was what really made the similarities stand out.

"Alex," Andrea said, "do you need me to get a nurse for you?"

"No. I'm gonna be okay. I just don't know what to do."

"About what?"

Alex looked for a second and then said, "You're that woman on TV that's been talkin' to Tommy and Jim, ain't ya?"

"Yeah. I guess that would be me."

"Well, I don't know nothin' about nothin', so just don't ask me nothin', okay?"

"I just want to know what happened to your leg. Could you help me out with a little info about that?"

"I don't think my leg thing is a TV news story. I got cut."

"I heard you told someone that Jim had done it. Is that true? Did Jim cut you?"

"Yep. That's what I told 'em. I ain't gonna tell you nothin' 'cause I don't wanna say nothin'. Please don't ask me to tell. I just want to go home. I don't know nothin' 'bout nothin', so I ain't gonna tell ya."

"Alex, I don't know what happened, but they put Jim in jail for killing his wife and daughter. They are also going to charge him with assault for your injuries. If you know anything, I need to know."

"So they ain't gonna fry Tommy?"

Andrea forced the surprised from her face and her voice. "Why would they want to fry Tommy, Alex?"

"'Cause that grub was found in his car. He didn't put her there." Alex paused for a few seconds before continuing. "I don't know nothin', so don't ask me no more questions."

"Alex, everyone I have talked to about you says you are a good person. They tell me that you are the best at what you do. I know that you want everything to come out good for Tommy because he is a good friend and he helped you when no one else would." Andrea noticed that Alex had begun to cry again. "You know that Jim saved your life when he brought you in. I also believe that you know Jim didn't cut you either. I won't tell anyone what you tell me. Please, Alex. I need to know the truth. I want you to tell me. Did Jim cut you?"

"Miss lady, do you promise you won't tell anyone?"

"I promise you, Alex. It is just between you and me."

"No, Jimbo didn't cut me. They made me say he did, but he didn't. I don't understand how this is supposed to help Tommy in his job. They said it would make people want him to stay as chief, but it don't make sense to me. I think it is going to end up bad for everyone."

"Alex, who cut you?"

"I really can't tell you that, miss lady. I just can't.

"Do you know who cut you?"

"Yes, ma'am, I do. But I can't tell you, okay? Please don't ask me no more."

"You know who killed Jim's wife and daughter too, don't you?"

Alex started crying uncontrollably. Andrea helped him stand on his feet and put her arms around him. He slowly put his arms around her as well. As they stood there, for the first time since arriving in Florida, Alex felt safe. He felt like he had when his mother used to hold him and tell him that everything would be okay. They stood, holding each other, for close to five minutes before either spoke.

"Miss lady, I didn't want nobody to die. The Grub was really cute and nice and all, and it wasn't supposed to be her time to die. I was startin' to like her. I didn't want nobody to die."

"Alex, did you kill both of them?"

"I ain't killed neither one of 'em," Alex said as he pushed himself away. "Jim did it, and that's that. I don't know nothin' else, so don't ask me nothin' 'bout it."

A voice came from behind Andrea. "Ma'am, I am going to have to ask you to leave. Mr. Carver needs to rest and not be so upset."

Andrea handed Alex a card and said with a gentle smile on her face, "Alex, if you want to talk, call me. Just know that anything you tell me is just between us."

Alex looked at the card and began to cry again. He wanted to tell Andrea everything. She had been so nice to him. She even reminded him of his mother. The problem was, he didn't want Tommy to get in trouble for this either, and Larry had said that he would if he didn't lie and say it was Jim.

Andrea pulled her microcassette recorder out of her purse when she got in her car and rewound it and replayed the whole conversation three times before reaching the police station. She was convinced that Alex knew everything and had been personally involved in it some way. She also believed that he would have told her if the nurse had not interrupted them.

A tall, dark-haired gentleman stood just inside the door, watching as Andrea walked up. Brock opened the door for her and let her in. Brock stood six foot six and was quite muscular. He had a stern look about him that most folks who did not know him found to be an intimidating appearance. One reason he was so successful in his practice was that he could put fear in the hearts of those on the stand just by leaning in close and looking into their eyes. Brock's friends knew that above all else, he wanted to see justice served, and he would take on many cases without pay because they were right. Whenever Brock was questioned about his success, he always gave God the credit.

"Brock, I just can't say thank you enough for coming down to take care of this. You really are a good friend."

"Hi, Andrea. Nice to see you too. That sure is a pretty dress you're wearing."

"Thanks." Andrea took Brock by the hand. "I know he didn't do it. There is no doubt in my mind."

"I talked to him for a few minutes, and I believe that he has resigned to the thought that no one can get him off. That makes it hard. I am afraid he will just confess to keep from having to go through any more fight."

"I can't tell you anything because I promised, but I know someone who knows the truth. I also know a lot of things that we need to sit down and discuss."

"I can get him out on bond tomorrow, but tonight he will have to spend in jail."

"Tomorrow will be fine."

"If you can go in with me and convince him that there is hope, maybe tomorrow will be okay. If he decides to confess tonight, tomorrow might be too late."

Dale escorted the pair back to the cell.

"Tell me, Dale, how hard would it be to find a phone number or address for Ms. Prevatt?" Brock asked.

"Not too hard. She is in the New Smyrna phone book."

"Off the record and from your personal point of view, is Jim guilty?"

"Actually, no. Although the evidence does not actually present a solid case against him, it does seem to gravitate toward him."

"What do you mean?"

"He seems to be tied to the majority of the evidence in some way. But there is so much that it would have been impossible for him to do or have unless…"

"Go on."

"Without help from someone on the force, he could not be guilty."

"Care to elaborate?"

"No. I know we said off the record, but I cannot tell you anything else. Tommy will when the time is right."

"If you decide otherwise, call me."

"Okay, that's not gonna happen. Here we are."

Jim, Andrea, and Brock sat down and talked about hope. In the circle of three, Brock led in prayer and asked God to reveal the truth in the situation. When they began to discuss the details and the things that Andrea had found out that the police didn't know, Brock became more confident that Jim would not go to prison over this. As much as Andrea wanted to tell Jim about what Alex had said, she didn't want to betray the trust that

Alex had given her. When the meeting was over, all three had an assurance that somehow the truth would come out and that whoever was behind all this would be revealed.

Brock left with a folder containing copies of all the files he could find on this case. Andrea left in a hurry to get to work for her evening broadcast. Jim stayed, knowing that he had three on his side: God, Andrea, and Brock. That was good enough for Jim. Despite the squeaking cot springs and the idea of being in jail, Jim rested well that night.

34

Tommy went home that evening, happy about the progress in the case that day. He had made the arrest without much of a fuss. A sense of satisfaction overcame him. He was sure that he had forgiven Jim for the broken nose. Susan was past history. Even so, it felt like revenge. He felt soothed to see Jim sitting on the edge of that cot in the smallest cell they had, looking defeated. He actually was beginning to think that his dad had been right.

When he walked in the door, Janet was running the vacuum in the living room. He was sure she hadn't seen him, so he eased up behind her and grabbed her. She let go of the vacuum handle and brought her elbow back hard into Tommy's ribs. When he let go, she spun around and placed her knee firmly between his legs, and Tommy hit the floor.

Janet had been glad that Tommy insisted she take self-defense classes. She had been a good student, but now she was afraid. When she saw that she had just put her husband on the floor, and knowing his temper, she knew something bad was about to happen. Immediately, she dropped to her knees next to him and started apologizing. She offered every piece of comfort she could.

When Tommy finally pulled himself together enough and stood back to his feet, he said nothing. He looked at Janet filled with anger. The look in his eyes made her even more afraid, so she began to back away.

Tommy could see the fear in her eyes, and that caused him to snap back into control. He never wanted his wife to be afraid of him. Holding out his hands, he said, "I'm sorry."

Surprised, Janet took his hands. "So am I."

Tommy smiled, "That was pretty impressive."

"I didn't even think. I just knew something had me."

"If the guys at work could do that, Port Suni would be on the news as the safest town in America." They both laughed.

Soon, the two were getting into the Crossfire and headed off to Los Fiesta for dinner. They enjoyed the time together and the food. The atmosphere in the restaurant seemed a little more romantic than usual to both of them.

Tommy stood at the counter waiting to pay when Kathy Prevatt walked up.

"Can we talk?"

"Cautiously, I suppose," he said trying to look as natural as he could.

"I'm worried. What if I answer wrong?"

"Then you won't win the prize. You'll do fine. We all have faith in you."

"I wish I was as confident as you are."

Moments later, Tommy and Janet were in the Crossfire headed home. Tommy reached across and rubbed Janet's neck. She smiled and closed her eyes.

Speaking softly he said, "I really enjoyed dinner and the company, especially the company."

"Me too. It does me good to spend time with you...Even if I have to throw you on the floor to get you to go out with me."

"Well, let's just not mention that to anyone, okay?"

"By the way, who was that woman at the register?"

"That was the big surprise that led to Jim's arrest."

"You arrested Jim?"

"Yep. This afternoon, Jim became a ward of Port Suni. His girlfriend there is going to testify against him."

When they got home, Tommy picked up Janet and carried her in.

"Wow, that was unexpected."

"Gotta mix it up a bit every now and then."

"So, what's got you in such a good mood?"

"I guess just knowing that a lot of the pressure will be off me now that Jim is in jail."

"Tommy, do you really think Jim is guilty?"

"Well, I can't say for sure he did it, but I can't say he didn't either."

"And you can't put a man in prison over an, 'I can't say for sure,' reply?"

"Janet, I am not putting him in prison, just jail. He will be tried, and if the jury thinks he is guilty, then they will send him to prison."

"Do you have any real evidence that would make you think he actually murdered anyone?"

Tommy was beginning to get angry with all the questions. The "Who's that woman?" and the, "Are you sure?" things were starting to get under his skin.

He looked her in the eye. "Listen. I don't care what you think. I don't care if he is guilty or not. He is all I have right now. I can do my investigation better if I don't have all the pressure of the media pushing for me to do something. I might even come out of this with a job."

"Tommy, I love you and know you are under a lot of pressure, but is it worth destroying a man over?"

"If that man is Jim Fender, yes and gladly so. He has ruined so many of my plans, and I don't care if he has to sit in there for the rest of his life. Whatever you think about this is your prerogative, but I am the chief of police, and I am putting him away. If I can help it, Jimbo will fry."

Janet reached out and touched Tommy on the shoulder. "Please don't do this. You know it is wrong."

Tommy shoved her away, and she tripped over the vacuum and fell. When she went down, her head hit the corner of the wall by the hall. She was knocked unconscious, and her head was bleeding. When Tommy saw her go down, he turned and put his first through the wall.

This wasn't the first time he had lost his temper and put his first through a wall. Several places throughout the house had been repaired due to his lack of control. This *was* the first time he had done anything to injure Janet. He didn't mean to cause her to fall. He just wanted away. He stormed across the room.

He turned and yelled at her, "Get up!" When she didn't move, he yelled again, "I said get up!" It was at this point that he realized she wasn't hearing him. He ran over and raised her head in his hand, and that was when he felt the blood. He checked her pulse. Careful to not hurt her, he turned her where she was laying straight. She opened her eyes as soon as he finished moving her.

"Are you okay?"

She tried to sit up but couldn't muster the energy. Her head felt light, and everything else felt heavy. The back of her head felt horrible. She looked at Tommy and asked him what had happened.

Tommy looked around quickly and said, "You tripped on the vacuum."

When he said that, she remembered. "You pushed me. You got mad and pushed me and made me fall."

"I didn't make you fall. You tripped on the stupid vacuum *you* left out in the middle of the floor. You tripped."

She tried to get up again. She made it to a sitting position this time and decided to stop there. She was afraid that she would black out if she went any farther. She looked around behind her and saw the puddle of blood, and fear engulfed her. She stood to her feet as quickly as she could and almost fell again.

Tommy reached out to catch her.

"Don't you touch me!"

Tommy grabbed her because he was afraid she would fall, and she kicked him again, this time on the shin. Again, Tommy put a fist in the wall. He turned around and said, "Let me help you."

Janet was running her fingers across the cut on the back of her head when Tommy placed his hand on her shoulder. She kicked him again.

Totally immersed in anger, he slapped her and yelled, "You need to stop kicking me and let me help you. Let me look at that. And if you need it, I will take you to the hospital."

"You are not going to touch me again. Just call an ambulance and stay away from me." Janet was so afraid that Tommy was going to try to touch her again that she pointed her finger in his face and said, "If you touch me again, you'll find yourself sitting right there in the cell next to your buddy, Jim. Maybe then you two can work out whatever it is between you two, and you can quit being so angry at everyone. But don't you think you will ever have the chance to do this to me again!"

When the ambulance came, the Suttons were standing on the front porch, waiting. Janet told the paramedic she had tripped over the vacuum and hit her head. Tommy was glad she hadn't said anything different and that the paramedics didn't insist that they come inside. They all headed off to the hospital a few minutes later. Tommy was in his car, following his wife in the ambulance.

It was close to midnight when they left the hospital. Janet had seven stitches in her head and a bottle of pills in her hand. Tommy had a bill in his hand and a load of guilt on his heart. When they were in the car, leaving the hospital, he discovered that they had different destinations in mind. Tommy wanted to head home, but Janet was looking for a hotel.

"Listen. You don't have a nightgown or anything. I ain't gonna hurt you, so let's just go home. If you still want to go to a hotel in the morning, I will help you pack."

"I am not going to go home with you. You pushed me down. You slapped me. I don't trust you."

"Okay. Then you go home, and I will go to the station and sleep. I am sure I can find a cot."

"No. I am not going in that house tonight. I don't know when or if I ever will, but definitely not tonight."

"Then let me bring you some clothes. I will pack you up a bag and bring it to you."

"I think I'd rather go naked for a while as have you do that. You just get me to a hotel and go away. I will take care of everything from there. When I am ready, if I get ready, I will come home. I might just come get my stuff, or I might come back to stay. Tonight I want to be away from you and that house."

Tommy was in his driveway, crying alone, by 1:00 a.m. He couldn't believe he had let his temper get the best of him again. Janet was right; he had been angry for years, but he didn't know how to get past it. He hung his head and prayed.

"God, I am sorry for my anger. I am sorry for hurting Janet. Help me."

35

August 12

The Harwoods arrived at the Fender home to find no one there. Jim had told them that they would be receiving friends at the funeral home this evening and that he would be at the house all day until it was time to go.

They went out back and sat on the deck and waited for Jim to arrive. Alfred had suggested that possibly Jim had run out to the store to get some food for the next few days. As they sat and talked, they discussed how unfair they had been to Jim when they were here last time. Maybe they should have given him the benefit of the doubt with Kathy Prevatt. How could they possibly think he had anything to do with his daughter's disappearance? They had been here long enough to realize that he would have had a hard time hiding it if he knew where Kristy was.

It was a beautiful day out. There was a nice, gentle breeze blowing in off the ocean. The waves were not too high. The Harwoods sat on the deck, enjoying the wonder of it all. They watched as people walked by. One boy had a kite attached to a fishing pole and was having a ball with it. Out on the water, about a quarter of a mile out, a sailboat sat anchored.

Several people stopped on the beach and took pictures of the house. A few reporters, with camera crews intact, had been by filming and trying to get an interview. The only thing that the Harwoods would say is that they knew nothing except that they were here for their granddaughter's funeral.

It was nearing 1:00 p.m. when they decided to get into their rented Impala to pick up some lunch. Just as they reached the end of the driveway, Andrea pulled in with Jim in the passenger's seat. They all decided to ride back into town in one car.

The news on the radio told about a hurricane brewing in the gulf.

"I wonder if that storm is gonna come after us or go for our home," Alfred said to try to break the tension.

"No tellin' right now. The computer has it going across New Orleans," Andrea interjected. "Just what they need, huh?"

"Have you been doing okay, Jim?" Inez asked.

"I could tell you I have. But that would be a lie. Nothing has been okay."

"I'm sorry, Jim. I know that. I meant you personally. Are you holding up?"

"Inez, I was going to wait, but I need to tell you. I spent most of the night in jail. Tommy charged me with both murders."

Alfred and Inez both sat, not speaking.

"Andrea found a lawyer who got me out on bond."

Alfred spoke up, "Jim, is there anything else we should know?"

"I am innocent. I don't know who, and I don't know why, but someone is trying to take me down for this."

"We actually have a couple of witnesses who know some things that will keep Jim free," Andrea spoke with a hint of doubt. "We just need them to be willing to talk."

As they sat at the Chinese buffet, it was obvious that they were recognized. All around the room, people were looking, pointing, and whispering. Andrea had grown used to the attention through the years of TV reporting, but Jim was not as well adapted. He did not like it at all. On one trip through the buffet line, he overheard another man say, "Child killer." It was all he could do to control himself. When he got back to his seat, all he could do was sit there and stir his food. His appetite was completely gone.

Inez had been watching Jim and suggested that they all just get a takeout box just as Sam Anderson walked in the door. Sam had been on the basketball team with Jim and Tommy in high school. He stood at the door and waited for a moment to be seated before he saw Jim sitting there. When he did, he walked over to the table and pulled up a chair from an empty table next to them. He looked at Jim and smiled.

"Man, you got a problem for real this time, don't you?" he said as he joined the group.

"Yeah, I do. By the way, you're welcome to pull up a chair and join us if you'd like to."

"If you're sure you don't mind, I think I will," he said with a smug look on his face.

They all laughed. That seemed to be just what it took to break the tension.

"So, Sam, what have you been doing with yourself? I haven't had a chance to talk to you in six months or so."

"One thing I've been doing is watching this good-looking woman on the TV."

Jim laughed at first and then realized he was looking for an introduction. Jim obliged and introduced everyone. It was good to have his attention off of all the potential jurors around the room.

"Well, Jimbo, I got something to tell you. I actually have some good news for a change. I bet you feel like you need some. Wanna know what it is?"

"I don't know. If this is one of your jokes about saving money on insurance or something, I don't think I am up for it."

"That's funny, Jimbo, but I have *great* news for you, something that could mean all the difference in the world for you."

"And what might that be? Please tell."

Sam stood up and lifted his voice to make sure that everyone in the room could hear. "I have positive proof that you are not guilty. I know who had your daughter." After he made his announcement, he sat back down with a giant grin on his face. The room was silent. Everyone at the table just stared. Sam knew they were waiting for the rest of the story but was savoring the moment of glory.

Finally, Jim forced himself to speak. "Sam, don't be messin' around like that. It's not funny."

"You're right, Jim. That wasn't funny. I'm sorry about my lack of humor. Not funny but true."

"Tell me what you know."

"After we eat, we can go somewhere quiet, and I will tell you what I have been trying to figure out, what small struggle I have been having, and what that struggle finally brought me to. But for now, let's eat."

Sam couldn't hold back his smile. He was enjoying knowing something that everyone else wanted to know. He even suggested that everything else they said while in the restaurant should be said in a whisper. Before he spoke, he would lean back and look around as if to make sure no one was within hearing distance. If they were speaking when the waiter came to refill a glass or take away and empty plate, he would hush them.

When they left, they decided to go to the park on the beach where Jim and Andrea had shared subs a few days earlier. Sam was insistent that they be as quiet as possible and as careful as possible. As all the preliminaries and pleasantries came to an end, Sam was ready to speak.

"Several days ago, I saw Ms. Everson here on the news talking to Tommy about Kristy. I'll be honest with you. I don't know everything that's going on, but I know you, Jim. There is no way you would ever be involved in anything like this. I should have called or come by, but I really didn't know what to say. I was at Susan's funeral, and I saw that look on your face when you found that picture in her casket. That started me thinking that there was something really strange with a lot of things. I started watching every piece of news related to this story that I could. I read every newspaper article, everything I could find. It all looked like phony stuff to me.

Apparently, Ms. Everson was asking questions over at Dipper Dan's the other day and got people started talking about seeing Kristy in the car with Tommy. That didn't make sense either. So I decided to keep an eye on Tommy. Here's what I found. Get ready. You will be surprised. Kristy was not in the car with Tommy. I don't believe Tommy knows what's going on, not a clue of anything." He trailed off and looked around again.

"But I found several witnesses who said they saw Tommy driving or standing with her. Too many to be wrong," Andrea said with a puzzled tone in her voice. "So what else did you find?"

"I know that Kristy and Tommy were seen together. That was the thing that got me until I started following Tommy. The day before they found Kristy, I followed Tommy when he left from the police department. You'll never guess where he went. I followed him to Alex's house. It was Alex driving, not Tommy. When he turned into the driveway and I could see his face, I could tell it wasn't Tommy."

"I can see how you could make that mistake. Yesterday, when I went to see him in the hospital, I thought it was Tommy at first glance," Andrea said.

Sam looked at her and smiled and said, "Here is the weird part. I parked down the street and waited for him to come back out. It didn't take long at all. When he drove by, he was wearing a police hat and sunglasses like the ones Tommy always wears, and he looked just like Tommy."

"Wow. I can't believe it," Jim said. "Alex pretending to be Tommy? Why would he do that?"

"Everyone in town knows that Alex would give anything to be a policeman, and Tommy is his hero. I am not sure if he had anyone with him or not when he went out. I was trying too hard not to be noticed and was so amazed at how much he looked like Tommy that I wasn't paying enough attention."

"Did you follow him to see where he went?" Alfred asked.

"No. I went to Alex's house. I left the car parked down the street and walked up. I looked around outside a while trying to find something. I really didn't know what to look for. What I found was a key to the house hidden inside a ceramic frog in the flower bed. I tell ya. I was scared to death when I opened the door and went in. I wasn't sure if there would be some kind of alarm or trap or what. You know how weird Alex is. I opened the door slowly and went in. Everything in the house amazed me at how perfectly clean it all was, not one crumb or speck of dust anywhere.

I did find something that looked wrong though. In the living room, a recliner was pulled out toward the center of the room. It looked as though it should have been pushed back against a door that I assumed was a closet. That door wasn't completely closed. With the rest of the house so in order, that looked weird. So I checked it. It wasn't a closet. It was a small bedroom that was neatly kept like the rest of the house, but something still wasn't right with it. On the dresser were pictures of your family. In a small box on the nightstand next to the bed was a note written in a child's handwriting. It said, 'I miss you, Daddy. Love, Kristy.' I almost wet my pants. I was afraid and excited and confused. I had no idea what to do."

"You found a letter with my daughter's name on it and you didn't tell me?" Jim asked with a touch of anger in his eyes.

"I wanted to call and tell you, but I think your phone is tapped. I thought about coming by, but I am not sure that there are not bugs planted everywhere. I didn't know what to do. I heard that you were arrested yesterday, so I went to talk to Tommy last night. But there was no one home. Later last night, I heard a call on the scanner that Janet had fallen and gotten hurt really bad. The ambulance people called in and said she had sustained a big cut on the back of her head. I called over to talk to him at the station this morning, and they told me that he had called in. Larry told me he said something about doing some cleaning up and painting. I went by his house and asked about Janet. He yelled at me and told me she was gone. I don't know if any of this makes any difference, but it is strange."

"Andrea, you went by and saw Alex yesterday. Did he give you any indication that he might know anything or might be involved?" Jim asked.

"Jim, I told you I can't tell you what I know. Alex did indicate that he could have some information, but that is all I can tell you. I promised."

"Wow! That is good news. Now we have to find some way to use it," Jim said as he stood to his feet. "You should be a private detective or something."

Andrea pointed out the time. "We need to get going. Thank you. I knew there had to be something that everyone else was missing."

"Jim, keep in mind that Alex isn't that smart. Someone had to put him up to this. Be careful," Sam said. "I can't keep an eye on you."

"I know. You be careful too. After that speech at the restaurant someone may come looking for you," Jim said as the two men shook hands.

"Kinda hopin' they do. Then I will know who they are. I am always careful."

The five parted, and each went their way to get ready for the evening viewing at the funeral parlor. All of them had more questions than answers. In some small way, the questions led them each to hope.

Jim and the Harwoods sat on the deck for a half an hour or so before leaving. They avoided the questions that were on their minds and spoke about life in general. None of them wanted to see Kristy in the coffin, yet they were each relieved that the mystery of her whereabouts was over.

Before they left, Jim led the group in a prayer. He thanked God for the time each of them had spent with Susan and Kristy. He offered thanks for the answers that were beginning to come to light. He lifted thanks for the promise of heaven and the comfort that he had in knowing he would see them again there. When he finished, he cried.

The funeral director met the family at the door when they arrived.

"Jim, Inez, Alfred, come on in," he said as he ushered them into his office. "Have a seat for just a moment."

"I am so sorry about your losses. Just a few days ago, Susan, and now Kristy. I know it is hard, but keep in mind that God can give you strength." He paused for a moment. "When we go in to see Kristy, I know we just went through this a few days ago, but if you need anything, please let me know."

Jim spoke up, "Does she look okay?"

"She is a beautiful girl. Whenever you are ready, we can go back."

Alfred stood first. Jim and Inez followed suit. As they started down the hall, Jim felt as if all his blood was being drained. All three followed the entrance with their eyes as they walked passed the viewing room that held Susan's body just a few days before.

The funeral director stopped. "If you are ready..."

They stepped inside.

The coffin was small.

They walked up together and looked in. Jim's face drew tight; burrows appeared on his forehead, and his lips closed. Inez leaned over and placed her hand on Kristy's and began to weep. Alfred draped his arms across his wife and son-in-law as he stared with tear-filled eyes into the lifeless face of his granddaughter.

Jim clinched his fists and held them in front of his chest. "It's not right. Why, God? Why?" He dropped to his knees and placed his head against the coffin.

Alfred could no longer hold back. He had fought so hard to be strong for Inez. He wanted to be a tower of refuge during the storm. His daughter and his grandchild were both gone. He turned his back and burst into tears. The tower had crumbled.

"She looks like she could just open her eyes and start talking," Inez spoke through her tears. "I keep watching for her to take a breath..."

The line of friends lasted for close to an hour and a half. As they were leaving Jim noticed three news crews taking pictures and filming. He put his hand on Alfred's shoulder and nodded toward the reporters. "I expect there to be a lot more of them tomorrow."

36

From his sailboat, Thomas could keep a close watch on Jim as he came and went. From here, he had seen a lot of goings on. He had brought Larry out to watch and time Susan many times before the day of Susan's "accident." Thomas had named his boat *Sutton's Magic* because that was what he called the extra money he had acquired from unsolved robberies.

He watched the Harwoods, using his high-powered binoculars, as they sat waiting for Jim. As they prepared to leave for town the first time, Thomas was watching. He used the scope on his deer rifle to line up the crosshairs on Jim's chest that afternoon as he and the Harwoods sat on the deck and talked. He wasn't able to stop the corners of his lips from turning up as Jim cried.

Thomas had convinced himself that every problem Tommy had ever had was somehow Jim's fault. When Tommy called him and told him that Janet had left him, he was sure that Jim had caused the problem. It was easy to overlook the temper tantrums and outbursts that haunted the Sutton household from the time Tommy was old enough to say no. What couldn't be overlooked was the continued pattern after the breakup with Susan and the breaking of his nose. In some way, they must all be Jim's fault.

Thomas would chuckle and make comments like, "Take that, you nose bustin' twerp," as he squeezed the trigger. The click of the firing pin in an empty chamber would be followed by such comments as, "You're lucky I am leaving you to the system." In his mind, he had already resolved himself to the idea that if somehow Jim did get off, he would put a bullet in his heart.

Thomas raised the anchor and headed for the harbor around sunset. He bought the boat with the idea that he would learn to sail, but for the most part, he would always crank up the motor to get to where he wanted. As a matter of fact, he rarely even raised the sails. At one point, he had almost convinced himself to trade it in on a different boat, but a thought wouldn't allow him to do that. The thought that all but brought him to shame every time it crossed his mind. In his mind, he could hear random voices say, "Them Sutton boys is too stupid to learn to sail. They have to do it the easy way." In this, as in most other things, the concern of what everyone else might think had made him choose poorly.

As he made his way in, the wind began to pick up. He looked around and could see a couple of other boats on their way in as well. One of them had his sails up and was cruising in at a good speed. The idea of what the man in the other boat might be thinking of him started taunting him. He could hear him saying, "Them Sutton boys can't even sail a boat."

He shut down the engine and raised the sails. He began to tack back and forth a little as he took aim on the inlet. The current was rushing out as fast as Thomas had ever seen it. It seemed that the harder he tried to enter the inlet, the farther off he veered. Thomas smiled and waved as the other sailboat cruised by seemingly without effort.

He worked as hard as he could and finally got the boat into the inlet. Fighting the current with all he had, he inched in. Darkness was falling, but the markers were lit. Thomas pressed on in, not noticing the party boat coming in from behind. Although the markers were lit, the lights on the small sailboat were not. Thomas had been so busy trying to get the *stupid* sails to take him where he wanted to go that he had forgotten to turn the lights on.

The party boat was less than ten yards from Thomas when he saw it coming. At just that moment, the driver of the party boat saw him and let out a blast of the horn and swerved left. Thomas jumped into the water as the party boat narrowly missed his boat. *Sutton's Magic* had passed the test, but the Sutton boy had not.

A voice yelled down from the upper deck of the party boat, "Hey, Buddy, you okay?"

"Yeah, I got it."

"Let me throw you a line, and we'll chase that boat of yours down."

"I said I got it! I like a challenge!" Thomas yelled. He knew he should have accepted but he didn't want people talking bad about him.

Thomas fought the current as hard as he could as he swam toward the sail that pointed upward. He was sure that if he hadn't put on his life vest, he would have drowned. Both the man and the boat were being carried back out to sea. It was all of midnight when Thomas guided his little, gas-powered boat into its appointed place of harbor in the Port Suni marina.

37

Jim woke up before the sun that morning. His dreams were filled with visions of times past with Susan and Kristy. Several times during the night, he had woken up and looked over at the pillow that used to hold Susan's head. He had revisited both funerals. A couple of times, he even walked to Kristy's room and made sure the covers were securely tucked in around Teddy.

He reflected on a few of the events from the day before. The funeral had been emotionally draining. So many people came over to speak to him, some that he knew and some that he did not.

Janet had been at the funeral, and she told Jim that she was sorry about Tommy arresting him. She also told him about the whole incident at their home the other night, and she said she was planning to go back to Tommy. She just wanted him to think about what he had done so he could get his temper under control. Jim wanted to tell her not to because he was probably going to go to jail, but he didn't.

Andrea stayed until after ten that night. They talked about how nice the funeral had been. She was still confident that with what Sam had found and with a little more investigation, Jim would be cleared altogether. The agreement was that Andrea would pick up Sam and Jim, and they would go look around a bit at Alex's house before they let the police in on everything.

Jim and the Harwoods headed off to bed soon after Andrea left. He heard Alfred and Inez talking and praying before they went to sleep. A short while later, he heard one of them get back up and go into the restroom. He was sure he could hear Alfred crying. Jim stared at the ceiling for a long time before he fell asleep.

———

Jim put on a pot of coffee and walked down to the beach. He was hopeful that the sound of the waves would soothe away the lonesomeness that he was feeling. Maybe he would even hear Susan's voice from the waves as he had in his dreams.

When he reached the water's edge, he turned northward. He walked, listened, and prayed. The waves were soothing. The gentle hissing of the bubbles washing up on shore had a calming effect. An occasional bird would call out as they prepared for the rising of the sun.

Colors began to fill the sky over the horizon as the sun made its way upward. Soon, the conversion from dark to light was complete. Once again the display of shapes and colors in the morning sky had been phenomenal. Jim thought that God had put them there just for him.

By the time Jim arrived back at his home, the temperature outside had already reached 84 degrees, and coffee was out of the question. He took a Pepsi from the fridge and opened it. Just as he turned it up, Alfred started down the stairs. Jim sat down his bottle and got a cup. When Mr. Harwood made his way to the kitchen, Jim was standing there with a cup ready for him. The two men sat down together to watch the morning news.

Unrest and turmoil filled the headlines, and sunshine filled the weather forecast.

"Seems like they could find a little good news." Alfred shook his head. "I'd gladly trade a bit of good weather for some good news."

"Amen to that." Neither of the men was aware that Inez had come downstairs until they smelled breakfast cooking.

Jim sniffed. "The news may be bad on TV, but I smell the aroma of good news drifting from the kitchen." It wasn't long before both men had all the news they wanted, and they went out to the deck. Alfred turned on the radio, adjusted the tuner, and within a few seconds, country music filled the air. The water was a bit choppy this morning, and there was a light breeze.

Inez walked out the door with a service tray decorated with breakfast burritos and orange juice for two. "All right gentlemen, this is gonna cost you."

"How much do we owe you for this wonderful labor of love you have set before us?" Alfred asked as he stood to his feet and placed one arm around her waist.

"Do you remember how much Susan and Kristy both loved to dance?"

"I think Kristy loved dancing about as much as anything," Jim answered.

"Probably about as much as Susan did," Alfred agreed. "When Susan was small, she would dance around the house with her stuffed toys all the time."

"Just one dance from each of you in their honor will be the price," she said while wiggling her eyebrows.

It was good to spend time together doing anything that relieved the stress, even if it was just a temporary fix. The music soothed away the worry, and the smiles eased the pain. Jim felt a touch of hope rise up in him that one day life would be bearable again.

The music from the radio covered the sound of the doorbell. Andrea could hear the voices and song coming from around the corner. She followed it as if she was a child hearing Pan's flute. She walked around the corner just in time to watch Jim dancing with Inez. She enjoyed spending time with Jim. His kind heart and gentle spirit reminded her of her deceased husband, Zack. She felt sympathetic toward Jim because she knew what it felt like to lose your life companion. Being there for Jim helped to heal her own hurt.

When that dance ended, she applauded and gave a small whistle. Both Jim and Inez felt a little embarrassed. "Don't just stand there," Jim said, motioning for her to come up. "There is plenty of room for everyone."

Andrea smiled. "I'd love to, but I won't crash your party unless someone will dance with me on the next song."

Alfred bowed. "Madam, I would be honored to dance with you."

Jim and Inez sat at the table and watched the two twirling about on the deck. Inez was enjoying watching Alfred dance. She loved to watch him almost as much as she loved actually dancing with him. That had always been one of the ways they found to resolve conflict when it would raise its head. The agreement was that if they could get some music that they could agree on, they would dance until they were finished talking it out. There had been a few times that she had just given in because she was too tired to keep dancing. She was also sure he had given in more times than she had for the same reason.

When that song ended, Jim and Inez both waited a turn. The two couples danced on the deck in the morning sun as the gulls danced in the sky above. When that song came to an end, all four felt unsettled. Jim was nervous because he was afraid of what the Harwoods would think. The Harwoods were nervous because they were unsure of how to deal with Jim enjoying the company of another woman that soon after the death of his wife. Andrea was nervous because the dance brought back even more memories of Zack. It was an awkward moment, each person waiting on the other to break out of it.

"That was fun, but I think I'm gonna sit the next one out," Jim said as he took a seat.

"Good idea. Let me reheat breakfast." Inez hurriedly picked up the service tray and headed back to the kitchen.

Alfred held a chair for Andrea.

"I though you were bringing Sam with you," Jim said as he took a sip of his Pepsi.

"Yeah. I know I was supposed to pick him up first, but I wanted to catch you before you got in the shower. That scruffy hair and beard makes you look cute."

"Very funny! I am sure *that* was the whole reason you came over this early."

"Okay. I confess. I got a call this morning from Sam, and he said that he has some kind of stomach stuff. He is going to take some medicine and maybe he will be up to going this afternoon."

"You could have called and saved yourself a trip over."

"I know, but I thought maybe you and I might do a little snooping of our own before we pick Sam up. If we go visit Alex at the hospital, he might give up a little more info. He might feel guilty and tell you what he told me if you are there. Or he might clam up tight. Either way, it is worth the try."

"You think I should go like this, or should I clean up a bit first?"

Andrea laughed, and so did everyone else.

Within twenty minutes, they were on their way to Daytona. Although both were anxious at what the day would hold, the conversation in the car was mostly about musical likes and dislikes. They discovered that they both enjoyed mostly the same genres. Country, contemporary Christian, and oldies topped the list. A few artists were debatable, but for the most part, they were a good match.

They walked to room 429 and found the bed empty.

"That's odd," Andrea said. "This is where he was before."

Jim looked around for a moment. "Maybe they moved him to a different room."

The two walked back to the nurse's station. Three women stood behind the counter talking about an upcoming party.

"Excuse me," Jim interrupted. "We are looking for Alex Carver. He was in 429."

"He left about thirty minutes ago with a police escort."

"So, he is doing that much better?"

"Mr. Carver will be fine once that leg heals."

Once they were back on the road, Andrea asked, "She said he had a police escort, didn't she?"

"Yeah, I assume Tommy came to give him a ride home."

"That's what I was thinking, too. I'm going to try again to give Sam call."

Jim stared out the window watching six pelicans flying in formation. They were flying southward parallel with the shoreline. The lead bird tucked his wings and dove from sight. Within seconds they were all gone.

"That's odd. Still no answer."

Jim redirected his attention back to Andrea. "May not be that odd. That stomach bug can make you spend time in places you don't really want to take the phone."

"Are you up to paying a home visit to Alex?"

"Let's do it."

When they turned on the street Alex lived on, they noticed Sam's car parked at the end of the street. Andrea pulled in behind it, and the two got out and walked up to the drivers' door. A feeling of dread rushed through them when they found it empty except the black leather jacket that was thrown in the backseat. They got back in the car and discussed their next move. A few moments later, they found themselves pulling into Alex's driveway.

They knocked, rang the doorbell, and called out to no avail. They tried the door, but it was locked. Jim remembered where Sam had said he found the key and went to the flowerbed. He could see the ceramic frog sitting there. He looked around and bent down to open it. Just as he placed his hand on it, he saw the police car turn onto the road a block down; and within a minute Jim, Andrea, Alex, and Larry all stood in the front yard, talking.

Jim extended his hand. "Hey, Alex. It's good to see that you are doing so well."

"I just got home. Thanks for takin' me over to the hospital."

"How's the leg?"

Larry stepped between them. "He needs to get some rest. He is home, but he is not well."

"Can I help you in or carry anything for you?"

"I will take care of Alex. He needs to be left alone," Larry said impatiently.

Andrea spoke up, "Do you know what happened to Kristy?"

Alex's eyes filled with tears, "Poor little Grub. I'm sorry."

"That's enough! Go, or I will arrest you for trespassing!" Larry's face glowed red as he pointed to the road. "Now!"

Larry rushed them off and refused to allow them to even get near the door of the house. As they were backing out of the driveway, Alex pulled out a large ring of keys and unlocked his door. Larry watched them as he hurried Alex to get inside.

They drove to the picnic table on the beach. Andrea had noticed that Jim had a very concerned look on his face. When they sat down, she led in prayer and then asked him what was troubling him so.

"It's just what he called my daughter."

"What do you mean?"

"He called her a little grub."

"I know she was your daughter, but I don't think he meant anything bad by it."

"I don't think he did either, but that is the same thing the guy on the phone called her. I don't know many other people who would use that particular word to describe a child."

"Does his voice sound like the caller?"

"Not really, but I am sure the caller had disguised his voice."

"I wonder what happened to Sam."

"Me too. It seems like if he was in the house, he would have answered the door when he heard our voices. If he wasn't in the house, where was he? His car was still there."

"Are you sure it was his car? Maybe we were just so into it that we decided it was him. I just hope he wasn't in the house somewhere when they went in."

Before Andrea took Jim back to his house, they went to check the car parked on Alex's street. It was gone. They went to Sam's house, and the car was there. In the backseat was a black leather jacket. They knocked and rang. No answer.

That afternoon, Jim tried on several occasions to call Sam on the phone. The answering machine announced that he was unavailable. He drove by a couple times and knocked. No answer.

38

Tommy had taken a little time off from work to get his mind together. He couldn't believe he had lost his temper so bad with Janet. Inside, he knew that he was struggling with pinning this on Jim, but after all, he deserved it. He was glad that today had been a better day. The ground work had been done to make sure all the evidence pointed as much as possible toward Jim. That looked as if it might actually work out.

The blood was cleaned up and the wall repaired and painted. Tommy was beginning to feel like he should have gone into the handyman business instead of law enforcement. After pondering that thought for a few minutes, he decided that there wasn't much difference between the two. It seemed to him that both jobs were basically to clean up after the human failings.

Janet had called to say that she would be by this evening, and Norm had called and said there were prints on the videotape case, and they were not Alex's. As good as the day had been, the evening promised to be better. If things worked out as he hoped they would, Janet would be staying, and the recent progress they had made in their relationship would continue.

Tommy sang along with the Tim McGraw CD as he showered, shaved, and dressed for the evening. He put on his western shirt, blue jeans, boots, and cowboy hat. His hope was that Janet would be up to a night of fun at the Starlight.

The doorbell rang. When he swung open the door, he was both surprised and disappointed to see his dad standing there. He was sure that it would be Janet.

"What's on your mind, Dad?" he asked as he motioned for Thomas to come in.

"Can't stay, boy, but I just needed to give you a heads-up."

"Okay, about what?"

"Boy, don't go playin' Super P.I. on that muggin'. Best to just let that one slide."

"What mugging?"

"If you hear about it, you'll know. Just don't be getting too anxious to be the hero and solve this one. Just say a drifter must have done it. There won't be any evidence anyway."

"What did you do, Dad?"

"I didn't come by to get you to ask a bunch of questions, just to keep you from askin' too many."

"Whatever. I really don't know what you're talkin' about, but thanks anyway."

"You goin' to the rodeo?" Thomas asked as he pointed at Tommy's hat.

"No. Janet is supposed to come by here in a few minutes, and I was going to take her to the Starlight."

"Boy, have you lost your mind?"

"What are you talking about now, Dad?"

"Takin' her to the same place she went with that Fender boy? If anyone saw her there with him and then sees you there with her, you know what they will say?"

"No, Dad, I don't. But I suppose you will tell me."

"They'll say, 'Them Sutton boys ain't even man enough to let a woman go when she has been messin' 'round with other guys.' You don't want 'em sayin' junk about you like that, do you?"

"I guess not, Dad. I'll keep that in mind."

"Okay, boy. I gotta run. You just let that muggin' thing ride. Ya hear me?"

"Got it."

Norm pulled into the drive just as Thomas pulled out. He hadn't really wanted to come by and bother Tommy when he had taken time off, but he felt that Tommy needed to know whose prints had been found on the tape package.

"That's right. You and Alex both left prints."

"Okay, no surprises. Thanks."

"Actually, I was just wondering how your prints got on it. They were Alex's tapes, so his were expected."

"I moved them around when I was looking for my yearbook."

"Alright, Boss, you have a good evening."

When Norm had left, Tommy went back to the bathroom and stood facing the mirror. Maybe his dad was right. Maybe he shouldn't take Janet back to the Starlight. After all, they hadn't been in a couple of years. Maybe it would bring back too many memories. Maybe knowing that she had gone there with Jerome would be more than he was ready to deal with. As he became aware that the country music was what they had gone to listen to, he started asking himself if he should even listen to it. The more he thought, the more questions came to mind. The more questions he pondered, the angrier he got.

Janet came in as quietly as she could. She watched as he stood there, staring at himself in the mirror. She could tell that something was really troubling him. She wanted to tell him that she was ready to come home for good. As she watched him, she felt her love for him rising in her. She hadn't seen him dress like that in a few years. She remembered when he used to take her out on a regular basis. She hoped that was what he wanted to do. Inside, she felt that if he would just allow himself the privilege of enjoying life a little, he could learn to deal with the stress of the job better.

She noticed his face begin to redden a little. Standing outside the bathroom door, she saw the expression go from troubled to angry. She watched as he took the CD from the player and smashed it on the counter. She cried as he pounded his fist against it. Her hopes of his getting past his anger were crushed with the CD. Tommy never noticed her at all. As quietly as she came in, she left.

39

August 15

The morning news told of a man's body that had been found overnight floating near the inlet. It appeared as if the man had been mugged and thrown in. He had nothing in his pockets that would identify him. Later on the radio, the reporter would say his pockets were empty other than one house key.

Jim tried again to call Sam, but there was still no answer. He wanted to call the police; but if Larry, Tommy, Alex, or possibly all three were involved, nothing but trouble could possibly come of that. He thought about sharing his concerns with the Harwoods, but he didn't want to stir up any more problems or hurt than was already there. He really wanted even needed someone to talk too.

As soon as he could, he called Andrea's cell phone. By ten, she was at his house. By eleven, they were at Sam's house. The car was still there, but there was no answer to the knocks on the door. At noon, the news on the radio gave the name of the mugged man found floating. It was Sam Anderson.

Both Andrea and Jim knew inside that he had not been mugged. He had been caught in Alex's house. They also came to the realization that Larry must have assisted in some way. After a little discussion, they were on their way back to Alex's house with hopes to catch him alone. Maybe he would be willing to talk.

When they arrived, the only car there belonged to Alex. After knocking on the door, they could hear some opening and closing of doors from the inside before Alex opened the one they had knocked on. He invited them in with a warning.

"If you come in, you can't tell no one nothin' about nothin' we say or it will be bad for everyone."

The agreement was made, and the three found themselves sitting around the living room.

"Alex," Andrea began, "I promised you I wouldn't tell anyone what we talked about at the hospital, and I haven't. Jim really needs to know anything you are willing to tell him. If you could find it in you to talk to him about anything you know about his daughter and his wife, it would really be helpful."

"Well, I don't really know nothin' 'bout it. I told you too much last time. I had to lie to Larry 'bout that anyway. Now with that other thing from yesterday, I just really don't know nothin'."

Jim spoke softly and calmly. He wasn't sure at first that he would be able to keep himself from showing his anger and frustration.

"Alex, I really don't know anything about you. From all I have heard, I understand that you are a really nice guy who wouldn't want to see anyone hurt. I also know that you feel a deep need to do what you can to make life better for Tommy because he saved your life. You are a true friend to those you choose to be friends with, but sometimes friends will let us and sometimes make us do things that are not good.

"Yesterday, when you talked to me, you called my daughter a little grub. That really caught me off guard because that was the same thing you called her when you called me and disguised your voice."

"How'd ya know it was me? I was real careful not to let anyone know 'bout it."

"Some people saw you with my daughter when you called me from the phone near Dipper Dan's. That was a good disguise to look like Tommy. Did you know that the people who saw you think it was Tommy? Those same people think Tommy is the man who killed both my wife and my daughter."

"They think Tommy did all this?"

"Yes. They think they saw Tommy riding with her in the car. They think that since she was found in Tommy's car, he killed her. They think he will go to jail for killing my wife too."

"Tommy don't even know nothin' 'bout it," Alex said as he began to cry again.

"My friend came by here yesterday, and now he is dead. His body was found floating near the inlet this morning. He had a lot of information that made it look like Tommy was guilty too. Do you know who killed him?"

"He was in my house when we got home from the hospital. When Larry saw him, he bumped him in the head with his stick and put him in his trunk. He made me go with him and drop him in the inlet. When we started to drop him, Larry saw him breathe and he hit his head with his stick a bunch more times. That guy said he thought it was his cousin's house, but he had some stuff in his pockets from in my secret room."

"Secret room?" Andrea asked, looking at Alex with a puzzled look on her face.

"I can't tell you nothin' else cause I don't know nothin'."

"Alex, you have already told us more than enough. I understand that Tommy is your friend, but he is going to go to prison unless someone tells the right people what really happened."

"Jimbo, miss lady, I don't really know what is going on. I was thinkin' at first that Larry wanted to make Tommy like a local hero kinda thing, but I don't know anymore. I think now he is trying to get Tommy in trouble. I also think he will kill me or make me go to jail if I don't do what he wants me to." Alex paused for a few moments before he continued. "I just can't do nothin' right. I was tryin' to help my only friend, and now I have got him in a bunch of trouble."

"Alex, Larry has been lying to you all along. He is not your friend or Tommy's." Jim continued. "We have a friend named Brock. If you will talk to him, he can help us make sure that Tommy doesn't go to jail and that Larry doesn't hurt you."

"Jimbo, miss lady, you need to promise me that you don't tell nobody nothin' 'cause I think he will kill me."

Both promised, and Alex pulled Andrea's card from his pocket and said he would think about it and call them when he was ready to talk. After a few more words of good-bye, Alex found himself alone.

He wanted to call and was sure he would. Death knocked on his door before he could.

As Jim and Andrea drove away, they were too busy discussing what they had heard to notice Larry's car parked at the end of the road. The discussion led them to Tommy's house.

Tommy answered the door, looking as if he hadn't slept in days. He was unshaven, and his eyes were bloodshot. Jim was terribly surprised when they were invited in. He was also surprised to see that Janet wasn't there.

Andrea, too, was amazed during this visit. She was astounded to see the two men pour out their hearts to each other. Years of bitterness that had eaten at them finally was set aside. She listened as they talked about the rape and the broken nose.

"I don't know what came over me. I wanted to have Susan. I wanted her to be my first, and I wanted to be hers. I just didn't think it would really go that far." Tommy spoke as a man broken by a reflection of his past.

"Tommy, that is over. It hurt when she told me. To be honest, if Susan wouldn't have told me to leave pay back to God, I would have come after you then."

"Somehow I convinced myself that she never told anyone. I imagined myself going back to her and apologizing. I never did, not really."

"Tommy, she told me. She told me every detail. She told me about your dad waiting with her clothes and about his threat. Even so, she chose to let it go."

"I wanted to make my dad proud. He wanted a son that was willing to do anything to get what he wanted. Just once I wanted him to tell me I did right."

"How would that be right?"

"My dad has a warped sense of right and wrong at times. I just thought that since he told me that he would cover for me…"

"All that is past. I want my thoughts and memories of Susan to be good. When I see you, I don't want to be angry. Let's put that in the past, okay?"

"Can you really do that?"

"I don't know. I am going to try. I have lived with hate and anger long enough."

Both men had damp trails down their cheeks.

"If you can do that…" Tommy looked away, "I will do my best to forgive the broken nose."

"Then I will say for the last time, I am sorry."

The conversation continued on with discussions of ballgames and life in general. Both men admitted that their lives had been good up until recently. The talk of recent events led them to reason for Jim and Andrea's visit.

"It seems that Alex has some information that he needs to share with you," Andrea said. "He knows the truth about most of what is going on here."

Tommy looked puzzled. "How is that possible? Alex, no way."

"Do you know a man named Sam Anderson?" she asked.

Tommy's heart skipped when he heard the name. "I have heard of him."

"It seems that he followed Alex around driving your patrol car. He thought he was following you until he got to his house."

"Why was he following me?"

Jim cut in, "It really doesn't matter why. Sam thinks he is some kind of detective or something. Anyway, he went in to Alex's house and guess what he found?"

"A spotless house?"

"No doubt, but he also found some things that indicated that Kristy had been there."

"That's a lie!" Tommy's mind rejected the idea that Alex could possibly be involved in any crime other than taping pay-per-views.

"Ask Alex. When I asked him about Kristy, he called her a little grub. The same thing the kidnapper called her."

"I can't. I don't believe he could possibly be involved."

"I would tell you to ask Sam, but I think someone killed him," Jim said.

"How did you know that?"

"I can't tell you that. But, I believe Larry had something to do with that."

"Alex and Larry?" Disbelief covered Tommy's face. "Sam was killed being mugged."

"It would probably be best to check that out a little closer," Andrea interjected. "I'll bet his head was beat in with something that would be consistent with a night stick."

"I'll check it, but I don't believe it."

After leaving, Jim and Andrea rode silently to the studio. They arrived just in time for News 7 at Seven.

40

The sun streaked the sky with red as the foam-covered water crashed with the rising and falling of the waves. The reflection of the sky against the foam gave the water the appearance of blood. From out there somewhere, Jim felt as if he was being watched.

Alex sat by Jim's side on the beach as the gulls dove in, looking for some free food. Jim picked up a bag of popcorn from the blanket beside him and started tossing it into the air one piece at a time. He had always been fascinated by the way the gulls would dive in and grab it mid-air.

As they dove in, they became more and more aggressive. Each dive, they would get closer and closer. As they ate the popcorn, they were growing larger and larger. One gull swooped down and grabbed the bag from his hand. He looked at Alex, and the gulls were all over him.

The gull that had grabbed the bag had grown and become enormous. Jim thought the wingspan must have been at least fourteen feet. Jim grabbed another bag and began tossing it, trying to lure some of the birds away from Alex. None of them went for the bait. Every piece he threw was caught by the megabird. Looking toward Alex, all he could see was a gray swarm of moving feathers as the birds covered him.

Jim ran toward Alex, yelling at the top of his lungs. The birds took to flight. They were gobbled up one by one by the mega bird. When Jim helped Alex to his feet, he noticed he was wearing a neck tie.

Jim and Alex began to run toward the house. The faster they ran, the farther away the house got. From behind them, they could hear a voice laughing over the crashing of the waves. When Jim looked over to tell Alex to run faster, he saw that Andrea was running with them. The mega bird grabbed Alex by the tie and flew high and dropped him over the water. As Alex fell, the mega bird chased him downward. Just inches above the water, Alex became lunch.

Andrea was carrying something in her arms that was wrapped in a blanket. They continued running toward the house as the mega bird flew toward them. Andrea fought with all her might to keep her grip on the blanket as the giant talons wrapped around it. Jim swung his arm toward the bird, and it turned its attention back toward him.

The sun was getting hotter and making it hard to run. The air was becoming thick and hard to breathe. Every step was becoming more and more of a challenge. His feet were sinking deeper into the sand with every step.

Noticing that she was falling behind, Jim took the blanket wrapped item from Andrea and looked at it as they ran. The face of Kristy looked back at him. She was so beautiful even through the fear that obviously covered her face. He could hear the voice screaming, "Jim, help me!"

Jim was even more confused now because the voice coming from the mouth of Kristy was muffled and belonged to Inez. It was all he could do to keep moving. The sun was too bright and too hot. He looked around to find that he was alone. The megabird burst into flames and vanished into a cloud of smoke. All that remained of Kristy was the voice of Inez screaming out as if she was in pain.

Jim forced himself awake. His room was engulfed in smoke. Flames danced around the perimeter of the room. He could still hear Inez screaming from the other room. Every breath felt heavy, hot, and labored. The orange glow of the fire illuminated the thick smoke like the fog of a bad dream. Finally realizing that the fire and the screaming were reality, he sat bolt upright and assessed the situation.

Jim grabbed his comforter from the bed, wrapped it around himself, and attempted to make it to the guest room, but the flames were too high. He called to Inez and asked her if she could see a way out. She screamed back that the whole room was filled with flames. Jim stopped in the bathroom, turned on the shower, soaked his comforter, and then proceeded toward the screaming voice of Inez.

When he finally made it to her, he found Alfred on the floor, not breathing and without pulse. He threw his comforter over Inez and picked her up and ran for the stairs. The flames were too high. He turned back to the guest room and ran as hard as he could and dove through the window.

When they hit the ground, Jim drug Inez away from the house. He could see that the entire house was being consumed with flames. He thought about trying to drive to the hospital; but his car was inside the garage, in lower part of the house and, along with everything else he owned, it was being destroyed.

Inez wasn't conscious as Jim tried to tend to her. He could see that much of her skin had been burned. She was breathing, and her pulse seemed strong, but he couldn't get a response from her no matter what he did. He could hear the sirens getting closer, and hope filled him. As the first fire truck entered the driveway, everything grew dark. Awareness of the sounds that filled the firelit night slipped away as Jim entered the world of nothingness.

41

August 16

Both Jim and Inez woke up in separate ambulances on the way to North Suni Hospital. Jim would be treated and released, but Inez would be kept and treated for burns and smoke inhalation. They were optimistic that with time and a few skin graphs, she would live to see a life of normality within a year.

Jim walked into Inez's room. "Mom, how are you feeling?"

"I hurt, Jimmy. I hurt everywhere. How about you?"

"I'm a little sore, got a few bruises and a burn or two. In light of jumping from the second story of a burning building, I am doing alright."

"Did Alfred get out?

Jim tried to answer but the words wouldn't come. "He was…" His eyes filled with tears. "I tried…" He reached for her left hand then realized it was bandaged, so he walked around and took Inez by her undamaged right hand.

"How can I go on?" Inez asked as tears dampened the bandages that covered the majority of her face.

"I…sorry." Jim was still unable to speak. He was fighting hard to retain enough composure to have the appearance of strength.

"God, no!" she cried, "Not my Alfred too! Jim, why? He was so good to me."

250

"You should probably come back later. Mrs. Harwood needs to get some rest." Jim had no idea how long the nurse had been standing there. "If you could give her a few hours at least." She reached under their hands and pressed the button that dispensed just enough morphine to take Inez from the land of consciousness.

Jim found his way to the restroom. He went into a stall and locked the door. His illusion of strength was gone. He was free to weep, and he did.

Jim called Andrea to take him to a room at a local hotel. When she dropped him off, she agreed to bring him some clothes as soon as she finished her morning broadcast. Jim found himself alone with no car, no ID, no home, no wife, no daughter, and not much hope. He cried himself asleep again.

The knock at the door brought Jim back into reality. He had been dreaming of stuffed animals on the water, of the rise and fall of the waves, of Susan and Kristy, of Alfred and Inez, and of fire and pain. He stood to his feet and headed toward the door, but the pain in his body caused him to fall to the floor. He forced himself back to his feet and continued on to the door.

When he looked through the peephole, he was surprised to see Tommy standing there.

"What brings you to Daytona?"

Holding up his clipboard, Tommy said, "A few questions that I need help answering."

Jim motioned for him to come in. "It's not much, but it's all I have right now." He pulled the lapel of the hotel bathrobe. "Even my clothes are borrowed."

"I need your brain for a few minutes. Keep the robe, please."

Jim tried to force a laugh. Tommy had at least tried to lighten the situation. "I believe I will. But before I answer any questions, I have one for you."

"Fair enough. Ask."

"Have you heard anything about the fire?"

"As a matter of fact, I have. It looks like it was possibly set on purpose. No clue who. Arson would be hard to prove anyway. Now it's my turn. What can you tell me about the fire?"

"I woke up from one nightmare into another. When I realized it was real, I did everything I could to get everyone out. It was too late for Alfred, so I grabbed Inez and jumped out the window. That's all I know."

"As for me, I have a few things about the rest of this case. Just keep in mind that it is speculation and nothing concrete."

"I understand. Just tell me what you can."

"Here goes. I talked to Alex. I am pretty sure you were right about Larry being involved. I think Sam was taken to the inlet in his patrol car. Oddly enough, a key to Alex's house was in Sam's pocket. That added some validity to what you told me." Tommy paused for a moment. "I want you to know that I really did not believe you were guilty from the start. When I first thought about charging you, I just needed some breathing room to be able to do my investigation. Then I saw it as a way to keep me from coming under the gun. I'm sorry. I will officially drop the charges today."

"Wow. I am surprised you admitted that. It almost sounds like you are moving to my side."

"I don't know that I would call it your side. I hope it is more to the side of truth. I've been thinking about everything. The clues as they really are. The talk from last night. Everything."

"Whatever brought you to where you are in this, I am glad for it."

Before the two men were finished talking, Andrea was knocking at the door. Tommy answered the door and let her in on his way out. In her hand, she held a blue plastic bag with some clothing in it.

"I picked you up some clothes. I hope you like what I picked out. Get a shower and try these on."

He took the bag and stopped. "Guess what?"

"Let me think. Tommy came over to visit because he is a concerned friend?" Andrea asked with a touch of sarcasm.

"Close. He told me that he had visited Alex, and he believes us."

"And what does that mean for you?"

"Let me get cleaned up and dressed, and we'll talk some more."

Andrea turned on the TV and watched the weather forecast while she waited. When she expected to hear him open the door to the bathroom, instead, she heard a bolt of laughter.

"Jim, you okay in there?"

"Yeah. Kinda. But I do have one little problem."

"And what would that be? Do they not fit?"

"You could say that. And if they did...I don't know. It might be interesting. I realize you probably felt a little uncomfortable buying men's clothes, but I really don't think I should wear these."

It was just about that time that Andrea realized she had brought in the wrong bag. While she had been shopping, she had bought a new outfit for herself as well, starting from undies up. She was embarrassed but decided to push it a bit.

"What, you don't like the lace?"

"Not on me. As buff as I am, I really don't think I need this upper body brace either."

"Just put it all back in the bag, and I will go get the right one out of the car," she said with a chuckle in her voice.

In less than thirty minutes, they were pulling up the drive to what remained of the Fender home. Sitting there in the place that used to hold such happiness was proof that everything was gone. Jim felt the void in his chest beginning to grow and rise into his throat. The smell of smoke and charred wood permeated the air.

The swing and monkey bars screamed out for Kristy to swing, but she could not. The gulls that flew overhead called for Susan to feed them, but they remained unfed. Everything cried for the life that was, but it was gone.

"You go on. I'll be there in a minute," Andrea said as she watched the unbelief on his face. She held up her phone and said, "I need to make a call."

Jim opened the door and stepped from the safety of the car into the nightmare of reality. He tried to walk, but his legs would not cooperate. He forced a few steps and sat on the hood of the car. He closed his eyes and lowered his head. He heard a familiar voice…

"Welcome home, Jim." He was sure it was Alfred. He raised his head. Standing on the walkway that led from the driveway to the deck was Alfred with his left hand on Susan's shoulder and holding Kristy's hand in his right.

"I missed you, Daddy," Kristy said as she ran toward him. He grabbed her up and spun her over his head, then softly placed her back on the ground. She put her arms around his legs and gave them a squeeze.

"He's the best dad in the world, isn't he, sweetie?" Susan asked as she walked up and took Jim by the hand. He took her in his arms and kissed her. She led him up to the steps that led up to the deck. He could hear music playing.

Inez called down, "Don't plan on coming up here unless you're ready to dance."

He looked around at the life he once had. A piece of glass crunched under Jim's foot. The sound and the feel of it drew him back. They were gone.

"God, why did you give them to me, just to take them away? How did I fail so badly that everything had to go?" Jim dropped to his knees. "I tried. I tried to do right. I tried to show them the love You showed me. I tried to give You credit for everything. Where did I fail so badly?"

Andrea watched from the car as Jim walked around for a couple of minutes. When he fell to his knees, she stepped out and started walking toward him. She overheard his prayer. She stood quietly behind Jim as he cried out to God. When he became silent, she placed her hand on his shoulder. "He let you keep them for a while. Now He has them with Him."

He knew in his mind that she was right. God had blessed his life beyond measure. He had what most people only dream of. He knew it. But knowing did not soothe the emptiness in his soul.

"It's not right." His voice quivered as he spoke. "My wife is gone. My daughter is gone. I can't find my parents. My father-in-law is dead. My mother-in-law is in the hospital. All of my pictures, everything, gone. Nothing is left."

It took several minutes for Jim to regain strength and composure enough to stand back to his feet. The soreness from jumping from the window made rising back to his feet slower than he anticipated. Andrea took his hand to offer any support she could.

Here and there were a few two-by-fours rising up from the perimeter. The concrete pad was covered with nails, miscellaneous glass, and metal objects. The stove, washer, dryer, refrigerator, bathtubs, and other items were scattered about. On top of the remains of the car were the skeletal remnants of the bed the Harwoods had been sleeping in. Near the back, under where Kristy's room would have been, were the springs from her bed. Closer inspection revealed a couple of the safety pins that had held Teddy's chest together. Jim's dresser was charred and busted. When he opened the drawers, everything in it was wet. In the top left drawer, Susan's Bible seemed to be untouched by the flames.

Jim held the Bible close to his chest and looked at Andrea. "She read her Bible every day. This one she carried to church and made notes in." He lowered it and looked at the cover. He pulled the ribbon that marked the place she had been studying. It fell open to 1 Kings 14. She had highlighted the last part of verse 8, "…my servant David, who kept my commandments, and who followed me with all his heart, to do that only that was right in mine eyes." She had circled the word David and written Jim in the column. He was frozen in time. Having taken in as much as he could handle, Jim asked Andrea to walk down to the beach with him. They walked northward just out of reach of the waves that rushed toward them and then backed off only to regroup and rush in again.

"Andrea, I understand more of the book of Job now than I ever wanted to. Job had it all. A wife, kids, land, servants—everything that spelled out success to the world around him."

"I haven't spent as much time studying his life as much as I should, I guess."

"What happened was Satan had to stand before God and give account of what he was up to. When he told God that he was destroying as many people as he could, God basically said, 'What about Job?'

"Job had more than just tangible goods; he had a relationship with God. He even sacrificed for his children just in case they had done something wrong. He tried hard to be the best he could be.

"Satan knew about Job. He also knew God had protected him and blessed him. Satan told God, "If you take away his stuff, he will curse you." So God let Satan loose on Job, but Job did not fail. So Satan told God, "Let me put some physical pain on him, and then he will fall." God let him do everything he could short of taking Job's life. In the midst of it all, Job praised God. He recognized that God was in control."

Jim stopped and took Andrea by the hand and said, "I feel like Satan has been turned loose on me. He has taken everything from me. He hasn't taken my health, but he took my wife. I am not Job. I want to be strong, but I fail."

"Jim, losing a spouse is hard. I know from experience. Losing a child is hard. You have been through a lot. The pain will not go away today or this month. The empty places cannot be filled with anything or anyone else. But they will become bearable."

"But it hurts so bad. I was supposed to be there to protect them, but I couldn't."

"Jim, I want to tell you something about me that most people don't know. Today is the second anniversary of my husband's death. He was on a charter boat fishing off the North Carolina coast when a gas leak caused the boat to explode. He was killed instantly."

"I am so sorry. I didn't know."

"There was no way you could have known. I haven't allowed myself the privilege of getting close to anyone since. It still hurts, and I am sure it always will. But Zack's memory is a friend. It soothes me."

As they topped the dune on the way back to the drive, they saw Jim's coworker, Ben Jackson, standing in the midst of the rubble. His back was turned to them and his face was well hidden. The way he stood with one hand on his hip and the bald spot on the back of his head left no doubt to his identity. In his other hand, he held an envelope.

"Ben, what are you doing?"

"Wow. Man, you scared the mess outta me," he said as he spun around. "I thought maybe you got burned up too."

"Maybe I shoulda, but I got out this time. I can't say as much for Susan's dad. He didn't make it."

"Sorry to hear that, Jimmy. Uh, I don't want to take up much of your time, but I have something for you."

Ben smiled as he held out the envelope. Just as Jim reached for it, he drew it back and put it in his pocket.

"I changed my mind. I guess I'll just keep it." He started to turn around, and then he pulled it back out and handed it over.

Jim almost collapsed when he opened the envelope. Inside was a check for five hundred thousand dollars. He just stood there and stared.

"The only way I could get those guys to seal the deal was if I promised that you would get this. I guess you deserve it anyway. You did all the work."

"Thanks, Jackson. You're a good man."

"Not true, Jimmy. I would have kept it all if they didn't make me promise. Now with the looks of your home and all, I guess you'll need it."

Thank-yous and good-byes were shared, and Ben hopped back in his car and was gone.

As Jim stood there, looking at the check, he couldn't help but think about how much he would rather have his family than the check. He wouldn't even mind having lost his house, car, job, and all the money in the world if he could have his family back.

They were soon in Andrea's car headed north on A1A. "There is one more thing I need to tell you."

"And that would be?" Jim asked.

"I am taking a couple of weeks off from work. It seems my boss wants me to back off on this story because I am getting a little too emotionally involved in it. I fully see his point. He suggested that I turn it over to some of our other people, but I can't. I have too much vested and know too many details to walk away at this point."

"Oh no, you're not gonna lose your job, are you?"

"Nah, just taking a short vacation."

The two sat quietly for a few minutes before Andrea decided to share about one of the strange dreams she had been having. "You and I are walking on the beach in front of your house. There is a small child there with us. It is a beautiful day, and I feel so happy. I don't know what it is, but all of the sudden I feel scared. I feel like someone or something is watching me. I look around, and there is no one. The feeling is like it is coming from the ocean. I start to run, and then I wake up."

"Sounds almost as strange as some of the dreams I have had recently."

42

When Tommy left from talking to Jim, he walked over to the room where Janet had stayed. He wasn't sure if she was still here; but inside, he knew he needed to try to work things out. He wasn't sure why she hadn't come by after saying she would, but he was truly sorry for everything he had done. Deep down, a feeling of frustration emerged with his uncontrolled anger. He realized that most of his anger and wrong choices had stemmed from trying to do the impossible, to live up to the expectations of the great Thomas Sutton.

He had tried with all that was in him to please his father and had failed every time. His desire was to once, just once, hear his dad say something that would make him feel worthy to be a Sutton. His failure to please his dad had caused him to believe himself to be a failure at everything else. On occasion, Tommy had seen the truth that his dad would never be satisfied, but somehow, his programming would override the truth. His pushing himself so hard kept Tommy on edge and always ready to snap. His time alone and honest, homegrown reflection had brought him to a point where he was finally ready to seek help.

He wanted the chance to tell Janet that he loved her and that he was sorry. He wanted her to know he was willing to see a counselor. He wanted to hold her and ask her to come home. Even if nothing else, he wanted to see her, if only for a minute.

He was still twenty yards from the door when it opened. Janet stood and looked at him for a few seconds before running to him. She put her arms around his neck, and the two joined in a series of kisses. The tenderness of her arms, the warmth of her body against his, and her eagerness to be near him was overwhelming. He felt loved, accepted, wanted, and even worthwhile for the first time since before he raped Susan. Tears filled his eyes, and a lump filled his throat. Tommy's love for Janet was stronger than ever. This new emotional high melted away the feeling of failure that had dominated his being just moments before.

Both were ready to start over, to forgive the past and to love each other, flaws and all. Tommy helped Janet get her things together and put them in the car. He held her door as she got in.

By the time Tommy was southbound on US-1, his mind was back at work. When he was getting dressed that morning, he had discovered that his police revolver was missing. He had placed his own .38 in his holster so that no one would notice. He hadn't worn it for a couple of days, but he was sure he had left it in his holster in the closet after wearing it last time. There had been no signs of forced entry, and as far as he knew, the only people with a key to his house were the two who lived there. They had at one time left a key hidden outside in case one of them were to get locked out, but they had the locks changed and stopped that when they found a few things missing a couple of years earlier.

Tommy waved at Larry when he saw him headed north. Being so preoccupied with thoughts of Janet and the whereabouts of his gun, he never once wondered why Larry would be in a red Mazda instead of his patrol car. Larry, realizing that he had been seen, changed his plan to pay Jim a visit.

Upon arrival at the police station, Tommy searched his office, the evidence room, the motor pool—everywhere he could think of that his gun might have been dropped. He finally broke down and asked Norm if he had seen it. The two men searched again before doing the paperwork to file the missing handgun.

Dale watched quietly from his desk. He had read over the reports Tommy filed on the Fender case and was convinced that some of the facts had been twisted. He also had spoken with Ms. Prevatt and was sure that someone had put her up to saying that she was seeing Jim. Some of the local townspeople were talking about how Tommy had been seen with Kristy and that Sam Anderson had made an announcement in a restaurant about knowing who had done it just before his body turned up. Now that Tommy was reporting his gun missing, he was expecting that someone related to the case would turn up with a bullet from Tommy's gun in them.

Norm and Dale had discussed, at length, the possibility that Tommy was the guilty person. The fact that Jim's house burned down on the heels of Tommy taking a couple days off and his wife leaving him struck them as strange. This morning, when Tommy had first arrived, he seemed so determined to set things right. Why had he not mentioned his gun being missing but instead tried to cover up it by putting a different gun in his holster?

Dale sat quietly until Norm and Tommy finished up the paperwork. Questions of the whos and whys just keep piling one on top of the other. The look of determination that planted itself within the features of the younger Sutton brought out the family resemblance to the elder. When Tommy started toward the door, he had to ask a couple of questions of his own.

"Hey, Tommy, do you think maybe someone came in your house and took your gun?"

"I don't see how that would be possible. I haven't seen any sign of anyone having been in. We changed the locks not so long ago. I keep the windows locked."

"You know how easy it is for someone to get in if they want to. A quick slide of a credit card, and boom, in."

"No. I keep the deadbolts turned. And besides that, I have been home most of the time since I last had it."

"Did you have it when you went to the hospital with Janet?"

"No. I left it at home. I changed while I waited for the ambulance."

"So it was left at home for several hours then?"

"Yes, but I doubt anyone went in then. I did have the house secured."

"Okay. I was just trying to offer some suggestions."

A couple of pleasantries were exchanged before Tommy went out the door. He didn't like having to tell his guys that his gun was missing, but sometimes you have to do what is right. Besides, if someone tried to hock it or if someone used it in a crime, the report would already be on file.

Tommy eased into his Crossfire and headed home. In the midst of all the unexplained events, the thought of Janet being there when he got home made everything else seem unimportant. He turned up the radio and sang along with Kenny Chesney.

He was vaguely aware of the red Mazda that followed him at a safe distance. When he noticed it behind him, it never registered that it could be the same car he had seen Larry driving earlier. The car pulled over for a moment and disappeared from sight. He never noticed the car park a block down from his house.

43

Thomas was not satisfied with the way things were going. Too many changes and way too many murders. The original plan was simple: Kill Susan, and make it look like Jim did it. Larry's suggestion of a small modification to the plan sounded good upfront and had added more to the mix than needed to be. Kidnapping Kristy and involving Alex had become a problem almost immediately. "We'll fill him with false hope and then snatch it out from under him…He'll go to the chair for both, and Tommy will be twice the hero."

Alex didn't have the heart for it. As much as he tried, he was just too careless and too soft. Now he too was dead. His carelessness had also cost Sam Anderson his life.

That stunt with burning down the Fender house to end it for once and for all was one more of Larry's changes that hadn't worked out. He hadn't even mentioned it until it was done. He had told Thomas that if Jim died in a fire that would divert the attention off of the recent talk that Kristy had been seen with Tommy. The house burned, and Alfred died, not Jim.

Once again, Larry had messed up. He knew something had to be done.

"He's gonna give us Sutton boys a bad name. People will be sayin', 'Them Sutton boys don't even make good cops.' Not while this Sutton boy can stop it."

Thomas followed him the rest of the day. He was watching when Larry parked at the end of Tommy's street.

Larry sat in his rental car watching Tommy's house as he worked on modifying the details of his plan. A few things had not gone as he had hoped. Although he had expected some difficulties when he had planted the seeds of this mess in Thomas's head, he never expected things to go as wrong as they had. Originally, he had just planned for Susan, Kristy, and Jim to die and for Tommy to go to prison; and he would be the new police chief. The version he had presented to Thomas left Jim alive and in prison. He also knew that any way this went, Thomas would have to be reckoned with. Larry was willing to use whatever means deemed applicable to do so.

Things really started veering off track when Alex decided to take Kristy on a picnic. At first, that wasn't even so bad. When people saw Kristy in Tommy's car and it looked like Tommy driving, that couldn't have been more perfect. People were talking all over town about having seen them. Even the place Alex had chosen to take her turned out to be perfect.

Who would have expected a little girl like that to think of using a knife? Even if she did, what was the likelihood of her actually doing anything that caused serious damage?

All that had almost worked out better than planned. Kristy was found dead in Tommy's car. Jim found Alex and had taken him to the hospital. With the planting of the yearbook and with Alex saying it was Jim who cut him, it was beginning to look like both Jim and Tommy would go down for working together on the murder and kidnapping.

That Anderson guy threw a wrench in the plan when he started talking; and then, when he was caught in Alex's house, he had to die. He was sure that Ms. Everson had suspected something was up when she had shown up with Jim at Alex's house.

He was glad they had gotten rid of the body as quickly as they did. It seemed that there was one kink after another.

One of those kinks was that other visit. Alex told him several times that he hadn't said anything. After a little encouragement, he had confessed that he had given some information.

Hanging Alex had been the hardest part of this whole thing. He didn't put up too big of a fight with a gun pointed at him. When Alex realized that he was actually going to die, he had told Larry that he and the Grub would be in his dreams, making him wake up screaming. The last thing Alex had said before he died was, "Okay, grub. I am sorry that I did bad stuff, but now comes my turn."

After that came the fire. Who would have believed that anyone could have survived that? He was sure it was too late for any escaping the inferno when he had left. According to the news, Jim had jumped through the glass of a second story window with Mrs. Harwood in his arms. He just couldn't see how it was possible for anyone to make it out alive.

If everyone had died, he could have taken Tommy down with manslaughter charges. He had intended to plant some evidence that would have proven his guilt. Thomas would believe his son had messed up one more time, and the job of police chief would finally be his.

When he left the fire, he had gone to Tommy's house to steal his gun. Tommy was sound asleep when his gun was taken. Getting in had been no problem because he had a key. On occasion, Alex would borrow Tommy's keys to work on his car. While he had them, he would make copies of any of them that he didn't already have. Alex had used his keys to go into Tommy's house many times. He would put on one of Tommy's police uniforms and walk around the house, pretending to be Tommy.

Larry had stolen the gun with the intention to shoot Janet— not to kill her, just to put a bullet in her somewhere. He would then come back at his next opportunity and place the gun back in Tommy's house. When he found out that Jim was still alive and in the hotel, he changed his plan. Instead of shooting Janet, he would shoot Jim. The bullet from Tommy's gun would indict him for the crime.

Nothing was going like he planned. All he wanted was to be Police Chief and to keep Thomas thinking that he was trying to help him. At this point, he was desperate. If something didn't go his way, this whole thing could turn on him, and he would be the one in prison. One more change of plans was in order. A bump on Tommy's head and a bullet in Janet's chest and Tommy would be the one going to prison.

An untimely auto accident and Mr. Fender would be out of the way and hopefully take Ms. Everson with him. Whether or not the accident was proven successful was not really an issue. If it looked to Thomas that he had tried, that would keep him at bay.

44

Tommy and Janet had a great evening together. They spent time talking and joking. No doubt, life was getting better. By the time the sun went down, Tommy was so tired he couldn't hold his eyes open. Janet stroked his eyebrows lightly and slowly until he was sleeping soundly. She eased her arm out from under his head and got up. She turned off the music and blew out the candles before she found her way to the bathroom. She closed the door, drew a hot bubble bath, and sank in.

She didn't turn on the light. The dark and the quiet helped her relax and enjoy her bath. She could hear Tommy snoring. It sounded more like a buzz. It was the sound that she missed so much while sleeping at the hotel.

Outside, she could hear the sounds of an occasional plane going over or car passing by. The crickets were even singing extra sweetly tonight. The sounds of home were good.

She closed her eyes to relax. Her mind drifted back to the events of the day. She could remember how excited she had been when she looked out of the hotel window and saw Tommy walking toward her. Tears of happiness had filled her eyes.

Janet sat bolt upright in the tub when the neighbor's dog broke into a fit of barking and growling. She settled back down into the water when the dog again became quiet. She smiled at her own jumpiness. She assumed that everything had been so perfect that she must have expected something bad to happen. Her eyes closed again.

The shadow cast on the window went unnoticed as Janet relaxed and reflected. The sounds of footsteps outside were dismissed as sounds of the night. She was determined not to let anything ruin her night. A second shadow passing by the window also went unseen. The buzzing of her sleeping husband in the next room over almost covered the second set of footsteps but not the rattling of keys. That was the sound that cut into the solitude and caused her belly button to pucker in sync with the raising of the hair on her arms.

Janet was now very aware that someone was outside her home, and whoever it was had found their way to the back door. She stood slowly and wrapped herself in a towel. She heard the key slide into the lock. She moved quickly to the bedroom and put one hand over Tommy's mouth and shook his arm with the other one. Tommy sat up and looked at Janet with a puzzled look on his face. Janet put a finger over her lips and pointed in the direction of the back door.

They both heard the pop as the deadbolt turned. Tommy eased to his closet and pulled his gun from the holster. He moved as quietly as he could toward the bedroom door. The back door opened and then slammed shut. Tommy dove for the far side of the bed.

Just outside the back door, they could hear some kind of commotion going on. Tommy moved toward the window and slowly stood to look out. Just as he touched the blind to open it, a thud and a yelp outside caused him to drop back to the floor. Two more thuds were followed by a gunshot.

Janet tried to speak, but the sound wouldn't come. Outside, they could hear the rapid, heavy footsteps as someone ran past the window and around to the front of the house. Tommy finally composed himself enough to run to the front window and look out. He could see a man running down the road. He went to the front door and ran out, hoping to see who it was. When a couple of his neighbors came out to see what was going on, he realized he was standing in his front yard in his underwear and ran back in the house.

From outside, they heard laughing. Tommy was scared and embarrassed. Janet was in the bedroom, getting dressed, when Tommy went in to get some clothes on. As he dressed, Larry got up from by the back door and headed back toward his rented car. His head was bleeding and hurting badly. When Tommy went out back to see what had happened, there wasn't much to go on.

Neither Tommy nor Janet slept any more that night.

Larry had been so confident of himself that he hadn't seen Thomas following him. The bullet that had rendered him unconscious for a couple of minutes was the one Thomas thought had killed him.

45

August 17

For the first time in years, Andrea woke up with a smile on her face. In her dreams, her late husband, Zack, had dropped in to see her. They had talked about life and plans. She really couldn't remember much of the conversation outside of a few specific comments. He had told her that he still loved her, that he was enjoying himself, that she was still as beautiful as she had ever been, that she needed to move on with her life, and that he was okay with her seeing Jim. He had also told her that Susan would be happy with Jim seeing her, even if it did take a while for him to adjust.

In her dream, Zack had held her close just like he used to. She had dreamed of Zack before, and he had told her some of the same things; but this time was different. This time, she was ready to hear and move on. She knew she would always love him more than she could explain, but she also knew that on this side of heaven, she could never really hold him outside of her dreams. This time, she knew she was falling in love, and he gave her the okay.

As she showered and dressed for the day, thoughts of possible ways to make Jim's day a little brighter ran through her mind. She had promised to pick him up at 8:00 a.m. to take him to see Inez in the hospital, so she was planning to be there at 7:30 with breakfast.

While she entered her morning blog for the station, Andrea also made reservations for dinner. A quick stop at Sandy's Café and she would be on her way. This promised to be a great day.

When she pulled into the hotel parking lot, she could see that the light was on in Jim's room. She thought that there weren't many cars for this time of year. One particular car did stand out, however. A red Mazda sat parked facing Jim's room. It was parked sideways and was taking up three spaces. The driver was in the car and had a bandage wrapped around his head.

She parked at the far end of the parking lot near the office where she could see the driver and Jim's room. She saw Jim open the curtain and look out. The driver raised a gun and pointed it in Jim's direction. Jim closed the curtain, and the gun went back down.

Andrea was afraid, not for herself, but for Jim. She looked around, trying to decide what to do. She thought about just running over to the car and telling the guy to leave, but it wouldn't help Jim if she died. She thought about cranking her car and ramming it into that little red Mazda, but if he survived, then what?

The curtain again was pulled back, and Jim stood looking out. The gun again was raised and pointed toward him. The door of the red Mazda popped open, and the driver's black-oxford-clad left foot touched the pavement. The curtain dropped, the foot retracted, the door shut, and the driver lowered the gun and slammed his fist into the steering wheel.

Andrea stepped out of her car, trying not to bring any attention to herself, and walked into the office. She tried to explain what was going on to the desk manager, and he laughed and told her to leave. She pointed to the red car and told him again.

Again, she was told to leave. He told her that security would take care of the red car.

She headed back to her car and pulled her cell phone out of her purse. As quickly as she could, she got Jim on the line. She was relieved to hear his voice.

"Jim, listen to me. There is a man outside in a red car with a gun."

"Outside where? At your house?"

"No. Outside your room."

"I've been looking out every couple of minutes for your car to pull in. I think I would have noticed it. Let me peek out…"

"No. Jim, stay away from the window. He is going to shoot you if you give him a chance."

"What are you talking about? How do you know?"

"I am watching him right now."

The man in the car looked at Andrea. He looked away and watched the window again. His door slowly opened.

"Jim, I don't know, but I think he just recognized me."

The man in the car looked back at her again. He had a smile on his face. She couldn't exactly place where , but she knew they had met. The door opened a little more.

"Andrea, are you okay?"

Again, she considered running back into the office, but she knew that wouldn't help, she would probably just get laughed at again. She looked around to see if there was anyone else who could help, but there was no one. Then she saw it. It was small and red. She leaped forward about ten yards and grabbed it and gave it a pull.

"Jim, do not come out," she yelled as she fell to the ground.

The fire alarm sounded, and the door of the red car once again closed. People began to run wildly out of rooms all over the hotel. The red Mazda cranked up and spun out of the parking lot. Security grabbed Andrea and took her inside.

Jim and Andrea tried to explain what had happened, but the hotel management felt like they needed to call the police and have them both arrested. They would have found themselves in jail except the surveillance tape revealed the gun in the driver's hand. The picture wasn't clear enough to make out the driver's face, but the gun was definitely there.

By the time they finished with the police reports and making amends with the hotel employees, it was almost lunchtime. The two decided to discard the breakfast that had been sitting in the car all morning and go on to the Mexican place for lunch.

"There is no doubt in my mind that I have met that guy before. I just can't place him. That bandage he had around his head, I don't know."

"That was one of those spy movie moves you pulled with that fire alarm."

"It worked, didn't it?"

"Sure did, turned the man with the gun into the man on the run!"

"What if he comes back? What if next time he doesn't run? Jim, you might want to consider another place to stay for a while."

"I agree. If you are sure you have met him, it is probably best if you don't go home either."

"You're right. I don't feel it would be safe at all."

After lunch, they went to the hospital to see Inez. She was burned pretty badly and hooked up to a morphine drip to help control the pain. She woke up to acknowledge their presence and then dozed right back off.

Jim and Andrea sat quietly in the room and stared at each other for a short period of time. Neither was up to sitting, especially considering that Inez wouldn't know if they were there or not.

They drove to the Daytona Beach boardwalk and went for a walk. They browsed several shops looking at trinkets and ornaments. For a while, the problems of life seemed forever away.

They found an empty picnic table and shared a soft pretzel, and Andrea shared her dream of Zack.

"He really said Susan would be okay with that?"

"It was a dream, but yes."

"Sounds like a good dream. I wish I could have a good dream. Mine are filled with giant birds and idiots with guns."

Andrea jumped to her feet when she noticed the time on her watch.

"Come on. I have a big surprise for you, and we are gonna be late if we don't hurry," she said as she held out her hand.

"What's goin' on? I don't know if I can handle too many more surprises."

"Just grab my hand, and let's go."

They drove on to the dinner cruise. The meal, the atmosphere, and the time together were all perfect. When they left the cruise, they stopped at the hotel and got Jim's stuff out of the room, checking the parking lot first for red Mazda, and then went to the new hotel.

46

Tommy had spent his day trying to understand what happened the night before. At several points throughout the day, he had considered going to talk to his dad to see if he knew what was going on. He was sure that somehow the great Mr. Sutton already knew everything. Somehow, he always did.

He had gone into his office for a while to see if anything unusual had happened during the night. Nothing outside of the usual trivial stuff. A few speeders and a drunk had been pulled, a domestic violence call, and one out-of-control party on the beach—just a typical night for the Port Suni Police Department. A note about false alarm at a hotel north of town caught his attention. He thought that somehow this might have been related to whatever was going on with Jim. A drive to the hotel found no one in Jim's room.

He was careful to log all the miles he was putting on his car. Every stop was logged and the actual mileage entered on the proper line. Even though he knew that just a brief note would have sufficed, he also knew that while Alex was out, he would be held a little closer to the rules that governed vehicle usage.

A trip to the beach house remains turned up nothing unexpected—no one, no clues, nothing to go on. While he stood looking at where the Fender home once stood, a news helicopter flew over. He had seen them do that many times over the years, usually when there had been a shark attack.

He continued his search for answers by going to the area where Kristy had been found in number 01. The recent news exposure had apparently turned this clearing into a popular party spot. The remnants of campfires and a hundred or more beer cans covered the sand. There was plenty of trash but no answers.

His head filled again with questions about why Alex had lied about everything. He knew that number 01 had not been to the carwash. He knew that Jim had not cut him. His questions lead him to question if Alex knew anything about what had happened at his house the night before. He wanted to ask Alex a few questions about what he might know, but there was no answer on the phone or at the door.

It seemed strange to Tommy that Alex hadn't called him or been by and stranger still that he wouldn't be home when his car was there. It might have been strange, but what hadn't been recently? Nothing seemed right. He walked around the house, hoping to see Alex outside, but to no avail. Peeking in the windows was out of the question because Alex always kept the shades pulled tight and the shutters closed.

Tommy started back toward the station when he noticed a red car behind him. At first, he didn't pay it much attention until he noticed the driver had his face mostly covered and had dark glasses on. Just the looks of him caused a chill to run down his spine. He made a sudden left turn to get the guy off his tail, but the red Mazda stayed with him. Tommy slowed to guide the car to pass, the car slowed more and left a larger space between them. Tommy sped up, and so did the Mazda. After a few more turns, Tommy found himself doing close to one hundred miles per hour southbound on a wide-open section of A1A. The rearview mirror showed the Mazda right behind him with a revolver in the driver's hand.

Had life not been so confusing over the last few days, Tommy probably would have remembered seeing Larry driving this same car a couple of days before. As for now, the main thing on his mind was survival. The demon in the car behind him was out to get him. If he kept going a few more miles, he was bound to come up on other traffic and endanger the lives of even more people. If he slowed, who knows how the red car would react. If he stopped, he was sure he would be shot.

The two cars blew past the charred markers where the Fender home once stood. The pull-off on the left flew by in a blur. Tommy took a deep breath and firmed his grip on the wheel. The Mazda was almost thirty yards behind him. His left foot found its way to the parking brake pedal. He swerved to the center of the road, and the left foot went down. Tommy's mind was moving as fast as the car when the rear brakes locked. He turned the wheel slightly, and the car began to turn. He could see the red car coming toward the front of his car as he released the parking brake and pressed the main brake. He was still traveling southbound backward when the red car flew past him.

As soon as he could get moving, he was wide-open northbound on A1A with no sign of the Mazda in his rearview. The last he had seen of demon-hauling red car, it was still headed south. His knuckles were white, and his heart was pounding.

As he made his way back to town, he started thinking about his drive home the day before. He remembered the red car that he had seen in his mirror. He thought about the ruckus outside his back door the night before. He didn't remember seeing Larry driving the red car.

He stopped by his father's house to find out what the great Mr. Sutton might know. Thomas's red Blazer sat in the drive and served as a beacon that said, "I am home. Come see me." Tommy all but ran to the door.

Thomas had the door open by the time he topped the steps. Just that was enough to cause Tommy to worry. His dad had never been one to get in to much of a hurry to get the door.

"Get in here, boy. We got ourselves a real problem. What took you so long?"

"I was…huh? What do you mean took me so long? I didn't tell you I was coming by."

"After that little racket behind your house last night, I really expected to see you early this morning."

"How'd you know about that?"

"Listen, boy. I ain't got time to mess with all the details. But here's what you need to know. Larry was supposed to be makin' everything that happened to those Fender folks look like Jim did it. That was what we first talked about. Then he let that dummy who works on the cars in on it, and that raised a small problem."

"Dad, what are you talkin' about?"

"Just listen to me, boy. Larry changed things up a bit. I think he has been trying to make everything look like you did it. I think he was gonna go in and kill that woman of yours last night and somehow frame you for it."

"That was Larry outside my house?"

"Me and Larry both. Good thing I came and showed him somethin' or he might o' made it. At first, the idea was he would kill that Fender woman and frame Jim for it. When he started doing the planning and the timing, he added the kidnapping of that girl too. I was okay with that 'cause he has sure enough caused you problems."

"Who has caused me problems?"

"Jim. Now shut up and listen. I don't know what he is planning on doing now. Instead of making sure you are seen as the local hero and guaranteeing you keeping your job, I think he started trying to put you away for it. He changed the plan, boy. And I think something bad is gonna happen. He don't plan to frame Jim anymore. That is obvious. But as for you, he might still be trying to frame you. But after last night, he might try to kill you. Now that he knows I am on to him, he might try to kill me too."

"I don't know who, but somebody just tried, I think."

"What do you mean?"

"Some idiot in a red car tried to chase me down. He had a gun."

"When I followed him to your place last night, he was drivin' a red Mazda."

Suddenly, Tommy remembered seeing Larry driving the red Mazda and waving at him. He was overcome with understanding. Everything started to make sense. Fear rushed over him—not fear for himself nor for his dad, but fear for his wife. Janet was home alone.

"Dad, I have to go. He might be going to get Janet now."

"Boy, why would he do that? Doing something to her at this point I don't think could come back on you."

"Maybe not, but if he took her, I would be at his mercy. And if I went to get her, he would kill us both. If I refuse, he will kill her. I don't know. I gotta go."

Tommy ran to his Crossfire and jumped in. Smoke rolled from the tires as Tommy headed home. He pulled his cell phone and called home. No answer. His imagination ran wild with what he might see when he got there.

The sun was going down as he pulled into his drive. A quick look around the neighborhood revealed no sign of the red Mazda.

"Hey, Tommy, you gonna be runnin' around outside in your undies again tonight?" the neighbor called from next door. "My wife says that if you are, she wants to have a chance to see before you go runnin' back in."

"Very funny. Hey, have you seen a red Mazda around here today? I think the guy that fired the shot last night was driving a red Mazda."

"Nah, but I just got in about twenty minutes ago. So what should I tell my wife?"

"Tell her to be very careful what she wishes for."

As Tommy turned to go toward his house, he noticed that there were no lights on. He ran to the door and grabbed the knob. It was locked. As fast as he could, he got his keys from his pocket and unlocked the door and went in.

The house was dark and quiet. He moved as silently as he could from room to room, afraid of what he might find. He left all the lights off as he moved. The bathroom held the fragrance of Janet's perfume but no Janet. The kitchen was clean and clutter free. When he walked in the bedroom, he could see the outline of a body under the covers. He stood quietly and watched for any movement that would indicate breathing or any sign of life. There was no movement.

He eased to the side of the bed and grabbed the covers and pulled them back. His emotions went wild. He saw nothing there but neatly arranged pillows.

Suddenly, he was tackled from behind. He found himself on the bed with the assailant on his back. He forced his way back to his feet, threw the attacker across the room, and pulled his gun.

Janet rose to her feet. She was wearing her nicest lingerie and a bloody nose. Anger filled her eyes.

"I can't believe you did that!" Tommy shouted. "I could have killed you!"

Janet just stared at him as she wiped the blood from her nose.

"Put on some clothes while I pack us a bag. We have to get away from here."

Janet's expression changed from anger to fear. "What's going on, Tommy?"

"I think Larry is gonna try to kill us."

"That's ridiculous. Larry couldn't hurt anyone."

"You might be surprised. I think he has already killed a couple of folks. Now get some clothes on or you are going like that. And why didn't you answer the stupid phone?"

"I heard it ringing, but I had just gotten out of the shower…"

Tommy was afraid to drive straight to any place, but by midnight, they were checked into a hotel in New Smyrna Beach. By 1:00 a.m., Larry was in Tommy's house, looking around.

47

August 18

Jim and Andrea met in the hotel restaurant for breakfast. They enjoyed the food, and the service was excellent. What they enjoyed most was having a peaceful moment away from all the stress and worry they had recently experienced. Not that is was forgotten or even in the past, just that it wasn't here. He missed his wife and daughter and wished they could have been at home having breakfast together. Even so, he was able to relax and loosen up a little. Jim opened the driver's door for Andrea before walking around to the passenger door to get in. As he opened the door, a red car on the far side of the parking lot caught his attention. He couldn't see inside the car very well because of the glare of the sun on the windshield, but he could see that the driver was in the car and holding something on top of the steering wheel with both hands. The sight of it caused the hair to stand up on the back of his neck. As quickly as he could, he slung the door open, jumped in, and slammed the door.

After he told Andrea what he had seen, they started out of the parking lot, trying to be noticed as little as possible. As they pulled onto the road, Jim could see the driver much more clearly. What his imagination had told him was a man with a gun was indeed a young woman with dark hair entering something in her

Palm Pilot. He laughed out loud when he realized the mistake he had made.

It didn't take long for his laughter to turn to anger. The stress of losing everything and the emotional roller coaster he had been on were taking their toll. He insisted that Andrea take him to where his old home used to stand, but Andrea refused.

Instead, she took him to the North Suni Hospital to see Inez. She was sedated and sleeping. The doctor came in and introduced himself as he looked at Inez and her IVs.

"That's my mother-in-law. How is she?"

"She's burned pretty bad, but from what I understand, she would have died if you hadn't acted so bravely. You could have easily been burned as bad as she is or even died."

"I did what I could, but it wasn't enough for Alfred."

"Listen son, there is no such thing as Superman. No one could have saved them both."

"If I would have woken up sooner…"

"She is healing. It will be a slow go, but she will be fine. Don't be so hard on yourself. She will need you to be there for her."

The doctor had been gone for a couple of minutes when they decided to pray. Joining hands over the bed, Jim led, "God. Have mercy on Inez. She has tried so hard to do right by her family and You. She needs a healing hand. If it is your will, Lord, send an angel to minister to her. Hold her in your arms and strengthen her. Minister to her loss with your love. Jesus, Scripture says, 'by your stripes we are healed'; let it be so, and you take the glory for it. Amen."

Andrea also prayed. Her prayer was silent, and Jim didn't know that she was praying; but God did. She gave thanks for her first husband. She asked for protection over Jim, physically and emotionally. She thanked God for Jim, for his courage and for his strength. Then she offered a word of praise to the God who not only promises but who truly does work everything to the good of those who love Him and are called according to His purpose.

As they left the hospital, both felt encouraged. Things were going to get better, and they knew it. All this was temporary and would soon pass.

They stopped at the Volusia Mall and bought them each a bathing suit and drove to Flagler Beach. Andrea felt it was best to keep Jim away from home as long as she could. She found a place to park that seemed to not be too crowded.

"Can you do me a small favor?" Andrea asked as they exited the car.

"I'm sure I can. Just not sure about which favor I can do."

"Promise me you'll at least try to have a good time?"

"I promise I will try, not that I will succeed."

The next few hours were spent wading in the water, walking on the shore, sitting in the sand, and just enjoying God's creation.

"I admit it. I have had a good time. Thanks for forcing it on me," he said as they built a sand castle. "I don't think I was ready to face 'home' again. Maybe now…"

The ocean seemed to smile on them that day.

He could hardly believe it had only been two weeks since he had last held Susan or Kristy in his arms. It was such a short period of time yet seemed to be an eternity. Time had lost its relevance. Days passed so quickly and drug by at the same time. As it is with life when nothing remains constant, everything needed to be carefully examined and yet nothing seemed to matter.

They stopped by the hotel and changed clothes and had an early dinner. When they finished eating, they left for the Fender property. Stepping out of the hotel lobby brought reality back to him. Jim still felt as though there was something there he needed to find that he had not yet found.

"I know it sounds strange, but there has to be something. I don't know what, but something that has been missed."

"What is it that you are trying to prove? Tommy seems to believe that Larry has something to do with all this."

"Maybe so, but Alex has some hand in it. And it is still possible that Tommy...I don't know what I am looking for. I just want to go look one more time."

Andrea was overcome with a deep sense of dread as they turned onto A1A in Port Suni. Her nerves got the best of her, and she had to stop about a mile north of the Fender property. Her hands were shaking, and her throat was dry. They sat and talked for close to fifteen minutes before driving on.

48

Janet listened intently as Tommy worked his way through the situation as he saw it. "Dad wanted me to have a big case to solve and to get rid of the Fenders for once and for all. He enlisted Larry to help with the actual hands on."

"Your dad? Why would he do that?"

"Because he thinks that everyone is out to get us and that I am not capable of holding the job without him."

"No, I mean the Fenders, why?"

"Because Jim's dad took his girlfriend a long time ago, and then Jim took mine. Somehow, he thinks that everything that has gone wrong in both of our lives has been because of a Fender. If you ask him, it probably goes back a generation or two further.

Anyway, Larry decided to take the girl, so he enlisted Alex. Something went wrong, and Alex got cut, and Kristy got locked in the car."

"You said you thought she cut him?"

"Yeah, she did. Then Sam found out too much, and he was found in the inlet.

That brings us to the fire. Larry wanted me to go down so he could have my job. He knew the case against Jim wouldn't stand, so if he could take him out, that would make Dad happy, and if I got framed for all the murders, he would be happy."

"Wow, good going, Sherlock."

When Tommy told Janet about everything that he had pieced together, she decided it best to stay away from Port Suni for a few days. They rented a car for her to keep in case she needed to go somewhere while Tommy was out trying to solve the crime of the century.

Tommy tried again to visit with Alex. He rang the bell and knocked on the door repeatedly to no avail. He used his cell phone to call Alex's phone. He could hear the phone ringing inside but got no answer.

He walked around to the houses closeby and asked if anyone had seen Alex recently. The couple in the house just to the west of Alex's home said they had seen Alex riding around with a cop a few days ago but not since. No one else had seen him at all since before his hospital stay.

He left a note on the door and started to leave when he thought to check the mailbox. It didn't appear to have been checked for several days.

He went by his dad's house to see if he could get some more information, but the red Blazer wasn't in the drive. He took a chance and took the key from the light fixture on the front porch and went in. The smell of beer was strong. As he walked through the house looking things over, he noticed that one of his dad's deer rifles was missing, as was his revolver and holster. On the kitchen table was a box of shells for the rifle with a few missing and a drill with a cutting blade in it. He picked up a few of the shells and found that the copper jackets had been cut.

Tommy was overcome with anxiety. He wasn't for sure what to do, but he knew that something had to be done soon. Too many people had been hurt; even more people had died, and it had to stop. Now his dad was gone with his guns, and Tommy didn't believe for a minute he was deer hunting.

He dialed his dad's cell phone just to find that it was sitting on the counter next to the microwave. He looked for anything that would give him a clue of where the great Mr. Sutton had gone. When he started for the door, he noticed that the hat Thomas used when he went out on his boat was gone. He turned on the marine radio and tried to call his dad and received no answer.

A quick drive to the marina proved his theory. Dock security confirmed that Thomas had left approximately thirty minutes earlier. After mentioning that he had carried a golf bag on board with him, the security guard said he had tried to convince him not to go during tide change because of what had happened a few nights ago. Tommy had no idea what he was talking about, but he agreed and went back to his car.

Tommy drove to the Fender property but saw that Andrea's car was in the drive, so he went on past. About a quarter of a mile past his drive, he saw something that caused his stomach to sink. Pulled off on the oceanside was a red Mazda. He was sure it was the same one that had followed him. He drove past it to find that there was no driver. He almost pulled in to stop and thought that the demon from behind the wheel might be somehow expecting him.

Tommy drove on, expecting to see the car pull out behind him; but it did not. He pulled in to the area where number 01 had been found and waited with anticipation, thinking that at any minute the red Mazda would show itself. The only other car he saw was the one that was already there and contained a young couple who were so deeply lost in each other's lips that they had no idea that Tommy was even there.

After no more than two minutes, Tommy pulled back out onto the road and headed north.

49

Jim and Andrea had arrived at the remnants of the Fender residence with much anticipation. They had dug and stirred the debris in hopes to find anything that might point them to the answer that would set Jim's mind at ease. They looked around the whole property and found nothing unusual.

A1A was not by any means a deserted road, and the stretch that serviced the Fender property was no exception. Many cars passed by while they continued looking and digging. Most of them would have meant nothing, but there was one that would have definitely received a second look if either of them had seen it. A red Mazda made its way southward. The driver was an experienced diver with plans to gain more experience today.

For Jim, the swing set brought back memories of laughter and dirty-blonde hair flowing in the breeze. The image of Kristy was almost real enough to touch. Inside his heart, he felt happy and sad at the same time. He missed her so much. He thought of how much she looked like Susan, and that brought the flood of emotions he had felt the day he last saw his wife—the love and the loss, the joy and the pain, the excitement and the confusion.

Andrea took his hand, and they walked toward the beach. She tried to comfort him with her words, but she wasn't sure of what to say. No words she could say felt adequate to soothe the pain she knew he was feeling.

They sat with their backs to the sand dune that had been just below the deck of Jim's house. They talked about life and death.

Jim's eyes began to puddle again. "I am beginning to understand the temporary nature of life here. That makes me appreciate the eternality of heaven even more."

"Just don't get in too big of a hurry to get there. Some people still need you here."

"No, I'm not rushing. I am just saying that I had never thought about how short life is here. All the pain and loss. Heaven just sounds better and better."

The sound of the waves crashing covered the sound of the car coming up the drive and the sound of the car door. The birds that circled overhead, looking for a handout, kept them from being aware of the movement as Tommy walked down to the beach. When Jim saw him, he jumped to his feet.

"Sorry, Jim, I didn't mean to scare you guys. I just wanted to take another look around."

"I kind of felt the same way."

"I don't know what you're going to want to do with Inez in the shape she's in, but I just talked with the coroner. He says that he'll be ready to release Alfred's body in the morning.

The three sat back down with their backs to the dune, and Tommy recounted the same account he had told Janet. He continued, "Yesterday a red car got behind me and chased me down the road out in front of your property. The driver had most of his face covered and held a gun."

"Wow!" Andrea said. "Sounds like the same car we saw."

They explained to Tommy what had happened at the hotel the morning before. They also gave the whole story a little levity when they told about the red car they had seen this morning whose driver wielded a double-barreled Palm Pilot.

Tommy told them about seeing a red car park just south of Jim's driveway.

"It could easily be the same car I saw yesterday."

They looked south and saw a couple walking along.

"There are a lot of red cars out there. I may not have been…"

They looked north, another couple and a family of three. About a quarter of a mile out, a small sailboat sat anchored.

Jim pointed toward the dune, "Let's find another place to talk. I'm getting a little spooked."

When he looked at the waves rising and falling, fear caused his heart to pound. He tried to talk, but the words wouldn't come. He grabbed Andrea by the hand and tried to pull her. His legs felt heavy and didn't want to cooperate. The three of them headed up the dune.

On the little sailboat that Thomas had decided to rename *Eyes of the Ocean,* a watchful eye was being kept on the threesome. The scope of his rifle followed every move. He had decided that although it would be easy enough to put a bullet through Jim's heart, for his son's sake, now was not the time. Thomas watched as the three reached the top of the dune, but the rising and crashing of the waves hid Larry as he eased up from the water.

Larry took Tommy's gun from the plastic zipper bag on his belt and raised it up.

"Hey, loser!" Larry shouted.

The three on the dune spun to see what was going on.

"Man, I had hoped to just have you put away, but now I'm gonna have to kill ya."

Larry walked a little farther in toward shore. He was now standing in less than a foot of water. He was also now visible from the sailboat.

"Listen, Larry. You've been a good cop. You don't have to do this. I will just quit, and you can have the job."

"Yeah right. Like you would just walk away from the job that your dad worked so hard to get you."

"My dad got me in it, but my wife wants me out."

"Too late. All three of you are history."

Tommy reached for his revolver that he didn't have on him. Larry panicked and pulled the trigger. The bullet ripped through Tommy's neck and continued on to make impact with Andrea's chest. Both fell to the ground.

Larry let out a laugh and yelled, "Man, I'm good. Two with a single shot."

He pointed the gun at Jim. "Now it's your turn to die."

Suddenly, Larry's head exploded as the hollow point with the cut copper jacket from Thomas' deer rifle mushroomed its way through his brain. Jim didn't hear the shot. He had no idea what had happened. He stood there and watched as the waves pulled Larry's body farther out.

He ran over to Andrea. The body in the sand and the blood reminded him of Susan. His knees gave way. Her cell phone was lying in the sand where it had fallen from her hand. He tried to feel a pulse, but the pounding of his own heart made it hard to tell. He listened for a breath and heard none. He took the phone and dialed 911. He fell to his knees and stared.

As he sat on the beach with his head in his hands, it was hard for him to believe that all these things had come to pass. It had only been two weeks since life seemed normal.

His mind wandered to that sunbathed morning when it all began. All of its images came back like an unbelievable flood that washed over him and drowned him in emotions. It had been less than five hundred yards from where he now sat. He turned his eyes that direction only to see the charred remains where his home used to stand. A few blackened two-by-fours stood ominously pointing toward the sky like solidified remnants of a bad dream.

He wasn't aware of how long he has sat there when he heard Andrea call out his name. There was a group of maybe a dozen people gathered around. Andrea had regained consciousness.

The bullet had caused her to black out. The doctor would later say she was lucky the bullet hit the breast bone at the angle it did or she would have been dead for sure.

Thomas jumped from his boat as it hit the beach. "Son, what have I done to you?" He fell on his knees next to Tommy. He frantically felt for a pulse and listened for a breath. He had just started CPR when the paramedics crossed the dune.

50

Three Years later

Jim and Andrea sat on a blanket on the beach and watched their one-year-old daughter, Alicia, teeter around as she walked in the sand. They had been happily married for almost two years. The house had been rebuilt and filled with love. Andrea held the top rating for local news anchors, and Jim's real estate business was booming.

The three walked hand in hand to the water's edge. Alicia was still a little afraid of the waves. As they walked along, Jim pointed out a few small fish as they swam by. As they walked and talked, they laughed at how the waves would push Alicia back and forth as if she was nothing at all. On a few occasions, Alicia laughed as Jim and Andrea lifted her into the air.

A short way south of where the little path went out to A1A, they walked out on the beach and built a small sand castle. As they dug, they came across a few sand fleas. Alicia seemed so amazed at how fast they would bury themselves back in the sand if you put them where the water had just gone out. It seemed to be natural progression for Jim to lay back and let Andrea and Alicia bury him in the sand. As they dug, Andrea had to keep a close eye on Alicia, or she would drop a handful of sand in Jim's face. After a few minutes, Jim noticed something shiny in Alicia's hand. Closer investigation revealed that she had dug up a ring. It was a class ring from Port Suni High. Inside were inscribed the letters TNS II.

Jim leapt to his feet. It was Tommy Sutton's ring, the one that had been lost the night Susan had been raped. He took the ring to the edge of the water and almost gave it a sling. He decided to put it in his pocket.

"What are you going to do with it?" Andrea asked with a concerned look on her face.

"I am really not sure. I hate that everything came out the way it did. To tell you the truth, I still don't like Thomas Sutton, but if it had been my son and someone found his ring, I would want it."

"I guess you're right. Do you think you are up to talking to him?"

"I think that might actually help me heal. I know he had to be hurting too. After all, he lost his wife to cancer and his son to…"

When the Fender family reached the deck, Jim walked over and turned on the radio. He bent down and picked up Alicia with his right arm and put his left around Andrea. The three danced together in the sun as Inez watched from the kitchen window.

On the water about a quarter of a mile out sat a small sailboat. The boat held only one person, Thomas Sutton. Thomas watched the Fenders as they danced through the scope on his deer rifle. When he was sure the crosshairs were lined up just right, he squeezed the trigger. He repeated the process three more times and began to laugh as he dropped his rifle into the water and raised the anchor.

Jim sat bolt upright in the bed, holding his chest where the bullet had entered in his dream. He looked at Andrea lying asleep next to him. He jumped from bed and ran to check on Alicia. She was sleeping soundly.

Thomas Sutton sat in his sixth-floor room and awaited the day he would be free from the Volusia Mental Health Center. For three years, he had plotted his revenge on the one who had caused his son to die. If he hadn't been overcome with emotions, Jim would have been found dead along with the rest of them.

The voices in his head tormented him. He could hear them day and night saying, "Them Sutton boys can't even protect their own. They let Tommy get killed and the bad guy get away."

Thomas dreamed of setting it right.